THE LOVE STORY THAT WOULD NOT DIE

In the swirl of intrigue that surrounded England's Civil War and the restoration of the Stuart monarchy, certain factions tried to destroy all record of the young King Charles II's marriage to the lovely commoner, Lucy Walter.

But this love story was too rich in passion, too historic to be suppressed. It lived on in the hearts of all who witnessed that unforgettable royal romance.

And now you, too, can read about it in a stirring novel filled with the sweep and drama of those turbulent years!

FIRST LOVE

Bethany Strong

A JOVE / HBJ BOOK

Copyright © 1976 by Bethany Strong
Published by arrangement with Parable Press

All rights reserved. No part of this publication may be reproduced or transmitted in any form or by any means, electronic or mechanical, including photocopy, recording, or any information storage and retrieval system, without permission in writing from the publisher.

First Jove/HBJ edition published March 1978

Library of Congress Catalog Card Number: 76-17950

Printed in the United States of America

Jove/HBJ books are published by Jove Publications, Inc.
(Harcourt Brace Jovanovich)
757 Third Avenue, New York, N.Y. 10017

PREFACE

Throughout history there have been mysteries that can never be solved because the documentation clarifying the affair was destroyed. Quite often it was done deliberately because some person stood in the way of the ambitions of politicians.

It appears that the love affair of Charles II and Lucy Walter is just such a mystery. In 1947, Lord George Scott, a descendant of the Duke of Monmouth, Lucy's son, gathered together all available information about his ancestress and documented it in his book, LUCY WALTER: WIFE OR MISTRESS, published by George C. Harrap and Co. Ltd., London.

The following story is based upon the evidence presented in that gallant and belated defense of a much "maligned" lady, as her biographer called her. In so many words our narrative implies that "maybe this is what happened." The known facts are interpreted in the weaving of the plot.

A selected biography is included at the end for those readers who would like to read more about the background of this fascinating affair which happened during the English Civil War and some years afterward before the Restoration in the middle of the seventeenth century.

Amherst, Massachusetts　　　　　　　　Bethany Strong

1

Lucy rode out through Brockhill's main gate at full speed so no one could catch up with her and stop her. She had been in the house for almost a week because of a rain storm that had battered the area. Now, it was glorious to be riding hard in the fresh air that was heavy with the fragrance of wet grass. The sun was breaking through the branches of the dripping trees and the mud of the road was beginning to dry. The storm was over.

She held her little spaniel on the saddle in front of her and he barked when they rode past the entrance to Bamfylde Park. He seemed to know that Poltimore Estate was the only place that Grandmother wanted them to ride, she thought. Well, she had to strike a blow for freedom today or she would lose her mind staying in the house with nothing to do but play games with Justus. She loved her twin brother but sometimes he bored her.

She saw several soldiers at the edge of the town near the church in Broadclyst. They were officers in the royal army, she thought, because their hair was long and curling to their shoulders under broad-brimmed hats decorated with long plumes. If they were Parliamentary soldiers, like Father and Richard, their hair would be chopped off just beneath stovepipe hats to show scorn for Cavalier lovelocks. Her heart beat a little faster as she thought of her grandmother's warning about what soldiers did when they found women alone, "They rape them," she had said with venom.

"There's nothing to be afraid of," Lucy assured herself, "I'll just go into the chapel and wait until they ride away." Anyway, Salvatore would like to run about for awhile in the churchyard.

She dismounted, tied her horse to the hitching post and set the spaniel on the ground. "Don't go far," she said as she gave him a loving little spank and then ran up the steps to the door of the church.

Inside, she sniffed the familiar musty, stale odor of old incense as she went down the center aisle and sat down in one of the front pews. She tried to calm herself by closing her eyes and starting to pray in the way Frances Vaughan had taught her. "I'm in the Presence of God," she murmured, but it was no good. She couldn't "feel that God is everywhere." All she could feel was a breathless terror. All she could think about was the soldiers outside and what they might do to her.

Suddenly, she heard the pounding of horses' hooves—a lot of them. They stopped, and she heard men's voices! She stood up and moved out of the pew into the aisle and stood still, listening. It must be more soldiers! She should hide—but where? She heard the church door creaking open and the tread of heavy boots with spurs clanking on the stone paving. There was a stomping as if guards were taking up a position at the door.

She ran to the altar and threw herself to her knees. "Oh, God, save me," she whispered.

They had probably seen her horse tethered outside. Why had she put her faith in hiding in the church? The rebels, she heard her mother say to Frances Vaughan, one day, had no respect for churches. They used St. Paul's in London to stable their horses—and her brother told her that the servants said that Cromwell's soldiers bragged that the baptismal fonts made excellent latrines! They laughed at the idea of sanctuary. She was trapped—what was going to happen to her?

"Oh, God, save me," she whispered, again.

She could feel eyes on her back, as if someone were waiting for her to turn around. He would have to wait a long time! She would stay there praying for help until he went away.

But he didn't go away. Finally, he said, "Lucy—Lucy Walter?"

Startled to hear her name she turned around and then, holding to the altar rail, pulled herself slowly to her feet. The blood rushed to her face. Not ten feet down the aisle stood Prince Charles, the King's son! His heavy black hair was dishevelled, and he had a puzzled but pleased expression on his swarthy face. She had met him the first time when they were children and her family was living with her other grandparents in London. She would know him anywhere. He was so handsome!

"Lucy?" he repeated. "I never forget a face as pretty as yours! Is it really you—or is it an angel that is making a fool of me in that bloody light?"

She took several steps toward him, and then sank into a curtsy at his feet. She was faint with surprise. "How gracious of you to remember my name, sir," she murmured.

"Oh, come now," Charles said. "We're not at court—we're in the middle of a filthy war!"

"Sir—!" Lucy stammered but couldn't go on. She kept her head lowered.

He reached forward and put his gloved hand on her elbow. "Rise, fair lady!" he said playfully. "Imagine seeing you after riding all day and half the night with my father's soldiers—for weeks at a time—" all I've seen are the dirty sluts who follow the army, he thought. "—what are you doing here, anyway? Why aren't you in London, or at Golden Grove where I remember seeing you?"

"My father brought us—my brother and me—to our

grandmother's house—" she hesitated because her father was fighting in the army of the King's enemies—"my father's mother is Mrs. Chappell of Brockhill."

"Ah, yes," Charles said as if he weren't listening to what she said for he was trying to remember where he had seen her before, and just who she was. Probably a relative of Carberry's he thought, because it was at Carberry's estate, Golden Grove, that he had seen her when he went there with his father on war business a year or two before.

"I first met you at Bedford House in London," Lucy said shyly. "It was a Christmas party for children. Lord Russell invited us because my other grandfather, Alfred Gwinne, is Her Majesty's equerry."

"Ah, yes," Charles said, "I remember now. I also remember that beastly little brother of yours—twins aren't you, and he always at your heels. The two of you look as much alike as peas in a pod," he said. "Where is he?"

She knew she was blushing with embarrassment. "He isn't always with me, now."

"That's something to be thankful for!"

"Sir," Lucy tried again, "you came in to worship—?"

He laughed but didn't answer the question. He put his hand on her elbow. "Let's go into the churchyard where we can talk in the daylight—and you'll look more like a woman than an angel!" He chuckled softly as he led her into the transept and out through the door into the churchyard. How delightfully naive she was. Obviously she was not used to the court—all that formality!

"You look more human out here without that ethereal light shining on you!"

How kind he is, and so handsome, Lucy thought. She smiled at him and felt more at ease.

"What are you doing here," he asked, "besides praying like mad at the communion rail?"

She looked down at the ground because she didn't want to tell him that she had been terrified.

"Lucy," Charles burst out, "I remember that Christmas party at Bedford House. I was—let's see—" He counted the years on his fingers, "—about eight or ten, I think. Remember the kissing bough?"

"Yes, I remember. I had never seen one before!"

"Remember how I kissed you?"

Yes, she remembered. How could she forget? She was standing looking up at the bough of mistletoe and holly and he had come up behind her and put his arms around her. His dark curls brushed her neck and sent a pleasant shiver over her. Then he had turned her around and kissed her on the lips.

"Yes, I remember," she whispered.

"Well, let's do it again!" He held out his arms to her.

"Sir," she murmured, "may I ask why you laughed when I asked if you had come in to worship—don't you believe in God?"

"Sure, I do, but I get a lecture every day from my chaplains; and that's enough!" What a strange girl she was to ask a question like that—when he was offering her love! It's not every day that the King's son offers love to a woman! Most of them jump at the chance, he thought arrogantly. "Why do you ask such a strange question?"

"I just wondered why you came into the church."

Charles smiled. "Well, it was a strange reason to go to church, I'll agree—but I have my favorite little spaniel bitch with me and when I dismounted and set her down—she ran away. I couldn't find her; she's in heat and I don't want her to be mated to another breed. I looked everywhere outside and thought she might have come in the church where it's dry and warm."

"Oh, I have a spaniel, too, that I take with me on the saddle when I ride."

"Actually, I don't know why I came into the church,

really," Charles muttered. "Certainly my dog couldn't open that heavy door! I seemed to be drawn in for some reason—maybe just to find you!" he said playfully. "I rode here from Exeter with some of my father's officers that had business here in Broadclyst."

"The King is in Exeter?" Lucy asked in surprise.

"Yes."

"Then Exeter hasn't been captured by Essex?"

"No, he moved on." He looked at her sharply. "How did you know of Essex' movements?"

"My father said that Her Majesty was in Exeter giving birth to a baby"—royal brat he had actually said—"and that Essex was going to capture her and put her in the Tower." She stopped, embarrassed, for she saw that Charles' black eyes blazed with anger and his jaw jutted out. She shouldn't have told him that! Her father had also said that the Queen had returned from Holland with money and soldiers for the King in Oxford and that, now, her health had failed. She had a rheumatic fever as well as being pregnant. Since there was the possibility of the Parliamentary armies closing in on Oxford and capturing the King, they had taken her to the Duke of Bedford's house in Exeter to give birth to the child.

"Essex underestimates my mother," Charles said coldly, "she escaped."

"Escaped? Was she able to travel so soon after the baby was born?"

"Probably not," Charles said, "but she went anyway. I hope that she is in France, but I doubt it—!"

Lucy knew that she shouldn't ask so many questions because it made him angry. She looked down and murmured, "Oh," and remained silent.

Charles stared at her as his anger subsided. Then suddenly he reached out and took her in his arms. "Lucy!" he murmured, "Lucy!" There was a muffled sob in his voice and Lucy knew that he felt helpless and frightened because of his mother's danger.

"I'm sorry," she breathed, and she said it sympathetically, the way Frances Vaughan would have said it! "She's a brave woman. I will pray that God protect her."

"Lucy!" he said again, almost desperately as he drank in her sympathy. He kissed her, then, timidly at first, and then when she didn't resist, again and again.

She heard someone coming out of the church and she drew away from him. Someone was watching them from the church door! When Charles became aware of it, too, he whispered in her ear. "Lucy, can you come to Exeter tomorrow? Someone has come for me. I'm sure that I won't be able to come here again, tomorrow."

"Yes," Lucy found herself saying, "I'll be there." How she could manage she didn't know but if he wished it she would get there somehow!

A tall nobleman with a scarlet cloak swinging from his shoulders and a plumed hat held in his gloved hand stood looking at them in surprise.

"Your Highness," he said sternly, "we have been worried about you."

"Very well, Arthur. I will be with you in a moment. Go back into the church and wait for me there."

Lord Capel glanced at Lucy disapprovingly, bowed to the Prince, and went inside.

"They guard me every moment," Charles said. "I know they have to but I get so tired of being watched!"

"I know, for I am watched, too, and I hate it—I like to do what I want to do! It must be much worse for you."

"I will have to go, now, but tomorrow——at St. Peter's in Exeter," he whispered. "I shall be waiting."

As they started to walk toward the door which opened into the transept—from behind a clump of

13

bushes walked Lucy's spaniel, Salvatore, and following him was Charles' little bitch.

"Oh, sir," Lucy said, "I'm sorry!"

"Is it your spaniel?"

She nodded.

He laughed. "It doesn't matter," he said. "Not important at all!"

He left her then, and rode away with the soldiers.

He dreamed about her that night. In the middle of it he woke suddenly and sat up in his bed in the quarters that had been assigned to him in the Deanery at Exeter. He reconstructed his meeting with her in the churchyard and remembered what they had said.

"Not important at all," he had said, and he meant the mating of the spaniels!

Maybe she would think that it was her visit that was not important. If she did she surely wouldn't come to Exeter. If only she could know how important it was to him that he see her again! Her violet eyes with the long lashes captivated him. Her skin was like ivory and her hair black—curly like his—and such a gentle spirit—not imperious and demanding like the ladies at court—and not rough and dirty like the women that followed the army!

The Prince had no cause for worry. Lucy was up at sunrise, restlessly waiting for the household to waken. She didn't dare leave the house until after morning prayers, and she must ask her grandmother's permission even then. She had been severely reprimanded for going off alone without telling anyone, the day before. If anything went wrong today a servant would be sent to find her; she would be brought back, punished, and confined to her room until she promised not to disobey again. But, she must go to Exeter! The Prince commanded it, and she wanted to go more than anything she had ever wanted.

At last the gong sounded for morning prayers. The

Chappells were Presbyterians and the exhortations of Nicholas Chappell were long and detailed; this morning they seemed interminable! Lucy squirmed in her chair until her grandmother frowned at her.

Nicholas had scarcely got his breath after a long "Amen" when Lucy asked permission to ride with Justus to Bamfylde Park. Since Mrs. Chappell was an ardent horsewoman herself, and believed that a canter in the fresh morning air would cure anything, especially a case of "female fidgets," she gave her permission at once, and without any questions. But Justus was not so agreeable. Lucy had whispered to him the night before that she wanted him to ride to Exeter with her.

"Exeter?" he had exclaimed in surprise. "We're not allowed to go any place like that!"

Lucy laughed at him but she had to listen to his objections. "We might lose our way," he said, "and Grandfather might send someone to find us, and we'll be punished! I don't like to be whipped," he whined. "Besides," he said, as the crowning point of his argument, "Exeter will be filled with soldiers!"

"Maybe," Lucy agreed.

"What do you want to ride to Exeter for, anyway?"

"I want to go to St. Peter's Cathedral, and you must go with me."

That was too much for Justus. Lucy was always going to church! "Are you going to see someone there—a famous churchman or something? Why can't you just go to church in Broadclyst?"

Lucy said, then, what she knew would vanquish him. "I must go—don't ask any more questions—but if you won't go with me I shall go alone!"

He knew that she meant what she said. He would have to go with her!

When they had Mrs. Chappell's permission to ride to Bamfylde Park they started out in the fresh morning air. They rode through the gates of Brockhill and onto the road to Broadclyst. When they reached the gates of Bamfylde Park Justus began protesting again.

"That's where Grandmother told us we could go," he said and he scowled fiercely at Lucy's back when she paid no attention to him and rode straight ahead.

Soon the road became very narrow with ditches on either side and steep-banked hedges, fragrant with honeysuckle tangled in their branches.

"Put on your cloak," Justus said. "It's damp."

She knew that Justus liked to think he was taking care of her. So, she put on the black cloak with a large hood that could be pulled up over her head and arranged to mask her face.

Justus didn't seem to be able to talk about anything but what would happen if they encountered a party of soldiers, royal or rebel. Since the countryside was full of both he had reason to be alarmed.

"What will we do if we meet soldiers?" he kept asking.

Finally she said, "I shall give a false name, and say that I am going to visit a sick relative in Exeter."

"Hmn, and who is it that we are going to see?"

She didn't answer, and Justus' attention was distracted because they were entering the town of Broadclyst. As they passed the church Justus stiffened with alarm because he saw two horses tied to the hitching post. They rode on only a little further before they heard the sound of horses behind them. There was no doubt about it—they were being followed—and there was no hope of escape.

"Keep close to me," Lucy said. She didn't alter the pace but rode steadily on. Soon, two men dressed as cavaliers drew up alongside of them.

"Madame," one of them said, "where are you going?"

"To visit a sick relative," she answered coldly, "and what right have you to ask?"

The man smirked. A sick relative indeed! The creature was charming. No wonder the Prince fell for her! "Is your name Lucy?"

She didn't answer so he said softly and persuasively as if it were a secret password, "Lucy, we have been sent to escort you to church—to St. Peter's."

"Very well," she said thoughtfully. "We'll go with you."

After that the two men fell back a little behind Justus and Lucy. It was as if they were guards that had no intention of letting their prisoner escape.

They rode in silence until they saw the great rounded towers of the South Gate of Exeter and the transeptal towers of St. Peter's, beyond. Then one of the officers told Lucy that they were going to enter the town and follow South Street to the Deanery. He included Justus in a careless jerk of his head and Justus frowned at the insult. He was more angry than frightened now.

Everywhere there were sentries armed with muskets, and on the highest tower of Bedford House the King's Royal Standard was flying. Justus saw Lucy look up to the tower of Rougemont Castle and he looked, too. Rougemont was the seat of the Duke of Cornwall, one of Prince Charles' lands and titles. His Standard was flying aloft. Justus' frown turned into a belligerent scowl. Charles Stuart was in residence and he had something to do with this strange journey!

They rode almost to the end of Bear Street and when the Chantry was just ahead they were told to halt and dismount. Soldiers took the horses and the officers led the way into the Hall of the Deanery.

Lucy looked up at the arch-braced ceiling with its delicate finials and, trying to distract his attention, said to Justus, "It's beautiful, isn't it?"

Justus didn't answer or look up. His face was scarlet and he clenched his teeth and opened and shut his hands convulsively.

17

A servant took Lucy's cloak and told her that she was to go into the chapel. Justus started to follow but the servant stopped him. "Good sir," the man said, "be so good as to wait here. Your sister will be back soon."

Lucy nodded to Justus in a way that he knew meant that he would have to do it. Then she went into the chapel, and just before the door closed Justus caught a glimpse of the Prince waiting for her. After that, there was nothing he could do but collapse helplessly on the bench that was offered to him.

Charles was over six feet tall. He was only fourteen but he had already reached his full height, and he had the sinewy appearance of an accomplished athlete: his shoulders were broad and his body slender. His features were coarse: his nose was large and the lips of his big mouth were full and sensual. More than that, his skin was swarthy and roughened by weather. He was dressed in tawny velvet and his heavy, black hair had been carefully arranged.

Lucy curtsied. "It was at your command, sir, that I came."

Charles smiled and held out his hand, a little hesitatingly because he was not sure of her meaning. Had she been offended by what he said the day before? Had she come only because he commanded it? Was that what she meant? And that formal curtsy—! Why that again? Was she that naive?

She didn't look at him directly but with a sidelong glance from under the fringe of her lashes when he put his arm around her shoulders and leaned forward to look into her eyes. He put his hand under her chin and made her look at him. After studying her face for a few seconds he led her into a small room adjoining the chapel.

"This is my home for the present," he said.

"All of Wales is yours, isn't it, Your Highness? You are Prince of Wales!"

"Yes, and that's about all that's left," he said. "The whole of the North was lost in the Battle at Marston Moor. Only the West remains loyal—but let's forget all about that," he said softly. "Let's think about us."

He took her hand into his large brown one. He stroked it, and then drew her to him and kissed her. Her head only reached his shoulder and she could feel his heart pounding in his chest as he held her tightly against him. She trembled because it was a new experience for her when he slid his hand down her arm and touched the roundness of her breast.

Then—someone pounded on the door. The Prince released her with a shrug of his shoulders and went to the door and jerked it open. Lucy could see a messenger with an orange battle-scarf tucked into his lace collar. She heard him say, "Urgent—from the King." Then seeing her, he lowered his voice to a whisper. Charles stepped outside and pulled the door closed behind him. He was back again in a moment.

"It's from His Majesty," he said when the door was shut again. "I must go immediately, but there will be other—many other days, dear Lucy."

He embraced her and held her close, putting his hand behind her head. He kissed her hard on the mouth, again and again. Then he lowered his head and kissed her throat. The perfume on his dark hair filled her nostrils. She put her cheek against his head.

"I must go," he said frantically. "But when I return I shall send for you as I did today."

"How can I be sure that a messenger is from you?"

Charles removed a ring from his finger. It was a circlet of gold, fashioned to resemble a golden cord tied into a bow-knot. The loops were set with diamonds and at the place which should have been the center of the knot, was the Prince's seal.

"This ring will be recognized by anyone of my

court," he said. "If all else fails you can use it to come to me when I send for you."

He hesitated and then said, "I will send the same officer if possible—and he will have the password—that which I thought of today. 'Come to church.' It's a good one, I think."

She nodded.

He thought a moment and then added, "Put the ring on a chain and wear it always out of sight."

He went to a jewel case and took out a long chain. He slipped the ring on it and put it around Lucy's neck and fastened the clasp. Then he dropped the ring into the bosom of her dress and crushed her to him before he kissed her, again, hard upon the lips and let her go.

"Go to your brother," he said hoarsely. "The guards will take you back to Broadclyst. As soon as possible I will be back." He led her into the Chapel and watched her go through the door to the Great Hall where Justus was waiting.

Justus sat where he had been commanded to wait. He had hardly moved and his teeth were clenched and his face red with rage. He stood up, glared at Lucy and roughly put the cloak on her shoulders. She looked at him in surprise but he said nothing as he followed her to the horses waiting for them in Bear Street. Lucy was silent, too, as they rode between the two officers back to Broadclyst where the guards left them in front of the church where they had found them.

Justus made a snarling sound between his clenched teeth when he saw one of the guards give Lucy an insolently appraising look. The officers took off their plumed hats without dismounting and with exaggerated courtesy. Then they put spur to their horses and were off.

Lucy led the way along the road to Brockhill but when they reached the lane that led to Bamfylde Park

Justus moved his horse up beside hers and grabbed the reins and turned him.

"Justus!" Lucy cried in alarm. She had never seen him so angry.

"We are going to Poltimore—to the Park at Bamfylde, where we said we were going. Remember? I want to talk to you and the Park will be a good place."

Lucy didn't answer as her horse followed his. She had reason to be surprised because she was used to having Justus do whatever she wanted him to do. When they were well into the Park he jumped off his horse and told her to dismount.

"Sit down," he ordered, when he had selected a dry spot under a tree for her. He paced back and forth in front of her, and he didn't seem to know how to begin. She watched him, amazed.

"Never do that again," he blurted out, "or I will kill him!"

Lucy gasped.

"Never ask me to take you on such a mission again! If you want to be a slut and steal into a man's room don't ask me to take you!" He stopped for he was close to bursting into tears. "My own sister—," he went on when he got control, "my own sister, no better than Kate in the kitchen!"

A blush crept over Lucy's face. Her eyes, with the voluptuous shadows under them, widened and her mouth drew into a pained little line. So that was what her brother thought!

"Oh, no!" Lucy said. "Oh, no, Justus, it wasn't like that!"

"Yes it was!" Justus cried out.

"He loves me," Lucy murmured. "I know he does." She touched the lace on the bosom of her dress and felt the ring where it lay between her firm little breasts.

Justus sank down on the grass beside her. "Fool! Fool!" he hissed. He sprang up again because he couldn't speak calmly sitting down. "Are you just plain stupid or are you fooling yourself? Think! Think! Think about what he did and what it was leading up to!"

Lucy looked up at him pathetically. Her eyes filled with tears. She didn't know what had happened with the Prince. She was very confused. He had been so wonderful. His kisses were so fervent!

"Answer me—what do you think Charles Stuart, the King's son, intends to do?"

The tears filling her eyes overflowed and ran down her cheeks. She let them go without brushing them away. "I don't know," she said helplessly.

"If you really don't know what's going on," he said, "you ought to realize that you should be careful about what you let him do. The Prince can do whatever he wants to and, because he is the King's son, no one can stop him or punish him. I would have to kill him—and I would!"

Horror filled her eyes. "Oh, no, Justus," she murmured. Her voice trembled, she turned pale and sobbed convulsively.

Justus softened. "Poor Lucy," he thought. "She doesn't know what she's doing or getting into!" He sighed. He didn't know, himself, really. He didn't care for girls but he had heard the men and boys at the stables talk and they said plenty—they bragged about the women they had laid in the straw and most of the boys were married—even those who were only fourteen. The Prince was fourteen, the same as he and Lucy. He knew what he was doing, all right. Charles was a grown man and had been around more than he and Lucy.

Helpless anger engulfed him again. "I'll tell you what he intends to do—he intends to lay you in the straw." That was the only way he knew how to express what he meant—and not use the vulgar words that he heard in the stables.

Lucy sat quietly until she had control of her tears and

then she smiled at him. "Justus, I don't think that what you are telling me about the Prince is the way it is. But—if it is, it's wrong, I know that! I promise that I will never permit such a thing to happen, and I know that the only thing to do is to stay completely away from His Highness—or at least never be in his presence alone." She stopped and was thoughtful. Was it wrong? She didn't know. Besides, maybe Charles really loved her!

Lucy and Justus had to stay at Brockhill all through the hot month of August. Lucy went to church in Broadclyst almost every day, and at first Justus insisted on going with her. As the days passed nothing happened. There were never any soldiers waiting outside of the church. At last Justus relaxed his vigilance. Besides, Lucy had convinced him that she saw things his way. She had come to her senses was the way he thought of it. By the beginning of September she was always alone. Justus had found other things to occupy him besides waiting for Lucy sitting in the church meditating—or whatever she was doing, as he put it.

The honeysuckle faded, the tall foxgloves began shedding their purple bells over the red soil of the hedgerow banks; it was autumn again. One morning when Lucy rode into the market square at Broadclyst she heard the townspeople saying that the King's Standard was flying over Bedford House, and that Exeter was full of the King's soldiers. The campaign in Wales was over. His Majesty was probably on the way back to his headquarters in Oxford!

Lucy's heart beat faster but she tried to be calm. She went into the church and kneeled to pray but she couldn't keep her mind on the prayer book. The words blurred and her thoughts strayed. What if the Prince sent for her that very morning? She was confused again! If only Frances Vaughan were there! She knew that she could talk to her—and then she would know whether she should see the Prince or not. But, how she longed to see him! She had a poignant memory of the perfume on his hair when he kissed her throat!

What if there were officers waiting for her when she went outside? Should she refuse to go with them? If she did that it would be the end of it, wouldn't it, unless the Prince came to her? But did she want it to end? Or would it be all right to go and see the Prince, once more, if she went back to Brockhill and insisted that Justus go with her? No, Justus would only be unreasonable! If she went it would be better to go alone, Yes, she knew she simply had to see the Prince again, if only to explain! She would go!

She went out of the church and was disappointed to find that there were no horses tied outside and no officers waiting for her. Maybe Charles didn't want to see her again! The longing to see him was excruciating. She couldn't think of anything because of her disappointment. Softly, she began to cry.

She mounted her horse and slowly turned him to go back to Brockhill. Then she saw two officers of the Prince's cavalry coming toward her, riding hard, on the road from Exeter. She recognized one of them as the officer that had come for her the first time. "Hugh," his companion called him.

"Madame," he said pulling up his horse and removing his hat cermoniously, "again I have come to fetch you. Come to church."

She recoiled at his playful tone. Was he disrespectful? She was so uncertain that she said the first thing that came into her mind in order to gain time to think. "Will you promise that my horse will be ready for me so that I may be back by midday? I must be back!"

"Anything you say, my lady."

The junior officer rolled his eyes and raised his eyebrows as the two riders fell in, one on each side of her. His superior frowned and shook his head; Lucy didn't notice. Cynical smiles passed over her head as she nodded that she would go and they started off. She was thinking about what she would tell Charles—memorizing the words that she must say to him—if what Justus said was true—or on the other hand if she were right—and he did love her! Beyond that her thoughts could not go. Vaguely, she thought that she must tell him that she would not see him again.

The ride was a silent one and at last they halted in Bear Street and dismounted, as on the first trip. Her horse was taken and she was ushered into the Deanery. This time the Prince, himself, waited for her in the Great Hall. He stood before a fire in the fireplace and the shadow of his tall figure flickered on the arch-braced ceiling above.

She tried to curtsy to him but he took her arm immediately, drew her close to him, and walked with her through the chapel to the small room beyond.

"I have something to show you," he said.

He led her into a sleeping apartment and pointed to a large wicker basket in one corner of the room. His spaniel lay on a silken cushion and all about her were five puppies, three black and two golden, their eyes not yet open.

Lucy looked at Charles. "In the churchyard?"

Charles nodded.

"Oh, Your Highness," Lucy said, "my spaniel is their father. I am sorry."

"I'm not," Charles said, as he shut the door. "They are beautiful puppies. It was a good mating!"

She looked up at him and her eyes filled with tears, "Yes," she whispered.

He took her in his arms and she did not resist. She forgot all about what she had convinced herself that she must say. He kissed her eyes, her mouth, her throat. Then he picked her up and carried her to his big bed.

It was first love for Lucy but for Charles—it was mostly amazement that he found that she was a virgin!

Again, someone came, knocked on the door and told Charles that His Majesty wanted to see him immediately.

"I must go," he told Lucy, as before, "but when I can—I will send for you, again."

Almost perfunctorily he summoned the officers that had brought her and sent them on their way back to Broadclyst where they left her in front of the church, the same as the first time.

Slowly, Lucy rode back toward Brockhill. She was lonely, frightened and confused. She felt humiliated by the Prince's behavior—she really couldn't be sure that Charles loved her. Maybe Justus was right. What was going to happen to her? She felt as if she had no home at all—no place that she "belonged."

There were so many things she didn't understand. It had been that way ever since Mother petitioned the House of Lords for a divorce from Father when she and Justus were eight years old. After that, they had been shunted back and forth between relatives. It all depended on who had the temporary custody of them—Mother or Father. Sometimes they lived with Father's mother and stepfather, the Chappells, and sometimes they were with Mother's cousin, the Earl of Carberry and his wife, Frances, at Golden Grove in Carmarthenshire.

If it weren't for Frances Vaughan she would think that there was nothing in the world but evil and hatred! Frances was an image of hope and love and patience. Her husband was becoming impoverished because of his loyalty to the King but she never complained and she was always ready to help other people. Some of the visitors that came to Golden Grove needed to have their battle wounds tended, some to hide from pursuers and some just to have their spirits buoyed up. Everyone was welcome and Frances was always serene. If she could do something for someone who was ill, wounded, or just afraid, she helped them joyfully.

Mother was different. She pointed out the worst in everybody, sometimes to them, and sometimes she just gossiped about them. There was more to it than that. Mother was so critical of people of loose morals. She constantly warned Lucy that she must not get "involved" with men until it was time to marry one of them. She must never let one of them "put his hands on her." Whatever did she mean? Then—what was Mother doing—sometimes—when she stayed so long in the summer house out in the apple orchard at Golden Grove with Thomas Byshfield? The door was always locked, and Mother wouldn't answer nor open the door when she knocked. Once when she was waiting, Richard Vaughan, the Earl's son, and Thom Howard, a visitor at Golden Grove came upon her sitting forlornly on the grass—waiting and wondering.

"Making love under the apple tree, oh, yes, oh, yes," Thom Howard jeered, pointing to the summer house with a leer.

"Oh, come on," Richard Vaughan had said, seeing Lucy's distress, "stop showing off, Thom. It's none of your business." He dragged Thom off but not before Lucy had burst into tears.

Once she had seen Thomas Byshfield kiss her mother in a way that shocked Frances when she asked her about it. She blushed and avoided answering Lucy's question. Why wouldn't she answer?

And Father! He almost never paid any attention to her. Sometimes, she thought he looked at her as if he hated her. Once, she heard him say, when he was quarreling with Mother, "They're not my children," referring to Justus and her, "they're your brats!" She had explained it to herself by thinking that he meant they were like Mother, and not him. But is that what he meant? Whenever she thought about it she felt anxious and miserable. Why would Father say that they were not his children? It would be so nice to have a loving father!

Lucy left her horse at the stable and walked slowly into the house. She must have had a stricken expression because Justus didn't ask any questions about where she had been. He just stared at her. Did she look different? Surely she did—because she felt different. She would never be quite the same again.

The next day the King and his army moved on in the direction of Oxford and Charles went with him. He didn't see Lucy again but he sent a messenger to the church in Broadclyst with a packet for the sexton to deliver to Lucy the next time she came into the church.

Lucy opened the packet with trembling fingers and found a pendant of one large pearl on a golden chain. A note said only, "To remember one perfect moment."

She stared at the pendant. "One perfect moment"—not to be repeated, or to be repeated at His Highness' pleasure. Was that what he meant? Her mind went blank for a moment then she said to herself, "Justus was right after all."

She felt terribly ashamed. She resolved not to let anyone know what had happened—especially Justus. She would remove the pearl from its setting, and hide it and the ring in her clothing to be worn at all times. She could sell them if she were ever in need! She tried to be vindictive but she couldn't. She was only sad and miserable as if she had been cheated or tricked when she really wanted to feel happy about the way her meeting Prince Charles had turned out.

The days dragged by and she thought almost constantly about the Prince. How she longed to see him! It would be so much easier if he were just an ordinary boy, and not the King's son. But in spite of the doubts about Charles and his intentions—she loved him, she told herself, and she would never love anyone else.

2

While Lucy went on living her dreary life at Brockhill, Charles was with his father at the King's headquarters in Oxford. The war had reached a crucial stage. Oliver Cromwell, a military genius who called himself "Liberator", as dictators usually do, had risen out of the New Movement, the name given to the people's longing for justice which had caused one riot after another in industrialized London Town. Cromwell's armies moved toward Oxford in a pincer movement and there was danger that the town would fall and the King captured.

His Majesty decided to send Charles to a safer place so that the heir to the throne would not be captured, too. He appointed Edward Hyde, his most able councilor, to take the Prince to Bristol, set up a court there, and keep a tight rein on the young man.

Lucy knew none of this, of course, for Charles never sent a letter or any other message to her. She excused his silence with imagined reasons and as she went miserably through the meager Christmas observances at Brockhill she thought of him constantly and longed to see him again.

The winter was very cold but in February of the new year the holly bushes withered and the "lamb's tails" began to swing on the hazel bushes. The streams were late in thawing and the primroses did not appear, even in the sheltered hedgerows, until the riverbanks were yellow with "Lent lilies."

Lucy was pale and thin: the shadows had deepened under her eyes and she rarely smiled. At the first signs of spring Mrs. Chappell insisted that she go outdoors and ride. It would restore her vitality, the ardent horsewoman said. One day late in March, Lucy obeyed somewhat listlessly. There was really nothing else to do. She mounted her horse and, taking her little spaniel with her, set off in the direction of Broadclyst. She didn't ask Justus to go with her for she knew that she couldn't keep from being irritable with him—and he would be hurt.

Occupied with her daydreams of balls, handsome cavaliers—and Charles Stuart—she didn't realize that she was being followed until four horsemen surrounded her on a desolate stretch of road. She tried to rein her horse and turn so she could ride through them and head for Brockhill; but one of the men caught hold of her horse's bridle and prevented her from doing so.

She knew that it was useless to scream. No one would hear her. Who were these horsemen? They were dressed as officers of the King's cavalry; but did they come from the Prince? They gave no indication that they knew the password, "Come to church." If they did not give that password, she thought, there would be no reason to trust them. When they reached Broadclyst she would cry out for help at the first opportunity.

The opportunity never came. Before they reached the town one of the men took the bridle of her horse and led him into a narrow lane. The ditches on either side, between the high banks and the road, were deep and half-filled with water. The branches of the trees growing on the banks had spread and met overhead. There was no hope of escape. It was as if they were riding in a tunnel.

Lucy's heart pounded. Salvatore, sensing her terror, began to bark.

"Who are you, and where are you taking me?"

The man riding ahead half-turned in his saddle and looked at her.

"To Bridgwater, ma'am," he said.

They avoided the question of who sent them.

Salvatore barked louder and louder. The man riding at Lucy's side said gruffly, "You'll have to silence the dog, ma'am, or we'll leave him behind."

Lucy stroked Salvatore's head and spoke soothingly to him. By the time she had quieted him they were riding out of the lane onto a thoroughfare. There were many thatched cottages on the hills of the countryside and Lucy tried to remember if she had ever seen any of them before. Had she been over this road at some time? It was a little like the road to Taunton, over which she had travelled several times—and which did go in the direction of Bridgwater, she thought, but she could not be sure. After they had travelled for several hours they came upon a coach waiting at the side of the road. Lucy knew it was of the type that was for hire in London. The men pulled up their horses, dismounted, and helped Lucy from hers. They told her to get into the coach.

"You may keep the dog," one of them said, "but you must keep him quiet." His voice was firm but not unfriendly.

The coach lurched ahead. Lucy was numb with fright and despair. What were they going to do with her? She didn't have anything of value except the pearl and Charles' ring. Did they know about that—and were they robbers? Or, was it time to use it? No—if they were highwaymen they might kill her and leave her by the side of the road. And yet, it could not be a casual holdup because of the waiting coach. Who had ordered it? She watched the scenery as they rode on and on, and at last she was sure that they were riding north.

"Bridgwater," they said. Had her mother arranged for her to be taken to Carmarthen—away from Father?

Her heart beat faster when she thought of that possibility. But why had they taken her without Justus if that were the case? She sobbed softly as she thought of being alone and unprotected. If only Justus were with her!

She was hungry and tired and cold when the coach stopped at sundown. She could see an inn ahead of them. One of the men left them and rode ahead. He returned with bread, cold meat and a pitcher of wine. He handed them in to Lucy. She ate and gave some of the meat to Salvatore. Then he watched her drink the wine with his little tongue hanging out and she knew that he was thirsty. Since there was no water she gave him some, too, and then they both fell asleep.

When she woke the sun was high overhead and the coach was still jerking along. They had travelled all night, she thought with alarm. They must be a long way from home! She had slept soundly—they must have put something in the wine, she thought. She parted the curtains of the coach and saw that they were still on a main thoroughfare. The country was wooded and flat and they seemed to be approaching a large town for she saw smoke rising from many chimneys. Soon they entered through a town gate and passed a square. The horses pulling the carriage clattered over a heavy stone bridge with triple arches and she caught a glimpse of a quai and the towers of a castle. Then she saw men getting water for their horses from a cistern which was in the top of a market cross. Only one place had such a cistern. There was no doubt about it. They were in Bridgwater. The horses were halted at the edge of a wide deep moat which surrounded the fortified castle.

"Yes," she said to herself, "the moat at Bridgwater fills and empties with the tide."

The coach door was opened and a tall cavalier helped her to the ground. She thought that she recognized him but she couldn't be sure, because he looked at her blankly as if he had never seen her before. Had the Prince sent for her? She had a momentary flash of joy—but then it subsided to a dull, aching fear. What was going to happen to her?

She was taken through the water gate into the castle yard, and she looked up at the towers. There were no flags unfurled anywhere. Her heart sank. That meant that no member of the royal family was in residence! A tall, blond woman stood in the doorway of the residence nearest the gate, and she came forward to Lucy as she was led into the castle yard.

"I am Anne Harvey," the woman said.

Lucy liked Mrs. Harvey, at once. Here, at last, was a ray of hope. "Madame," she said. "Why have I been brought here?"

"Come in, my dear," Mrs. Harvey said gently, "Come into my house. You must be weary and frightened."

Lucy burst into tears, and Mrs. Harvey put her arms around her and led her through the door.

"My dear, I can't tell you why you are here because I don't know."

Lucy sobbed convulsively.

"I know your mother, Lucy. My husband is a cousin of Dr. Harvey who knows all your mother's family, especially Frances Vaughan and the Earl."

"Has my mother arranged for me to be taken to Frances Vaughan, and stolen me away so my father would not find out about it?"

"No," Mrs. Harvey said, drawing her brows together in a frown. "It was Mrs. Wyndham, the Governor's wife, who sent for you. I was told only this morning that they were bringing you here; and I was asked to receive you in my house."

"Mrs. Wyndham? She doesn't know me. Why would she have had me abducted?"

"I don't know."

"Mrs. Wyndham? Mrs. Wyndham?" Lucy tried to

think of where she had heard of Mrs. Wyndham. "Of course! Christabella Wyndham of Bridgwater, the nurse-governess from Wales who took care of Prince Charles when he was a baby." She had heard of her when they lived in London.

"Yes," Mrs. Harvey said drily, "and never for one moment does she let anyone forget it!"

Lucy felt only despair. What was going to happen to her? Did all this have something to do with Prince Charles? She could not believe that he would have had her brought to him in this way. Yet, she had recognized one of the Prince's officers in the castle yard, she thought, but she couldn't be sure. She felt that she was in some sort of great danger and she shivered.

"You are chilled, aren't you, my dear?" Mrs. Harvey led her into a room warmed by a fire and summoned a servant to take care of her. Her hair was combed and a gown of yellow satin laid out for her. After she was dressed, Mrs. Harvey came to her again and said, "Mrs. Wyndham has sent a servant to take you to her. Will you go?"

"Do I have a choice?" Mrs. Harvey had been kind to her, Lucy said to herself, but she was trusting no one!

Mrs. Harvey looked distressed at the abrupt remark. She waited a moment and then said, "I don't think that you have anything to fear, Lucy." She lowered her voice so the servant could not hear. "Christabella Wyndham is a foolish woman, but she isn't evil. I don't know what this is all about but if you need help you can trust me. My husband owns the castle and leases it to the Governor—and we have influence. Go now, but remember, we are here."

"I am ready," Lucy said, close to tears. "And thank you, Madame, for your kindness."

Lucy went with the servant out into the castle yard and stood transfixed because of the confusion that she saw there. Officers with swords were stamping about in

35

their cavalry boots directing the disposition of horses and packs from horses. She looked up to the thick castle walls and saw that soldiers were manning the cannons in the crenelated embattlements but there was no sign of action. It was not an attack! She looked up to the domed towers of the castle and as she watched—on the uppermost tower was unfurled a standard that she knew was that of the Prince of Wales. It was probably being raised by the Governor out of courtesy to His Highness. Prince Charles was in residence!

Mrs. Wyndham received Lucy in one of the rooms of the Governor's quarters. Tapestries on the stone walls and on the floor did little to relieve the austereness of the room. A fire in the great fireplace absorbed only a little of the chill from the dank air of the sturdy old castle.

Christabella Wyndham was a heavy woman with a low forehead. Her eyebrows were heavy and black and her dark hair, that she wore pulled back from her face, had a white streak in it. It gave her a sort of cat-like expression, Lucy thought. At Mrs. Wyndham's side stood the mysterious cavalier who had been in the castle yard. A mocking smile played upon his handsome face. He had only pretended not to recognize her, Lucy thought. He was one of the officers that had twice taken her to Exeter from Broadclyst to see the Prince.

"I am Christabella Wyndham, my dear," the woman said. Her black eyes travelled appraisingly over Lucy, from head to toe, and she seemed immensely pleased by what she saw. She nodded to the cavalier. "And this is my son, Hugh Wyndham," she said.

Hugh Wyndham! Hugh Wyndham, who knew of her two visits to Exeter! What could it mean? Lucy dropped her eyes in confusion. Was it Charles, after all, that was responsible for this trickery? She was about to turn and run desperately to Mrs. Harvey—to ask her to take her to a ship at the quai—so she could go to Car-

36

marthen—to Frances Vaughan or to her mother. Her mother? How would she feel about all this? Maybe she would be delighted with her daughter's having attracted the Prince!

Her mother had warned her so often to be careful— to use all her charms for one purpose only—to make a suitable marriage. But was she, herself, so chaste? It was not only the garden house in the apple orchard at Golden Grove, where the door was locked when Lucy tried to go to her mother. There were times when she was locked in a room alone with some friend of Alfred Gwinne's, too, and Father had accused her of repeated adultery. Then, there was Mother's cousin, Thomas Byshfield, the famous swordsman, always in attendance. And Mother wore a miniature portrait of him in a locket. Maybe she would be pleased with her daughter for making an alliance with the King's son, even an immoral one, she thought angrily. Maybe marriage wasn't so necessary as she insisted! She checked herself. What wicked thoughts and at a time like this! She had a wobbly feeling as if the ground were swaying under her. She was helpless! The Prince—she almost hated him! Yet, she still couldn't believe that he would do such a thing as order her abduction.

Christabella broke into her thoughts. "My dear, you look like a frightened bird—and the loveliest one that I have ever seen." Her broad mouth parted into a sensual smile. She looked sidewise at her son. "We understand, don't we?"

He nodded and looked boldly at Lucy.

"My son has told me of your visits to the Prince—!"

Lucy cried out in dismay but Mrs. Wyndham would not let her say anything. "The Prince doesn't keep secrets from me, his old nurse," she said.

Lucy looked from mother to son. What had these two done? She was convinced, now, that Charles didn't have anything to do with it.

"My dear," Christabella went on, "you need not be frightened. We were sure that you would guess that we were helping things along when we had you brought here. You can count on us to be discreet."

Lucy lifted her eyes and studied Mrs. Wyndham. "Discreet! About what?" she said angrily.

"The Prince, as you know, has very little of what normal boys should have," Christabella said, and her full mouth, with its moustached upper lip, pulled into a half-stubborn pout and her black eyes flashed. "He is under the iron thumb of that fat Edward Hyde, who has no heart—no mind for anything but business—business—business! Even a King's son should have some fun! Fortunately, Hyde is not with His Highness—but will undoubtedly come later. He will follow as soon as possible—to stick his nose in everything that goes on."

"Did His Highness command you to send for me?" Lucy's heart pounded and she didn't know whether it was because she hoped that he had or that he hadn't!

"Lordy no," Mrs. Wyndham laughed. "He doesn't know a thing about it yet. I don't have to be told what to do—nor do I have to be hit over the head with a three-legged stool to know what the boy would like. Was I not his nurse-governess?" Pride puffed out her large bosom.

This was worse than anything that Lucy had imagined. The Prince didn't know that she was there. Maybe he didn't even want to see her! That stupid, meddling woman! Mrs. Harvey was correct. Mrs. Wyndham was just plain foolish!

"There's no harm in it," Mrs. Wyndham pouted. "I merely helped things along. Hugh said it would please the Prince, so I sent for you."

Tears sprang to Lucy's eyes. No harm in it except that her life could be ruined. Mrs. Wyndham hadn't given a thought about that apparently! Her grandparents would never believe that she had not run away of her own accord.

Mrs. Wyndham thought that she guessed the reason for Lucy's distress. "We will see that you are safely returned to your home in Broadclyst when the Prince wishes you to go."

"When the Prince wishes me to go, indeed," Lucy said to herself. Where could she go—who would protect her? Was she utterly ruined?

"Come with me, my dear," Mrs. Wyndham said. She took Lucy by the hand and ignoring the fact that she recoiled from her touch, led her into another apartment. Hugh knocked upon the door of an inner room and pushed it open. There stood Prince Charles, and a look of amazement spread over his dark face when he saw Lucy.

He has changed, Lucy thought. He is a man and yet he is only sixteen! His bearing was, indeed, that of a man of affairs; he had seen battles won and lost and he had learned to take responsibilities that his father could no longer meet. With it all there was a wistful expression in his dark eyes, as if he regretted his lost childhood! And it was that wistfulness that made Lucy say to herself that she loved him—she couldn't help it—she loved him! She knew that her face was flushing from her strong emotion and she kept her eyes down so that he could not look into them.

"Lucy, my darling," he said, as he went to her with his long arms outstretched, "you have come to me."

How wonderful to be in his arms again, pressed close to him! Again and again he kissed her. Then he released her and held her at arm's length and murmured, "My beautiful Lucy—you have come to me when I need you more than ever—when so much depends upon me and I am so alone!"

Mrs. Wyndham smiled. She signaled Hugh to follow her, and they left the room.

"Your Highness," Lucy said, "I didn't come to you of my own free will."

Charles stepped back and looked at her in amazement.

"What?" he asked savagely. "You didn't come here because you wanted to come?"

"No," she said. Her eyes filled with tears. Her cheeks burned as she thought of their last meeting and the note that Charles had sent her. She wouldn't tell him how much she loved him until she knew how he really felt about her!

Charles studied her face with a mixture of disappointment and disbelief. "What happened?"

"Four men, your officers, I think," Lucy began slowly, "surprised me as I rode through the gate at Brockhill, my grandmother's home in Broadclyst, and forced me to go with them."

"Did they harm you?" His black eyes flashed.

"No, sir," she said. "They had a coach waiting on the road to Taunton. I think that they gave me a sleeping potion because I slept all the way to Bridgwater."

"Thank God for that," he said, and then he paced up and down the room.

"Who would do such a thing?" he muttered. "Even Ned Villiers didn't find out about you."

"Mrs. Wyndham," Lucy said.

"Mrs. Wyndham? Christabella Wyndham?" He was astonished. "She knew nothing about you!"

And yet—he stopped—his thoughts raced back to the secret letter he had received from her. She had sent a rider with a letter that was received by Mrs. Fanshawe, his private secretary's wife. He had realized that by persuading Mrs. Fanshawe to deliver the letter to her husband she was circumventing Edward Hyde! They all tried to do that, he thought grimly. For once Richard Fanshawe had passed it on to him without opening it. He was probably tired of Hyde's incessant vigilance, too! So, Mrs. Wyndham had escaped the watchful eyes of Edward Hyde—Charles smiled in spite of himself. His old nurse was irrepressible! Even his discerning secretary had been duped. He, himself, was getting a little tired of being under the constant surveillance of Edward Hyde and he had deliberately read the letter and threw it into the fire without telling Sir Richard what was in it. And the next morning he had announced that he was making a trip to Bridgwater without asking anybody's advice—and certainly not letting Edward Hyde know why he was going. After all, he was a grown man, now! The expression on Hyde's face was worth the blow for freedom, he thought.

"A surprise," Christabella had written, "a surprise when you come." The surprise was Lucy! How could she have known about Lucy? He sat down upon a bench and put his head in his hands. Then he sprang up—"Hugh—Hugh Wyndham!" He groaned. He began pacing again, and after a while he stopped and put his hands on Lucy's shoulders and looked down into her eyes.

"Lucy, my dear, I'm sorry. I am fast learning to trust no man beyond his own interest! Wyndham, the fool, thinks he can ingratiate himself with me. He should know that I will not tolerate any meddling by my officers."

"I think," said Lucy, "that it was Mrs. Wyndham's idea."

"That's worse than ever!"

He looked at her in dismay. "What shall I do? Shall I arrange to have you escorted back to Broadclyst?"

"I am not sure that I can go back," Lucy said. "Justus—and my grandmother—I doubt if they would believe me—"

"I see. There's no doubt that your brother believes the worst of me."

Lucy shook her head.

41

"Oh, yes, I know he does. Why shouldn't he? He has reason for it. How about your grandmother at Brockhill—?"

"—an enemy of the King—and a Presbyterian."

"Oh," he groaned, "it couldn't be worse. There is nothing else for you to do, then, but stay with Mrs. Wyndham until we can decide upon something else."

"I would rather stay with Mrs. Harvey. She knows my mother's family. Maybe Mr. Harvey can find a way to put me on a ship bound for Carmarthen. I could go to my cousin, Frances Vaughan, at Golden Grove."

"The very thing! Anne Harvey will take care of you here. And I promise you that a way will be found to do whatever you wish. I swear it. I'll even see that Mrs. Harvey takes you to Carmarthen, if that is what you wish. You do understand that I had nothing to do with it? I would never do such a thing to any woman—without her consent."

Lucy smiled through tears, and nodded.

He smiled. "Do you wish to go to Mrs. Harvey now?"

"No," said Lucy, "unless you wish it, sir. Since it can't be helped, I would like to stay with you until you command me to go." She could not keep the longing and the desire from her voice.

Charles laughed faintly. How charming and naive she was! He took her by the hand and led her to a chair close to the fire.

"Lucy," he said, "I have thought of you often since I saw you in Exeter. I could not forget you."

"I, too," said Lucy, "have thought of you."

"I love you enough to make you my mistress, officially and with all the privileges that would be granted to you," he said impetuously and he grinned. He was a little naive, himself, to make such a speech! He couldn't refrain from more embroidery. She was so gullible! "I know that you would be as dear to me as Gabrielle d'Estrees was to my grandfather, Henry of Navarre."

"Yes," she said. "I think I understand what you mean."

Lucy wanted to believe him but she sensed his insincerity. He didn't seem to be thinking much about her feelings—or something! Maybe when he knew her better he would understand. He didn't know that she could never endure living what she thought of as "second best." Besides, as Justus told her, when Charles became King, or maybe sooner, if he tired of her he could very easily cast her aside. She wouldn't do it! She didn't know what to say. Her lips trembled and a sob escaped from them. "I cannot—will not be any man's mistress, not even yours," she said.

"I don't understand."

"If you don't, Your Highness, I can't explain it to you."

"Then, that's the way it is," Charles said with a shrug of his shoulders and the mental reservation "for the present." He didn't think that she knew what she was talking about. She was confused! Why all this fuss about a sexual encounter! But in any event there seemed to be no other way but for Lucy to stay with Mrs. Harvey in the little house inside the Fortress until an arrangement could be made for her to be taken to her mother's family in Carmarthen.

Charles knew that he would have to leave when Edward Hyde and the other councilors came for him. They would follow him, he thought grimly. They couldn't leave him in peace, to enjoy himself! He went to the Harveys' house as often as he could and sent the servants away. Then he would take Lucy's hand and kiss it tenderly. Then he would fondle the black ringlets that lay so tantalizingly on the white neck, and slip his arm around her waist and press her to him. Soon he was kissing the white neck and when she closed her eyes he kissed her mouth and throat. He nestled his head upon her lace-covered bosom on the pretext that he wished to see if her heart was beating as fast as his. The next time he came he made no excuse and slid the slender fingers of one hand inside the bosom of her dress while he lifted her skirt with the other and caressed her thigh. She had been too inexperienced to know what to do before, but this time she broke from his embrace and pushed him away.

A flush of anger spread over the Prince's dark face. Lucy drew back in fear for he had an animal-like expression. His nostrils were dilated and his eyes had no tenderness in them. "If you really loved me you would be willing and would not push me away," he said. His voice was gruff and he drew down the corners of his ugly mouth. He was beginning to be bored with this stupid game.

She believed him. She herself was overcome by a desire to fulfill the sensation which shivered through her. "Yes, my love," she said as she permitted his embrace. She forgot everything and was willing to surrender to him. Furiously he kissed her, pressing his large, ugly mouth hard upon her soft eager lips.

There was a knock at the door and without a pause, it was opened.

" 'Od's blood," Charles said.

Hugh Wyndham smiled at what he saw. Too bad that the sport had to be interrupted, he thought. He told Charles that his secretary was looking for him. Four noblemen had ridden into the castle yard, and they had demanded that Sir Richard bring the Prince to them at once. They ignored the Wyndhams, including the Governor himself.

"Why didn't you come sooner to tell me?" Charles asked.

"You were busy," Hugh said insolently. "I didn't want to interrupt you."

"Who are they?" asked Charles, forced to ignore the insolence.

"Edward Hyde," said Hugh, "and he's livid. Somehow he's learned about her." He nodded toward Lucy.

With a nod to Lucy, Charles followed Hugh out the door.

Hyde had brought the terrible news that the enemy had closed in on Oxford. The King had been able to leave the town before they could capture him and, taking only his chaplain, Dr. Hudson, surrendered to the Scottish general, Leslie, at Newark.

Hyde had lost his temper when he heard about Lucy. "Incredible," he stormed, "in the light of His Majesty's peril." He was contemptuous and outraged and he let the Prince know it. The evening passed and the councilors and the Prince remained behind closed doors.

Lucy didn't leave the room where Charles had left her. Finally, Anne Harvey, curious and not a little worried, went to the apartments of Christabella Wyndham. She returned with a report for Lucy. "It's Edward Hyde," she said. "He has been severe with the Prince. He has accused him of being disobedient to the council appointed by His Majesty."

"Oh," gasped Lucy, "how dreadful!"

"He knows that you are here. He reprimanded Mrs. Wyndham and accused her of encouraging the 'waywardness', as he called it, of the Prince. Christabella is furious and is storming about like a wild woman."

"And what did the Prince say?" asked Lucy.

"I don't know."

It was midnight when the Prince walked out of the council meeting in Governor Wyndham's quarters. His head ached from clenching his teeth. His eyes were angry and his jaw protruded. The beauty and serenity of the evening seemed to heighten his anger. He looked at the full moon and saw the round face of the hateful Mr. Hyde. He wished he could tear it from the sky.

"Fat, fatuous fool!" Charles muttered. "Accusing me of 'lack of control—of untrammelled self-indulgence'!" Those smooth, polished, insulting words were infuriating. "The girl," Hyde had said, "is a beautiful, bold strumpet who has captivated His Highness." Anger boiled up in Charles. He would get even with all of them. He would marry Lucy. There was no law in England which forbade the heir to the throne marrying a commoner. To do it without the King's consent was unthinkable, he knew, but what difference did it make, now? His father had failed. He was in the hands of the enemy. Soon, maybe sooner than anyone expected, he, himself, would be King. He would begin, now, to make his own decisions. He would marry Lucy!

He went in to Lucy and she watched him with fear and anxiety in her shadowed eyes. She trusts me, he thought. She depends upon me to know what to do. I must have her. It is Hyde's fault that I am forced to take action, immediately; it will be Hyde's fault if things go wrong, he assured himself.

"Lucy," he said, "Lucy, I am going to marry you."

She gasped in surprise. "Oh, no!" she murmured. "It's impossible!"

"If I say it is possible, it is," Charles said. His jaw jutted out and his black eyes snapped. "Tomorrow I must ride back to Bristol with my nobles. You are to stay here until a ship can be found to take you to Golden Grove. I will send for you as soon as I can."

Next morning Charles said to Sir Richard, "I am going to marry Lucy Walter. Will you help me?"

Sir Richard was stunned. He hadn't expected that the Prince would go that far. He didn't know what to say.

"I shall do it secretly," said Charles, "and I need your help. Will you do it?"

"I will think about it," Sir Richard said, playing for time, but he saw a sudden flash of anger in Charles' black eyes and the jutting out of his jaw, so he added hastily, "The arrangements will not be easy."

Charles eyed him suspiciously as if he wondered if Sir Richard would betray him.

Later, Sir Richard said to his wife, "I have no choice but to tell him that I will help him. If I don't he will rebel against me, too." He paced up and down the room, thinking out loud. "Hyde should have known better! I cannot understand how he could have lost his head. It is not like him."

"Perhaps," said Lady Fanshawe, "he thought that he was being firm with the Prince and didn't realize that he was treating him like a child."

"I think you're right, my dear," Sir Richard said. "Unfortunately, the damage was done because of that misjudgment."

"Would it be possible for you to mend the situation by talking to His Highness? He has always followed your advice before."

"He won't this time unless I do what he wishes me to do."

"It's all my fault. I shouldn't have accepted that letter."

"Not at all! Christabella Wyndham would have found another way if you had not. Don't worry. Perhaps it is better that we know about it."

"How so?"

"Our only hope is that circumstance may prevent the marriage. Time is what we need."

"What do you plan to do? What is to be done with the girl?"

"She's to stay with Mrs. Harvey until a ship can be found to take her to Carmarthen—to the Earl of Carberry—until the Prince sends for her to marry him. So he says now!"

"Oh," said Mary Fanshawe, "you mean that, because

of the state of the kingdom, a long time may pass before His Highness will find the marriage possible?"

Sir Richard smiled. "Yes, my dear. As much as a year, or two, could pass because of the way the war is going. And, it is almost certain that, given time enough to mature, the boy will not only see the folly of the marriage but he will no longer think about the girl at all."

"It would be the best thing for her, too. No doubt she will outgrow the infatuation at the same time," Lady Fanshawe said.

"That's not our problem," Sir Richard answered curtly, but seeing the expression on his wife's face, added gently, "I hope that it will work out that way."

She nodded. "So do I. When do you leave for Bristol?"

"Early tomorrow morning. Your coach is being prepared to follow, day after tomorrow."

"Very well," she said. "I will be ready."

Next morning the Prince and the councilors, who had come for him, rode out of the castle yard. Lord Culpepper and Lord Hopton led the way. They talked incessantly about the details of the arrangements for the Prince's comfort on the journey. Where could they quarter him for the night, and which noblemen with residences on the way, would be most likely to have adequate food supplies?

Lord Capel rode at one side of the Prince. He was silent but every now and then he glanced at Charles as if wondering what was on the boy's mind.

Charles stared straight ahead. Under his wide-brimmed hat, pulled low on his forehead, the black eyes smoldered as he kept thinking of his parting embrace with Lucy. His nostrils dilated as he remembered the perfume of her hair.

Sir Richard rode on the other side of the Prince, and he watched him anxiously. If Hyde were not riding behind, at the end of the party, he thought, he would see for himself that Charles' rebellion had not been resolved. It was written all over his face!

Spring was bursting upon the countryside as they left Bridgwater. The fragrance of blossoms and the early-morning songs of birds filled the air It was hard to believe that death stalked the kingdom; that failure, even tragedy, lay ahead for most of them.

In the castle, Henry Harvey was left with a difficult task. The Bristol Channel was full of enemy ships lying in wait for Royalist craft. Not only that, there were many pirates taking advantage of the situation to plunder cargoes of munitions and supplies. It wouldn't be easy to find a captain foolhardy enough to take two women across the infested water to Carmarthen, but Harvey had promised to try; he had reluctantly agreed to let his wife go with Lucy.

Henry was a slender, partly bald man with piercing blue eyes that seemed to stare straight through a lying servant or thieving steward. He had large estates to manage. Not only did he own the castle that he had leased to the King's Governor, Colonel Wyndham, but he had lands and tenants in Haygrove, Durleigh, Chilton and North Petherton. The people from these lands brought their silver plate, and other goods of value, to the castle for safekeeping, not so much because of Wyndham's boast that the castle and garrison could withstand any siege that was laid against it, but because they had confidence in Henry Harvey.

It took him two months, but at last he found a captain willing to attempt a crossing of the Channel. The two women passengers were told to go aboard with their baggage because the ship was already riding at anchor at the quai; the captain was waiting for the tide to go out.

As Mrs. Harvey and Lucy came out of the house they had to stand back because of a courier who rode into the castle yard with his horse covered with mud,

49

churned up by hard riding over wet roads. He dismounted and, taking a dispatch case with him, went into the Governor's quarters.

"Let's wait," said Mrs. Harvey. "He probably carries important news. It will only take a few minutes."

He did come out again in a few moments, and Mrs. Harvey went to him and asked if he could tell them what news he carried.

"It's no secret, madame," he said. "Bristol is full of the plague!" He lowered his voice and added, "This I should not tell you, but you will learn of it soon enough. Governor Wyndham has been commanded to prepare the castle for the arrival of His Highness and his retinue. They are on the way to Barnstaple to set up new headquarters."

Lucy put her hand on Mrs. Harvey's arm. "Please, please," she begged, "don't send me away before he comes!"

"Let's go back inside," said Anne. "I'll see what Henry says about it."

Henry Harvey thought it over. The ship had given him the opportunity of getting rid of Lucy by sending her to the Earl of Carberry before the Prince returned, and with Lucy out of the way there would be no danger of Edward Hyde reporting the affair to His Majesty. That would be fortunate for all of them. On the other hand, if the Prince's desire for the girl had cooled, which Henry had every inclination to believe would happen sooner or later, she could be sent back to Broadclyst. If this were done his wife would not have to make the dangerous trip across the Channel. It was for that reason that Harvey decided to let Lucy remain in the castle. The Prince would be with them only while the royal yacht was being provisioned for the precarious trip to Barnstaple. Surely, not more than twenty-four hours would be needed.

He went to the quai, at once, to make arrangements

for the captain that he had engaged, to wait a few days, but the man had already gone. When he found that his passengers were not coming aboard he shipped his anchor and went out with the tide. Henry turned his attention, then, to speeding up the work on the Prince's yacht. At least he would get rid of the royal party as soon as possible and then he could take up the problem of what to do with Lucy.

Governor Wyndham was annoyed that he had to receive His Highness again. He grumbled that he had enough to do to maintain the defenses of the castle without having to entertain royalty! His wife, Christabella, was in a transport of delight. She began making elaborate plans for a trysting place for the lovers. She told Hugh that he was to make it possible for the Prince to disappear into the Harveys' house as soon as he arrived and stand guard at the door while Charles was there.

There was not a person within the castle walls who did not know that Lucy was hidden in the Harveys' house. It was inevitable that someone would seize the opportunity of informing Edward Hyde for pay. The Governor and Henry knew that Hyde would probably be informed about the whole affair the minute he rode in through the water gate.

So, Henry did the only thing he could do. He sent a messenger to Bristol with a letter for Sir Richard, hoping to reach him before the party left the town because he wanted him to know that Lucy was still in the castle. Maybe he could think of something to divert Hyde's suspicions when they arose.

"Will we ever get rid of that girl?" the secretary muttered when he read it just before they left Bristol.

Sir Richard made a suggestion to Lord Culpepper that they spend the night at Wells instead of riding posthaste with the result that they would arrive in Bridgwater in the middle of the night. Culpepper agreed and when the secretary told the Prince of their decision, Charles seemed pleased. He sighed with relief when his secretary explained that the stopover would avoid any impression of undue haste on the Prince's part which might arouse Hyde's suspicions. It was almost as if Charles were reluctant to see Lucy again. Sir Richard had a twinge of disappointment that Charles was in no hurry. He was glad that he was willing to comply, but he would have liked to find that it was necessary to persuade him to do so! Somehow, it would have been more gallant on the Prince's part.

Charles assumed his usual air of indifference about where he would be quartered. At sunset, when they rode through the ancient gates into the town of Wells he seemed to be giving no thought to where they were taking him. They crossed the bridge spanning the pentagon-shaped moat of the castle and his secretary watched Charles and wondered what he was thinking.

They were quartered in the Deanery for the night and when they left the next morning, Charles was still preoccupied. When they passed an exquisite rose garden where the gardener was on his knees, digging in the soft earth, it would have been customary for the Prince to stop a moment and compliment the man upon his work but he didn't. When the fellow jumped up, anyway, and began bowing, Charles passed him without so much as a glance.

To Sir Richard's dismay, he saw that Hyde was observing all this. He was obviously wondering what ailed the boy. That was unfortunate! When a question arose in Edward Hyde's mind, he did not rest until he had the answer to it!

They reached Bridgwater and the people in the castle were outwardly calm but most of them were disturbed because they were worried about their own fate when not only Hyde but the King knew what had happened.

Anne Harvey was not so much afraid as unhappy about the role that she was expected to play. Reluctantly, she did what Christabella had asked her to do. As soon as the royal party rode into the castle yard she sent her servants away from the house. She opened the door, herself, when the Prince came to see Lucy, and she lowered her eyes when she greeted him. She didn't wish to reveal how much she disapproved. He probably wouldn't have noticed, anyway, because he had his eyes upon the door behind which he knew that Lucy was waiting for him.

Lucy wore a gown of blue satin, and black curls lay upon bare white shoulders. Her heart-shaped face was pale and her large, shadowed eyes were wistful. She scarcely had time to greet Charles before he took her in his arms, crushed her to him, and kissed her hard upon the lips.

Mrs. Harvey stood in the doorway and an angry flush mounted her cheeks. She hesitated a few moments and then, deciding that there was nothing that she could do to change the situation, she left the room, shutting the door behind her. When the door closed Charles held Lucy at arm's length and looked down into her eyes.

"Lucy," he said, "Lucy, I will wait no longer. I'm not going to send you to Carmarthen. I have thought about it all the way from Bristol, and I have decided to marry you at once. The kingdom has collapsed. At least I will have you!"

Before she could reply there was an insistent tapping on the door. The Prince frowned but went to it and jerked it open. It was Hugh Wyndham.

"Your Highness," he said, "Edward Hyde is asking why you left them so abruptly and where you are at the moment."

"Oh," said Charles, "so that's it."

"Sir Richard sent me to tell you that you must come

at once. The ship is ready and waiting at the quai. Come, before it is discovered that you are here," he said nervously.

"Very well, Hugh, I will go at once. See that the way is clear, and I will follow you." When the door closed behind him, Charles took Lucy in his arms and kissed her again. "Lucy," he said, "there is not much time. Listen carefully. I must go aboard my yacht at once, but when I reach Barnstaple the rest will be easy. Lady Fanshawe is ill and not able to make the sea voyage. She will remain here for a few days' rest, and my yacht will come back for her. You are to come to Barnstaple with her."

"I will be ready."

He left her, then, and went back to his councilors. They told him that the yacht was ready and waiting at the quai. He raised his eyebrows in simulated surprise and politely commended Henry Harvey on the speed with which he had completed the arrangements.

They told him that his craft was provided with all the guns that she could carry, and they were all manned and ready to shoot it out with any enemy ship that accosted them. Again, Charles complimented Henry Harvey before he said, "I, too, am ready. Let's go to the quai." In less than an hour the Prince and his councilors were aboard, and the ship went down the River Parret and out into the Bristol Channel.

Christabella was the only one in the castle who was ecstatic about the change of plans. "If the darlings are to be married in Barnstaple, Lucy must have a wedding gown," she said. Seamstresses were brought in to work around the clock. Christabella took a length of cloth, shot with silver, from one of her chests, and said that it was to be used for the gown. Other ladies in the castle contributed laces and jewels. Henry Harvey dispatched a messenger with a carefully worded letter, addressed to the Earl of Carberry at Golden Grove, Carmarthenshire. The letter said, in effect, "Lucy can be found in Barnstaple, under royal protection." That was all.

A week went by, and the yacht didn't return. A man was sent to watch at the quai and he inquired of every captain, that got his ship safely ashore, if he had news of the fate of a ship resembling the royal yacht. The wedding dress was completed, and the ladies were ready to go. Their clothing remained packed for two weeks and still there was no news. Then one morning Mr. Harvey was summoned to the quai. A small ship had made it in with her mast torn into shreds and her deck scarred with cannon balls. The captain had news.

Henry heard him out and then went back to the castle and told the anxious group that was waiting for him, "The royal yacht made it safely to Barnstaple."

Lucy murmured, "Thank God!" At least Charles was safe!

"But on the way back," Henry went on, "it was captured. It was taken by pirates."

" 'Od's blood!" burst out Christabella as roughly as any man could have said it. "Will fortune never smile on us!"

Lady Fanshawe began to sob because she was afraid that she would never see her husband again.

"I'm afraid that it will be impossible to find another captain willing to take women passengers," Henry said.

"You must," Mrs. Fanshawe insisted between sobs. "I shall die if I cannot join my husband!"

"I shall try, but I can't promise anything."

The days passed, and Harvey's effort ended in failure after failure. It seemed that he would never find a vessel, and the whole castle was steeped in boredom and despair. Then, one steamy, humid day in the third week of July, everything changed. It had rained during the night and the heat of a bright sun drew the moisture that lay on the cobbles back up into the air; one could actually see the steam rising. The sentries at their posts

55

mopped their hot faces but never once did they relax their vigilance. The air seemed to be electrified. The castle was spellbound in an ominous expectant waiting for it knew not what.

In the afternoon word came from the quai that an unidentified vessel had arrived. Hugh Wyndham went to investigate and when he came back at sunset he told them that the craft had been dispatched from the Prince's court at Barnstaple. The captain had been commanded to bring back Lady Fanshawe and Lucy; they were to go aboard before the tide went out in the morning.

"Thank God," Governor Wyndham said when he heard this news. "The enemy is too close for comfort!"

Hugh went back to the ship that evening with the baggage, including Lucy's wedding gown and the other clothes that had been made for her. The ladies were to stay in the castle until early the next morning so Hugh could have everything ready for their comfort. He slept on board ship and was up at sunrise expecting to go back to the castle but he couldn't do it! Governor Wyndham had been surprised in his impregnable fortress! He had had every reason to have confidence in the garrison for the castle was surrounded by a moat, thirty feet wide, which filled and emptied with the tide: cannons were mounted in the crenelations of the fifty-foot walls and they were kept manned and alerted at all times. More than that, the town both on the castle side and beyond the river was defended by strong earthworks. The Governor was aware that the main body of the King's army had been destroyed at the Battle of Naseby and that all that was left were the scattered defenses in Wales of which Bridgwater was the strongest. He knew that the town of Langport, not far away, had fallen a short time before and that he would probably be attacked at any moment—but he thought that he was ready. He was unprepared for the way that it happened.

In the middle of the night, long before sunrise, when the tide was out and the people of the town were asleep and the sentries on the walls not too vigilant, a storming party of soldiers effected a lodgment with portable bridges and ladders. At the same time, Fort Royal was reduced and its guns turned on the town. The top of the Market Cross was blown to bits and a house near the bridgehead occupied and armed. Cromwell's men, under General Fairfax, let down the drawbridge at St. John's in Eastover, expecting a stiff engagement to clear out the defenders but, instead, five hundred Royalists from Pembroke surrendered without a fight!

Hugh started out from the ship to go to the castle and was caught in the middle of the holocaust. It was only luck that he was able to make it back to the ship where he found the captain getting ready to go out with the tide whether the passengers were aboard or not. Hugh overcame him and locked him in his cabin. After that the crew was no problem. The men knew that if they left the ship they would be captured but Hugh held them at pistol point, anyway, to be sure. Then, though the sun was still bright enough for fighting, the enemy ceased operations. The castle was intact but the Governor was restricted to a very small area around it.

The next morning the guns were still quiet but after the sun rose a white flag was run up by the attackers and a rider approached the castle. When he was within shouting distance a sentry in one of the towers commanded him to halt. The man shouted that he carried an order for the Governor to surrender.

"Never!" was the immediate reply.

This was taken back to General Fairfax and he answered that in that case he would show no mercy. He would permit the women and children to leave the castle but they would have to come out, at once. Wyndham accepted that offer.

Several hours passed in these negotiations. The sun

was high in the sky when the great water gate of the castle was thrown open, the drawbridge let down and a procession began moving over the moat toward the three-arched bridge. There were old women and young women and children. Some of them were in their mothers' arms, some were clinging to skirts, and some were dragged by hand. A soldier was posted at the bridge and he scrutinized each woman as she passed. If she carried anything of value he took it away from her and threw it into a wagon.

From the deck of the ship Hugh watched the procession through the captain's glass. At the same time he never relaxed his observation of the captain and his men, and he ordered them to make the ship ready. They were poised for flight when the tide went out and it was almost time. Hugh wondered what he should do if the ladies weren't aboard. Should he overpower the captain again and keep the ship at the quai or should he let him sail with orders to return as soon as possible? There was little hope that he would do it! If he let him go should he go with him, or leave the ship and try to find the ladies? He looked carefully at each figure as the women went over the bridge from the castle gate. Mrs. Fanshawe and Lucy must be together somewhere in that procession. At last a familiar figure caught his eye. It was the statuesque Anne Harvey. Following her was a diminutive figure with a hood over her head. That had to be Lucy Walter. Behind her was Lady Fanshawe. Hugh grinned when he saw that the very last woman was his mother, Christabella. She came out like a captain that was the last to leave his ill-fated ship. Her heavy figure moved with belligerence. The hood of her cape had fallen off and it flapped on her square shoulders. He didn't take his eye from the glass. He watched every move the four women made. They reached the soldier at the bridge. Then, as if by prearranged plan, they broke away from the procession and ran together toward the quai.

The soldier on the bridge shouted for help. Several men joined him to run after the women but they were handicapped by heavy boots and firearms. Soon, all but one stopped. That poor fellow caught up with Christabella Wyndham! As he reached out to grab her she turned and blasted away at him with a pistol that she carried under her cloak.

The man staggered, dropped his weapon, and clutched at his shoulder. This gave the women the time that they needed to reach the ship. Hugh, with the help of a sailor, pulled them aboard. The captain bawled out an order to ship the anchor and the little craft slipped into the outgoing water. A volley of shot came over its mast, but that was all. The commanders of the New Model Army decided that they had more important business at hand than the pursuit of four refugee women. The command was given to let the ship go, and it went down the River Parret without further harassment.

Fairfax's men concentrated on the attack upon the castle—all, that is, except the soldier whose sword arm was hanging uselessly at his side because of the wound that Christabella had inflicted upon him. "The Governor's lady is a demon in women's clothing!" he groaned.

Governor Wyndham gave the order to close the gate. It clanged shut as a flare of red-hot shot came over the walls. The attack on the fortress was under way. But that was not all. All over town, both on the castle side and beyond the river, houses burst into flame. The residents had agreed among themselves to set fire to them rather than let them be occupied and used by the enemy. Miraculously, the ship carrying Lucy to Charles went across the Bristol Channel without encounter. The captain was able to thread the way through enemy craft, and in record time, they sailed into Barnstaple Bay.

The anchor was dropped at the quai, and Hugh and the women disembarked. Mrs. Fanshawe went, at once, to the house of the merchant, Palmer, where her husband waited for her. Hugh took the others to an inn at the foot of Boutpor Street. Its sign swung gently in the mild breeze that blew in from the bay, and it creaked rhythmically, accompanied by the guttural quacking and complaining of the sea gulls when they rose from the edge of the water each time they were disturbed. The innkeeper was standing under his sign; he was short and rotund and his ruddy face beamed and grimaced with hospitality and excitement. He protested vigorously when Hugh said that he wished to inspect the inn before the ladies went to their rooms.

"No other guests have been admitted, nor will be, sir," he complained.

His protest made Hugh even more resolved to look in the common rooms, the upstairs chambers, and even the kitchen. When he returned, satisfied, he took his mother, Lucy, and Mrs. Harvey to the rooms that had been prepared for them. They were on the second floor at the front of the house, and their windows had a view of the mansion directly across the street. It was a massively elegant residence and, aloft over its roof, fluttered the Royal Standard of the Prince of Wales.

Christabelia removed her cloak with its black hood, laid aside her pistol, and smoothed her hair with her hand. She was ready to go to work. She loved to take care of young people and she bustled with importance.

Lucy stood still in the middle of the room. The hood of the black cloak was over her head and she clutched her little spaniel to her as if she would never let him go. A loud knock on the door made her jump and cry out in alarm.

"It's only a servant," Christabella said cheerfully.

She let in a very frightened porter, carrying a chest on his shoulders. He dropped it to the floor and ran out as if he were afraid for his life.

"Stupid bumpkin!" Christabella hissed. "Obviously, he's overwhelmed by royalty!" She raised the lid of the chest. "H-m-m," she said, "it's your wedding gown. It's a good thing that Hugh put our baggage aboard before those devils attacked us."

Lucy didn't move. Christabella looked at her appraisingly. The girl was nervous. She would have to do something about that.

"Give me Salvatore," she said.

Lucy's hands shook as she handed him over. Christabella set the dog on the floor and gave his small flank a little spank as she pushed him out of the way. Then she gently removed Lucy's cloak. "You must get some sleep," she said.

She helped Lucy remove her clothes and put her into bed, as if she were a child. She took some lotions and oils from a large handbag and set them on a table. She bathed Lucy's face. "Now, turn over," she said. "I'll rub your back and you will fall asleep."

Lucy drifted off to sleep and while she slept the preparations for the wedding were completed. As the innkeeper had promised, no other guests were admitted. The shutters were closed and a servant posted at the entrance to send away anyone who tried to enter the public rooms. Whenever a few curious townspeople gathered in the street they were hustled on by the sentries stationed in the doorways of the mansion across the way.

Hugh Wyndham was in charge of arrangements. He chose a small room off the main hall and transformed it into a chapel. A large oak table from Spain was covered with a cloth of fine lace which Christabella had brought along with the wedding gown. In the center of the table they placed a vase of wildflowers which the innkeeper's servants had found among the sparse vegetation on the countryside. Lady Fanshawe came with two silver candelabras, borrowed from the merchant, Palmer; they were placed one on each side of the vase of flowers.

"It will make a good altar," Hugh said to Lady Fanshawe as he stood back and admired the arrangement. "The clergyman will bring a Bible, along with his Prayer Book."

"And who is the clergyman?" asked Lady Fanshawe.

"William Wheeler," he said. "He will bring vestments with him from the local church, I presume."

"Who invited him?"

"Thom Rogers and Rob Marsh," Hugh said. "Their families live here, and they are well acquainted with the clergy."

Lady Fanshawe was a little dismayed by this news. She knew Rogers and Marsh. They were minor courtiers in the retinue of the Prince and both of them were sly opportunists. She wondered if their families could be trusted to select a suitable clergyman for the wedding of the Prince! She wouldn't trust either of them, she thought, as she went up the stairs to join the other women.

Rogers and Marsh came with William Wheeler, Marsh carrying the vestments over one arm. He followed the clergyman into the improvised chapel and Hugh took Rogers into the common room. Lady Fanshawe had planted a seed of anxiety in his mind.

"You are sure," he asked Rogers, "that Wheeler is honest and will not reveal the marriage?"

"Absolutely," said Rogers. He pursed his small mouth primly. "He will never tell that he married them though they put him to the torture."

"I doubt if it will come to that," Hugh said drily. Rogers was a little melodramatic!

Marsh came out of the small room. "We're ready," he said.

"Yes," Hugh said. "Everything is ready. Thom," he said, and his voice shook with excitement, "you go inform His Highness that all is ready. Rob, you stay with the clergyman."

Thom and Rob exchanged glances and if Roger's pencil-thin eyebrows in the round, flabby face, elevated just a bit Hugh didn't notice for he had turned his back to go upstairs to tell his mother that all was ready.

Lucy cried out sharply when Christabella opened the curtains around the bed, bent over, and kissed her on the forehead to waken her. Lucy had slept soundly because she was exhausted but when wakened she was overcome with a feeling of coldness and fear. What was she doing? She wasn't sure she really wanted to marry Charles. It was going to change her whole life and she hadn't really made a decision to let it happen. She had been swept along by what Charles wanted—was it really necessary for her to do what he wanted? But how could she stop it now? She couldn't, she thought. She had already caused so much trouble she couldn't change it, now!

Anne Harvey seemed to sense Lucy's fear and indecision. She was overcome with sadness as she watched and she found it difficult to restrain the tears that came to her eyes. Lucy looked like a child, she thought. Her round little face, with its small chin, was very pale, and the violet shadows under her eyes had deepened. It was tragic! No other word could adequately express how she felt about what was going on; she couldn't approve and she could not prevent it. She wondered about Lucy's mother and father. What would they think of all this?

"My dear," said Christabella, "it is time for us to dress you. Everything is arranged. The Prince will be here soon. The clergyman is waiting."

"You are very kind," said Lucy.

"On the contrary," said Mrs. Wyndham. "I have

never done anything in my whole life that gave me so much pleasure." Under her breath she added, "I can't wait to see Hyde's face when he finds out!"

Christabella and Anne Harvey lifted the gown of cloth of silver, and lowered it over Lucy's head. The heavy train fell on the floor and lay in shimmering folds.

"H-m-m," said Christabella putting her hands on her broad hips. "I hope that she will be able to walk." Thoughtfully she cocked her head. "Take a step, child," she said.

Lucy did so. "It's heavy," she said.

"Can you sit down?" asked Christabella. "Here—try it—" she pushed a bench toward Lucy. "It would be dreadful not to be able to sit down at the wedding feast!" She chuckled. "However, you'll not eat much," she added. "You'll be too excited."

Lucy smiled and sat down on the bench. She remained stiffly erect.

"Excellent!" said Christabella. "The dress will hold you up when you're standing," she said. "A royal bride must learn that. No matter how tired you are, my dear, you must always remember to conduct yourself with dignity now. Often,—" she said with an outbreak of boastfulness, "I have seen the great ladies at court nearly fainting with fatigue but still standing erect, supported by their gowns!" Her black eyes shone beneath the heavy brows. She could imagine Lucy with a heavy crown upon her dark curls!

Anne Harvey brushed Lucy's hair while she was sitting on the bench. She smoothed strands of it over her finger and arranged each curl carefully so that they lay in a pattern upon the white shoulders. Next, came the garland of flowers into which had been woven a filament of gold. Christabella held it up to be admired and then set it on Lucy's head. "The bride is ready," she said dramatically.

Anne Harvey said nothing but she could restrain the tears no longer. She brushed them away with the back of her hand and tried to smile. Then she saw that Lucy's face had turned white and that she trembled from head to foot. Anne went down on her knees beside her and took her in her arms.

"What is it, child?" she asked.

"I don't want to do it," Lucy whispered in Anne's ear. "It's madness! It's impossible!"

Anne drew back and studied Lucy's face. "Why?" she asked. "Are you frightened? Or don't you love him?"

"I don't know," said Lucy. "It will only cause trouble."

"Then don't do it," whispered Anne. That would solve everything, if Lucy changed her mind. They could placate the Prince!

Lucy took one of Anne's hands and pressed it in her own. "I'm all right," she said. "The dress is too tight here." She pressed her little stomach. "I feel faint."

"Oh," Anne said disappointed. "So that's it. You'll get used to it."

Christabella chuckled. "It is that way with all brides," she said.

Hugh was waiting for them at the foot of the stairs. His eyes twinkled as he watched Lucy descend with his mother who was holding up the long train of the gown. What a clever girl she was! Mentally, he congratulated himself for his part in the intrigue which was now bearing fruit. He thought of the reward that he had every reason to expect and he wondered if the Prince would ask what he preferred. Would it be money or land—or a title?

What a joke they had played on Edward Hyde! The competent, passionless Mr. Hyde who never permitted himself to be influenced by anything romantic and who was the first to learn of every enemy intrigue, had been outdone by a slip of a girl! The way he figured it was that the girl had been clever enough to restrain the Prince's lust until he was helpless in her grasp and then had shrewdly demanded that he marry her! He and his mother had helped her do it! He really thought that was the way it happened.

Sir Richard didn't give up hope that the Prince would come to his senses and change his mind until Thom Rogers came to tell them that all was ready. No matter how hard he tried he could not smile; he exchanged anguished glances with his wife as they prepared to follow the Prince from the mansion to the inn across the road.

Charles was dressed in white satin with a collar of fine Italian lace covering his muscular shoulders; his coarse black hair contrasted dramatically with the delicate fabric of the costume. He had a dazed expression on his swarthy face and he didn't smile until he saw Lucy. Then his whole face softened. He took her hand and with her led the wedding party waiting in the common room into the small chapel where the candles had been lit upon the improvised altar. William Wheeler waited, Prayer Book in hand.

Sir Richard muttered to himself as he went, "It is like one lamb leading another to the slaughter!"

Charles and Lucy knelt together, eyes uplifted.

"Dearly beloved, we are gathered here in the sight of God—"

Wheeler had a beautiful voice, well trained for sermons but Sir Richard thought that he looked ill and distracted. He seemed to find it difficult to remember the words or even to follow the text with his finger. He fumbled the words several times and had to repeat them. Maybe, Sir Richard thought, he was worrying about the possibility of being reprimanded by his bishop. Bitterly he said to himself, "He should be."

At last Wheeler reached the final blessing:

"God the Father, God the Son, God the Holy Ghost, bless, preserve, and keep you; the Lord mercifully with his favor look upon you, and fill you with all spiritual benediction and grace; that ye may so live together in this life, that in the world to come ye may have life everlasting. Amen."

Wheeler closed his eyes as if in silent prayer and then slowly lowered his uplifted arms and held his hands, palms down, over the couple. It was done. Charles kissed Lucy and the moment of silence that followed was punctuated by a loud and dramatic sob from Christabella Wyndham.

The Prince gave the signal for the party to go into the great hall and he led the way, holding Lucy's hand. The room was filled with the aroma of roast meat and pastries. The innkeeper and his servants had been forbidden to enter the room so it had been decided that Rogers and Marsh should carry the food in from the kitchen on large platters. Hugh served it to Charles and Lucy in the manner required for royalty. Each time he offered them a dish, he lowered himself to one knee and held it up to them.

The food was good and the wine plentiful, and each gentleman offered a toast to the couple's happiness. Overshadowing the graceful words and uplifted glasses was an uneasiness, a foreboding, that evil hung over the rash event. It was almost midnight when the Prince rose from the table and announced that he would go to his quarters in the mansion across the way. Lucy's cloak with the hood was put on her shoulders and the party groped its way across the street in the darkness. Sir Richard led the way and he was so irritated by the whole event that he spoke sharply to the sentry who let them pass into the corridor which led to the Prince's private quarters.

"It was beautiful," Lucy said. "It was like my dreams of how it would be!" Her eyes shone.

"Lucy my love—" the Prince began. He put one arm around her shoulders and looked down into her eyes. Sir Richard watched him closely. He saw that the Prince's face turned pale and that he passed his hand across his brow as he looked away from Lucy's trusting eyes. It was as if an ominous darkness had flooded his brain and Sir Richard wondered if doubt of the wisdom of the act had come to Charles too late! The Prince shook his head as if to dispel the dark mood, embraced Lucy and kissed her.

"You must promise," he said to her, "that you won't tell anyone about the ceremony."

She nodded.

Charles motioned for Sir Richard to bring him a velvet covered box. The secretary touched a spring which opened the lid before he held the box for the Prince to take out a heavy gold chain from which hung a pendant. It was a portrait of himself, set in diamonds. He clasped the chain around Lucy's neck.

She lifted the pendant and looked at the portrait. "It is very beautiful," she said. "Your penniless bride has nothing to give you but herself."

"For that," said the Prince, "I would forfeit my kingdom."

"That," Sir Richard thought as he followed the Prince into his dressing room to help him prepare for the night, "may very well be what you are doing!"

Christabella Wyndham and Anne Harvey removed Lucy's heavy gown of cloth of silver, and a lovely night dress of azure satin, shot with golden threads, was slipped over her head. They brushed her hair and placed her in the great bed and each of them kissed her tenderly.

"God bless you, my child," Anne Harvey whispered,

"I wish your mother were here. I shall send a messenger to her, at once, so she will know that all is well."

"Thank you, dear Anne, for all that you have done."

There was no Benediction Posset. The reason was that William Wheeler had closed the Prayer Book, took off the robes and left the inn immediately after the ceremony. He disappeared into the night without saying goodbye to anyone, much less drinking to the couple's health and happiness.

Early the next morning Lucy was taken back to the rooms on the second floor of the inn. For seven days she lived there attended by Anne Harvey and Christabella Wyndham, and with Hugh guarding the entrance to the inn to be sure that no strangers were admitted. Every evening the Prince came to Lucy after his councilors thought that he had retired for the night, and had gone to bed themselves.

It was so cleverly done that the snoopers, who made it their business to spy upon the Prince, learned nothing more than that something unusual was going on. Most of them came to the conclusion that the Prince was keeping a lady of pleasure in the inn, and the air was full of ribald remarks. The fact that she was never seen added to the mystery and the gossip. Even Edward Hyde misjudged the situation. He was led to believe that the Prince was having an affair with a local girl. Each morning he watched Charles come into the council meetings, half-awake, and his eyes puffy as if he had had too much wine the evening before.

"The lust of the young is appalling," Hyde said to himself.

One morning he spoke to Sir Richard about it. "He is beginning young. The Bourbon blood is beginning to tell! I shall be glad to be relieved of the responsibility of the personal life of His Highness." Sir Richard flushed with anger. He resented Hyde's arrogance and the implication that Charles was degenerating. But then he had to admit that he, too, would be glad to be relieved of the responsibility of the Prince.

It was a real possibility that it would not be long before Charles would have to go into exile, and he became more and more distraught as the signs of the King's total defeat increased. Every day brought closer the day when he, himself, would have to leave the country to avoid being captured by Cromwell. A ship stood ready at Falmouth.

But what would happen to Lucy? He couldn't abandon her in Barnstaple and certainly none of his attendants would be willing to provide for her. Once more he appealed to his secretary to help him. Could Lucy be taken to Carmarthen where she would be under the protection of the Earl of Carberry? Fanshawe agreed immediately because he thought that it would be an excellent way to get rid of her. He hold his wife that he fully expected that when the Prince was aboard the ship and on his way to the Island of Jersey, where they had decided to send him, that he would forget all about Lucy.

"There is nothing that I can do about it," he apologized, guiltily, when he saw that his remark saddened his wife. "There is no way that I could have prevented this affair," he added almost angrily. "Now let the Earl of Carberry be charged with the welfare of his relative!"

It was decided that Lucy would have to cross the Channel alone with only a servant to accompany her. A small yacht was commissioned and a lady attendant engaged. Sir Richard sent a letter to Golden Grove, addressed to the Earl, telling him that the Prince commanded that he receive Lucy and care for her. When all was ready Lucy went aboard and the little vessel set sail with Charles watching until it was out of sight.

The next day he began preparations to join his troops that were going to make one more attempt to relieve Exeter, that was under siege, and if that failed he would go to the Island of Jersey.

On the morning of Charles' departure Brian Duppa, who was one of the King's chaplains, drew rein and dismounted in front of the Prince's residence. He had ridden all night and the sun was just beginning to rise. The stiff yellow clay of the marshes had been touched by an early frost during the night and he was cold and exhausted. He asked to see the Prince at once. Sir Richard was called and he came and took the clergyman to Charles' bedroom.

"Your Highness," Sir Richard said, "Brian Duppa is here, and His Grace wishes to speak to you at once."

"Very well, very well! What news can be so important that I am waked at this ungodly hour?"

"Your Highness!" exclaimed Sir Richard, hoping that Charles would take the hint that he should conduct himself with more dignity.

Charles sat bolt upright. "What is it?" he asked, looking at his former chaplain. "What is it? Has something happened to my father?"

"No, Your Highness, but I have come about a matter that would be a sad blow to your father in all his trouble, if he knew about it."

He stared at the Prince before he began. The boy had been under his guidance from the time that the doll that he slept with had been taken from him. Had he failed in the moulding of the Prince's character? Charles should have had more personal direction, he thought with consternation. A fleeting prayer rose in his thoughts; a petition that the young man who had been in his care would not be a spiritual casualty of the war.

"Two men have come to me," he said slowly, "one, Thomas Rogers, and the other, Robert Marsh. Their purpose is blackmail." He stopped and searched the Prince's face for an expression of guilt before he went on. "For some reason these men have threatened to go to Edward Hyde if I do not pay their price."

The Prince's face was impassive but his black eyes

never wavered or left Brian Duppa's, as he waited for him to continue.

"Do you know these men?"

Charles nodded. Of course he knew Thomas Rogers and Robert Marsh. They were members of his retinue.

"They have told me that you permitted the staging of a sham marriage," he said, "the diversion that is popular in degenerate society, today." His voice broke, and he paused before going on. "They told me," he said, "that the young woman who took part in it, Lucy Walter, left Barnstaple several days ago." He stopped and studied Charles again.

"Sham marriage?" the Prince said in an unnaturally high voice.

"If there was such an event, it couldn't have been anything but a mockery of marriage."

The Prince turned pale. He looked at Sir Richard and the stricken expression of his secretary's face confirmed what the chaplain was saying.

"This description of the event seems to shock Your Highness," Brian Duppa said grimly. "But if it is true that William Wheeler wore the vestments of the church, as Rogers and Marsh told me that he did, and if he read the ceremony of marriage from the Book of Prayer, it was worse than a mockery. It was of the foulest sacrilege."

The Prince gasped.

"Wheeler," said Duppa, "because of unspeakable behavior, was unfrocked long ago. He is not a priest of the Church of England and never could be."

"I did not intend to make a mockery of marriage," the Prince said. His voice had a wooden, empty sound to it. "I know it's fashionable but I didn't do it," he said, stubbornly. "It's not what I intended at all."

Brian Duppa sighed with relief. It was not as bad as he had been informed, but the boy was guilty of lustful behavior. He needed chastisement and guidance.

"I shall expect you to come to me for spiritual guidance in the matter of the girl who has been with you," he said sternly. Then he left the room.

"Stay here," the Prince commanded, as Sir Richard started to follow Brian Duppa out of the room.

The Prince walked to the window and looked out upon the sleeping town. Across the way the Blackamoor's Head was swinging in the early morning breeze above the door of the inn. He thought of the ceremony. Those despicable fellows! That ceremony had been a farce, a trick, something to be used for blackmail! He had been so concerned with the keeping of the romantic secret that he hadn't considered the possibility of baser motives. He should have known—he should have known! He turned on Sir Richard. His dark face flushed with anger. His jaw was thrust forward and the underlip of his large, ugly mouth protruded.

"You know of this? Is it true?"

Miserably, Sir Richard nodded.

"Did Hugh Wyndham know of this impersonation by Wheeler?"

"No," said Sir Richard, "I am sure that Hugh is completely honest. He didn't know—any more than I did, but there is no doubt that he was foolish and indiscreet."

"Stupidity can be worse than deceit in such matters," the Prince said.

"Yes, verily," agreed Sir Richard.

"See to it that Hugh and his mother are removed somewhere, somewhere that their stupidity and meddling can do me no further harm!"

Sir Richard nodded.

"And as for William Wheeler and his confederates—," he paused and his black eyes flashed, and his jaw jutted out again. "Deny the whole affair of the wedding," he said. "Report the matter to Hyde and the council. Tell them that the scoundrels have attempted blackmail and there is no truth to their statements. See to it that they are frightened into silence, and I don't care how you do it. If possible, don't let Lucy know what has happened."

Sir Richard was astonished. He hadn't expected that the Prince would completely deny the facts. It was a solution, of course, but he had not expected that the Prince would be ready to renounce Lucy so soon—and was he intending to completely deceive her? He knew that he should rejoice that the affair was to be ended with safety for all concerned, but he couldn't get rid of a feeling of disappointment in the cold-blooded, self-centered attitude of His Highness. These thoughts left him unprepared for what came next.

"And before God, my good friend, Richard, I swear that when next I meet Lucy Walter, a ceremony will be performed that will leave no doubt in anyone's mind. I don't care where the axe will fall! I shall do it if it ruins the kingdom! They cannot make a fool of me!"

Sir Richard left the room in dismay. The boy was angry, it was true. Could that be a worthy explanation of the fact that he exhibited an almost maniacal egocentricity? He would do it "if it ruined the kingdom" and for the reason that he didn't wish to look the fool! Sir Richard could scarcely believe his ears. He had hoped that the Prince would lose interest in Lucy, but never that he would be a cad! And more than that—what would Charles do next?

3

The Earl of Carberry's coach was waiting when Lucy disembarked from the ship with her maidservant. A footman put them in, tended to the luggage and they were off, going smoothly and quickly over the road to Golden Grove.

The first thing that Lucy learned was that her mother was living permanently at Golden Grove, completely dependent upon the Earl. Elizabeth had aged; her face was pale and wan, her eyes tragic. She coughed a great deal and spent most of the day in bed or sitting in the garden in the sunshine.

When Lucy had an opportunity to talk with Frances Vaughan she made no explanation of her own situation but went straight to the point and asked questions about her mother.

"Mother is ill, isn't she?"

Frances hesitated before she said, "Yes, but more than that, Lucy, affairs have not been going well for your mother. Alfred Gwinne and your grandmother are still in London but since the Queen is no longer there they have little livelihood. The House of Lords handed down its final decision in the divorce suit, and it was in favor of your father. We know that the decision was influenced by the fact that we are all loyal to the King and that His Majesty has been defeated. The judges were afraid to do anything else."

"What about Justus?"

"William has the custody of him—and legally, you too, but I don't think there will be trouble if we keep you here."

"Where is Justus?"

"In London, studying law."

"Does Mother have a specific illness?"

"Yes," Frances said, sadly. "Her lungs, but she is ill both in body and in spirit." She studied Lucy and decided that she was mature enough to know everything. "Elizabeth was not only abandoned by William but by Thomas Byshfield, too; he is married to someone else."

Lucy caught her breath and was silent for a few moments and then murmured, "Poor Mother."

"Yes," Frances said quietly. "And how about you, Lucy?"

Lucy wanted to tell her everything but she remembered her promise to Charles that she would not reveal their marriage. She did tell her about her meetings with him in Exeter and about the abduction and the siege of Bridgwater. She stopped short of telling her about going to Barnstaple and the wedding, though she longed to do so. Frances listened quietly and when Lucy stopped and looked at her pleadingly as if begging for understanding she put her hand over Lucy's and said, "I have a letter from Anne Harvey. She is an old friend and she has explained everything to me."

"Oh, then you know."

"Yes." Frances would have liked to express concern that Lucy was getting herself into an even worse predicament than that of her mother but she didn't. In order to keep Lucy's confidence she should say nothing, for the present.

Even though she enjoyed being at Golden Grove time passed slowly for Lucy. At Christmastime Justus was allowed to come there for the holidays and he stared at Lucy as if he didn't know what to say to her. He tried to resume their old familiar relationship. "After all, we're twins," he kept saying but somehow the old intimacy didn't develop. They were like strangers.

After a while the situation was taken for granted and Lucy settled down to wait, as patiently as she could, for Charles to lift the siege at Exeter and then send for her to come to him. The siege at Exeter was not lifted. The Prince's army was defeated. There was no summons for Lucy to come to him. The Earl of Carberry received a formal letter from Sir Richard Fanshawe, one that all the King's noblemen received, telling him that the Prince had landed safely in Jersey and that he was under the protection of Governor Carteret and would stay there waiting for favorable developments. That was all. No mention was made of Lucy and no invitation was received for her to join the Prince in Jersey or anywhere else.

When Exeter fell Edward Hyde was on hand to see the Prince put aboard the yacht waiting at Falmouth but he didn't go aboard himself. It was Carteret's turn, now, he thought grimly; he, himself, was in the process of making arrangements for the safety of his own family; he was taking them to Holland. He was going there himself, to set up his own spy system and begin to work on restoring the monarchy. He was exasperated when the King surrendered to the Scots for he knew that the only sensible course for His Majesty to follow was to escape and go into exile—but Charles wouldn't do it. "I will live as a King or die as a Christian gentleman," he said.

Lucy thought only of Charles and how much she loved him. Completely trusting, she took it for granted that the regard for her welfare was uppermost in his mind. How could she know that while Charles was intrigued by her when she was with him—because she was unlike the women he knew at court, sweet and naive and undemanding—he had many other things to occupy him and there were many women that were only too glad to attract his attention. She had no inkling of the dilemma that her marriage to the heir to the throne would pose for the heads of state when they found out about it. She thought that Charles could make everything possible. She couldn't know what a disaster the marriage would be for Queen Henrietta who had all the responsibilities of the royal family and even the monarchy, itself, since the King had been imprisoned. In addition there were hundreds of retainers who had no support at all that she had to provide for. Innocent Lucy knew nothing of all this.

When the Queen had reached France after escaping capture by Essex at Exeter she was welcomed by the royal family of France. They gave her the chateau at St. Germain-en-laye to live in as long as she wished. Her brother, Louis XIII, gave orders that the wine cellars and the areas assigned to food storage were to be kept well stocked at all times and that Henrietta was to have every comfort and luxury that befitted a Queen.

Every day she walked upon the Pavillion of Henry of Navarre and enjoyed the sunshine; every day her health improved. She looked out across the Seine to the peaceful fields and orchards beyond and thought of King Charles. What were they doing with him? Was he comfortable or was he living in privation? The Royal Treasury of France had granted her a generous pension with no restrictions on how it could be spent; she sent every coin she could spare to her husband. The days crawled by this way for two years as they did for Lucy, waiting at Golden Grove. Henrietta gradually dispensed with her carriages; then the number of attendants was reduced; servants were discharged; but most of all, she refused to buy any more clothes for the people who remained in her household and even for herself.

Anne, the Queen Regent of France, tried to reason with her, from time to time, about the condition of her wardrobe and the shabbiness of her attendants. "If your pension is not large enough—?" she suggested at first, but when an increase was secured Henrietta sent that to her husband, too, and she and her attendants were as shabby as ever. Often Anne pointed out that Henrietta's gowns were frayed at the edges and that the fur lining of the hood of her only cloak was sparse and worn. Every time, Henrietta replied that such things were trivial compared to the dire needs of her husband. With that answer the French Queen could only sigh and let the matter rest.

The fashionable ladies and gentlemen of the French court were embarrassed by Henrietta's appearance. Some of them remembered her as she was when she went to England at fifteen to marry King Charles. When she left them, they said, she was a scintillating little beauty. Now she had returned, twenty years later, a solemn woman with wrinkled face and prematurely white hair. They looked at her hands and averted their eyes. Her fingers were swollen and discolored by rheumatism.

"It must be the foul climate of England that changed her," one of them whispered as she passed them, staring straight ahead and not seeing them, in a corridor of the Louvre one day.

"She does nothing all day, every day, but compose letters to all the governments of Europe begging for military aid," said another.

"Her loyalty is commendable but it is not very prudent. The monarchy in England is finished. No one will be grateful."

St. Germain-en-laye was an ancient castle, completed in the time of Francis I and Henrietta's father had added the famous terrace built upon the crest of land overlooking the River Seine. Directly below this Pavillion the gardens descended steeply to the river and they were as well kept as they had been a quarter of a century before when they were laid out. The parterres, broderies and carreaux were handsome and the gravelled paths were straight and well-edged.

One day late in autumn Henrietta came to the Pavillion followed by her faithful majordomo, Henry Jermyn. Her eyes rested, wistfully, upon the magnificent view across the river where the vineyards and orchards of the valley beyond St. Germain Forest stretched as far as the eye could see. The last leaves were falling in the forest and the bare branches of the fruit trees had been pruned for winter. A sudden breeze blew in from the river and Henrietta shivered. It reminded her of the coldness and dampness in England and of how she had suffered in Exeter when Henriette Anne was born. She walked slowly and thought over her present situation.

Her family was divided: the two younger children, Elizabeth and Henry, were confined in London as hostages of the Parliament, and the King had left James with his attendants in Oxford; only Mary was safe in Holland. And Charles—how he exasperated her! He had, after a long time and many entreaties, obeyed her and come to St. Germain. She could forgive him for his delay in coming if he would only cooperate with her plans now. If Charles married his cousin, Mademoiselle de Montpensier, the royal houses of France and England would be united; with France's support the English monarchy could be saved. She was sure of it!

Mademoiselle was not only her niece, and cousin of the King of France, but the richest woman in the kingdom. More than that, Mademoiselle made no secret of her intention of marrying a crown. She was so desperate she had even expressed hope of capturing the decrepit old Austrian Emperor when his wife died. What if the prospects of the British throne and a handsome young husband were dangled before her ambitious eyes? It wouldn't be difficult to persuade her that the restoration of the Stuarts was only a matter of time especially with her cooperation. Henrietta knew that it was a dream—

but still, Edward Hyde believed that a restoration was possible!

"Why is Charles refusing to do what he should do; he insults Mademoiselle continually because he doesn't like her. What difference does that make? What is wrong with him?"

"Perhaps," Jermyn said, "his affections lie elsewhere." He dropped his eyes respectfully and then raised them again, waiting for her reply.

"Is it Mademoiselle Carteret?" she asked reluctantly. "I have been informed that she expects a child by Charles."

"No," Jermyn scoffed. "Carteret has already married his daughter to a local curate in Jersey."

Henrietta was silent for a few moments and then burst out, "Was it Edward Hyde that kept Charles in Jersey when we needed him here so desperately?"

"No, Your Majesty."

"As you know, it is said that Charles spent his time sailing, hawking, dancing, and otherwise enjoying himself at the Governor's expense. Is Carteret such a fool that he expects to ingratiate himself with the Crown by these tactics?"

"I think not, Your Majesty. Carteret is generously loyal. That is all."

"Then it's not Mademoiselle Carteret who is causing the confusion in my son's mind?"

"No," Henry said softly. "That was but a momentary infatuation. Marguerite Carteret is ten years older than His Highness."

"If that's the way it is," she asked, "why won't he pay proper attention to Mademoiselle now that the affair has been resolved?"

"That was a good question," Henry said to himself.

She looked at him shivering in the autumn air; he needed a new cloak. She also saw, by the expression on his lean face, that he had something to tell her. He wouldn't blurt it out but would inform her methodically, without haste, so that she would understand every step of his thinking.

"Is His Highness having an affair with one of my ladies?" she asked bluntly.

"No, Your Majesty," he said. "It would be easier if he were."

"What then? Surely it is not that girl, Lucy Walter?"

Henry was silent for a moment. He hadn't realized that Henrietta knew about that disgraceful affair. Certainly he hadn't informed her. He nodded and murmured, "Yes, Your Majesty."

The Queen gasped. She could scarcely believe that her son would be so foolish.

"He must forget her," she said sharply. "He is the heir to the throne. Courting Mademoiselle is a delicate, diplomatic task which must be undertaken."

Henry lowered his eyes to conceal his amusement. The Queen was not as naive as her son, he thought, but she didn't understand that the Prince's behavior was to be expected. He hadn't been trained to sacrifice himself in abstaining from pleasure.

"This 'anguish fever' that he affects," Henrietta said, "moping around quoting poetry about his lady love. I will not have it. He must come to his senses. Tell him that it is my command that he court Mademoiselle de Montpensier and ask her hand in marriage."

"With Your Majesty's permission, I must say that it would be imprudent to try to coerce His Highness at the moment. It would only increase his rebellion." He paused and stroked the points of his moustache. He mustn't go too fast.

"That's true," she said. "I know that it would only make him more defiant. But what are we to do?"

"Since he cannot be forced to do your will, Your Majesty, perhaps circumstances can be arranged so that he will choose to do it."

The Queen studied his face. "Come, come, Henry, you have information or a plan. What is it?"

"I have both. With your permission—?"

"Yes, yes," she said impatiently, "proceed."

"Your Majesty is aware of the rumor that His Highness married Lucy Walter before he left Wales?"

She nodded with a frown.

"It is true."

Painfully, the Queen drew in her breath.

Before she could say anything he went on. "Our agents have discovered that there was a ceremony performed, but it was a fraud. The service was read by an unfrocked priest of the Church of England."

Henrietta stared at Jermyn. She couldn't believe that her son would do such a thing.

"His Highness was not a part of the mockery. He was sincere in his intention of marrying the girl."

Henrietta didn't know which made her suffer more; that her son was foolishly imprudent, or relief that he hadn't been deliberately sacrilegious. Henry thought that she was going to faint. He put out his hand to support her but she motioned him back.

"The stupid, immature boy," she cried out, passing her hand over her eyes. "I suppose now he wants to marry her again." She was being facetious with no thought that she was making a true evaluation of the situation.

"Yes, he does." Henry paused a moment before he went on, making an appraisal of her reaction. "It's most honorable of His Highness," he said in a simpering tone and then remained silent, his eyes on his boots.

Henrietta reflected that the wicked little smile playing on his lips meant that cynical thoughts were passing through his mind to the effect that the Prince need not marry every wench that he slept with. When Henry was impertinent, even in his thoughts, it offended her.

"Go on, Henry," she said coldly. "Complete what you have to say. You mentioned a plan. What is it?"

Henry cleared his throat softly before he began.

"Perhaps, the girl could be brought here from Carmarthen. As long as she is 'at large' so to speak, the Prince may find a way to go to her, and we will completely lose control of him."

"Did she try to go to Jersey?"

"Not that I know of."

"Or to come here?"

"Probably not."

"She must be very naive, or for some reason is afraid of being involved with royalty. It can't be that she is blessed with common sense! If so she wouldn't have consented to marry Charles."

Jermyn smiled a wicked little grin. "What female wouldn't be willing to sell her soul to be 'involved' with a royal prince!"

I wouldn't, Henrietta thought. "Don't take liberties, Henry. I won't tolerate it." He knew she meant it; he quietly lowered his eyes as if he were crestfallen. So far so good, he thought, but he still must allay her scruples by proceeding slowly. That was obvious. But he must be very careful!

"If it can't be avoided," he said, "a marriage ceremony could be performed—an honest one," he added hastily when the Queen cried out in protest, "—a Protestant ceremony by an Anglican clergyman," he said with a smirk.

She was displeased and she was puzzled. What was he leading up to?

"Later, when His Highness comes to his senses, it can be annulled. I hope Your Majesty will forgive me for the necessity of speaking boldly," he said. "But, the situation must be resolved. His Highness must be rid of her once and for all—or there will be trouble later."

The Queen was already committed to overlooking his "boldness."

"When this madness is all out of his blood," Henry went on, "His Highness will be willing to consider a suitable marriage." He paused until he thought she had accepted that idea. "The Walter girl comes from a family of fanatic heretics," he went on. "Puritan on her father's side and the English church on her mother's." He paused to admire his choice of words that he hoped would provoke the response that he wanted from the Queen. "The time will come when His Highness will consent to an annulment."

"I still don't understand why Lucy hasn't made an attempt to come to Charles."

"I think," Henry said, slowly, "that she is childish. I think that Charles is her lover—but she also looks to him as the father she never had. She has been waiting for him to send for her."

"Oh, no!" Henrietta said. "The poor child—but that is not our responsibility!" She set her lips in a firm line. "It is not our responsibility!" she repeated.

"No," Henry agreed, and again he smiled his cynical little smile beneath the pointed moustache. "But we must take it into account—and it is reason enough to have her here so we can end the affair."

"I see what you mean." The Queen sighed. "How could all this be arranged?"

"By delay, chiefly," he said. "These things cannot be hurried."

"We have so little time," she said anxiously. "Mademoiselle may find a husband elsewhere."

"True enough," said Henry, "but we will get nowhere if we try to force the Prince to do our will in his present mood."

"Yes, I know that's true. I see that I must consent but I will do so only if Charles, himself, promises to be agreeable enough to Mademoiselle that she will believe that he is courting her."

Jermyn rubbed his chilled hands together. "That's exactly what I was hoping that Your Majesty would say," he said.

"Where is the girl at this moment?"

"At Golden Grove, the estate of Lord Vaughan, Earl of Carberry, who is her mother's kinsman."

"Mm," said Henrietta. As he often did, Henry had distorted the truth. He had implied that Lucy was of no consequence—a "nobody." "She is well connected after all. It was at Golden Grove that Jeremy Taylor, the King's favorite chaplain, took refuge," she said.

She remained lost in thought trying to consider every aspect of the situation that Henry was leading her into. She took into account that he was never known to lie to her but he would do everything short of it to convince her to permit an intrigue that he planned. It was true that there was a great risk involved if Charles did marry the girl in the Church of England. If the time came for him to succeed his father—Charles might even decide to abdicate in favor of his son—a marriage in the Church of England would be embarrassing; it would preclude a more favorable marriage with a royal house and he might need that desperately to stabilize his government! On the other hand, when Charles became head of the State Church it might be impossible to annul the marriage. They must prevent it.

At the same time, it might be true that there would be less risk if she could have the situation under her surveillance with Jermyn's help. She knew all too well how rebellious Charles could be if he were not handled with tact. He could not be forced! More than that, Lucy had been with the Earl of Carberry and his wife all this time and while the Earl was loyal to the King and Frances Vaughan was a woman of high principles, who could be sure what Carberry might do under pressing circumstances or if he became maliciously ambitious. The war had caused some strange defections.

Henry watched her face for a hint of her thoughts. The Queen's moral scruples were something that had to be taken into account, he knew. She could spoil the best laid plans with a sudden reversal of attitude if she thought that there was something in them which was against her conscience. But she could act relentlessly if she were convinced that there were no moral principles involved. He felt a little guilty about the plans that he had made! He wondered if she sensed his uneasiness.

"I wouldn't have His Majesty know of the plans," she said.

So that was it, he thought with amusement, and congratulated himself that he had won her over. She was his partner in crime to the point of worrying about the King discovering it! He caressed the points of his moustache, first on one side and then the other, waiting until he had control of himself again.

"Of course not, Your Majesty." Skillfully he transferred the object of their deception to someone other than the King. "The Earl of Carberry," he said, "is in no position to object to anything that we do. If we send for the girl he will release her and not even ask why we want her."

"What about her father?"

"Of no consequence—a nobody—a Roundhead!" Again Henry congratulated himself on the choice of a derogatory word. "It is reported that he died in a skirmish at Tavistock."

"What is your plan?"

"Lucy's grandmother was Elenor Vaughan, sister of the first Earl of Carberry. One of her maternal aunts married John Barlow of Slebech."

Again the seemingly unrelated fact. That was Henry's way. Henrietta sighed and waited.

87

"John Barlow of Slebech is a trusted partisan of My Lord Glamorgan."

"I remember now," said Henrietta. "John Barlow was taken prisoner at Pill Fort, and his lands were given to Rowland Laugharne."

"Yes," said Henry, "but he was one of the prisoners exchanged, and he is in Kilkenny with Glamorgan at this moment."

"I see, and what is the plan?"

"In brief, a secret messenger will be sent to Golden Grove from the Prince to take the girl to Barlow."

Henrietta listened with a worried expression.

"In the meantime we shall send an envoy, perhaps George Leybourn, to Lord Glamorgan with instructions that he receive the girl and permit her to join his party when it leaves for the Continent. The rest will be easy!"

Again Henry's fingers went to the points of his moustache. He fondled them thoughtfully before he went on. "The girl's twin brother is in London studying for the bar. He should be sent for. He may be useful."

"How will the girl be known?"

"It could be said that she is the widow of some relative of Barlow's," he said. " 'Mrs. Lucy Barlow' would sound convincing."

Henrietta sighed. "This affair must be conducted with the greatest secrecy."

Jermyn nodded. "There's no need to confide in anyone. We need make no explanation, even to Lord Glamorgan, why we want the girl here."

"Henry," she said, "I don't like all this but we must do something before it is too late."

They had been walking slowly along the Pavillion as they talked, and her capitulation seemed to conclude the matter. She still had faith in him! He dropped to one knee on the cold stones of the gravelled path and kissed the hem of her threadbare cloak.

"To the death, Your Majesty," he murmured his devotion.

It was melodramatic and it was overdone, but Henry Jermyn knew that the Queen loved it.

Day after day Charles had sulked in his apartments in his mother's chateau. He was trapped; he was completely dependent upon her financially and she treated him like a child! He had known what it was like to be the King's commander-in-chief in Wales. He had lived like a King in Jersey. He had finally come to his mother's court only because Marguerite Carteret had told him that he was bankrupting her father; that the noblemen quartered on the people were a burden; that he should leave the island! In royal arrogance he agreed. If it didn't disturb her that she was going to bear his child and only thought of the welfare of the people of the island he didn't see why he should let it trouble him. Her father could marry her to a local curate to avoid scandal.

Charles had expected that his mother would treat him like a man and an ally when he came to Paris. She didn't even ask his advice! She demanded that he obey her without question. The most galling of all was her demand that he court his cousin, Mademoiselle de Montpensier, whom he detested because she was oversized, clumsy and arrogant! His mother told him over and over what he already knew: that Mademoiselle was the richest woman in France. What did he care if she would bring to her husband four duchies, the Seigneuris of Dombes, the Palace of Luxembourg and a fortune of twenty million francs? It only made him think of Lucy who had nothing at all. When Mademoiselle looked at him coldly, shrugged her shoulders and turned her back on him, he thought of Jersey and the governor's daughter. Marguerite Carteret always smiled at him and was anxious to please him.

He stopped answering when the Queen commanded him to escort his cousin to some affair in one of the royal palaces. He obeyed because he had to but the lower lip of his large mouth was thrust forward and his eyes glinted rebellion. When the French courtiers pretended to swoon at the sight of the beautiful Mademoiselle he was disgusted and he showed it. Since his tutor wasn't there to deny it, Charles pretended that he couldn't understand or speak French.

Mademoiselle suspected that this was the case so one day she spoke in rapid French to her friend, the Duchesse de Châtillon, in his presence. "My dear Aunt confided to one of my ladies that Prince Charles is dying for love of me," she said coyly. She looked sidewise under her lashes at Charles but he returned the look with a blank stare. "If only he said it himself," she went on, "I cannot say what might happen; but I value little all that they say to me on behalf of a man who can say nothing for himself."

Charles grinned as he turned his back on her. He had no intention of admitting that he understood every word she said.

The social season in the French court was an especially gay one. Balls, concerts and masques followed one after the other. Only the appearance of the threadbare English Queen and her morose son with the jutting jaw and tousled hair was a reminder that across the English Channel a revolution was dethroning a royal house.

The French courtiers felt compassion for the English Queen but they had only contempt for her untidy son. His tall swarthiness dwarfed them and his long feet, accustomed to military boots, walked all over his partner's shoes when he condescended to take part in the dancing. He was always hungry. At dinner he attacked a joint of beef like a hungry wolf while the French courtiers nibbled daintily on ortolan. This never failed to set off a titter of giggling behind the fans of elegantly coiffeured ladies.

One evening after Lord Jermyn's plan had been set into action, and there was an exceptionally brilliant affair scheduled for the evening, Henrietta sent for Charles. He appeared before her expecting to be given the usual command to appear at the fete and make himself agreeable to Mademoiselle. There was a warning glint in his eyes; he stared at his mother as if he were contemplating the idea of refusing to go at all.

The Queen smiled at him. "My son," she said, "we have had a misunderstanding."

The Prince was astonished. He had expected a frown.

"In my preoccupation with diplomacy and the desperate situation of His Majesty I have overlooked your feelings." Henrietta was trying to keep criticism out of her voice.

Charles looked quickly at Henry Jermyn standing at the Queen's side. Henry's face was impassive. The Prince's eyes returned to his mother. She was no longer smiling. Her eyes burned with fanaticism. "It is absolutely necessary that we secure aid from France," she said. "You must help me!"

Charles' eyes flashed with sudden anger.

"But—" said Henrietta. Her eyes were flashing, too. "It is obvious that you are not yet mature enough to accept responsibilities."

Softly, Henry Jermyn cleared his throat. The warning came just in time for Henrietta halted the torrent of words that was about to come out. Silently she stared at her sullen son until she regained her composure. Then she went on.

"You must make yourself agreeable and popular in the French court. There is no other way. However, if you will do this I promise that you may have your— Lucy." It took all the self-control that the Queen could muster to say this! "You could make her your mistress and marry Mademoiselle."

Jermyn sighed with relief.

Again Charles looked away from his mother to Jermyn. Henry was quick to take up the challenge. By a silent gesture he indicated that he was on the side of Charles in this matter and that the Prince should act before the Queen changed her mind.

"You mean," said Charles, "that if I pretend to fall in love with Mademoiselle and become popular with those stupid French courtiers you will send for Lucy Walter?"

"Exactly," said Jermyn.

"How will she get here?" Charles asked suspiciously.

"We will arrange to have her join a party which is under the protection of Lord Glamorgan. My lord is leaving Ireland for Paris soon, and he can bring her with him. She can assume the name, 'Mrs. Barlow'." Cynical amusement lit up Jermyn's eyes.

The Prince was astonished and indeed a little chagrined. He wasn't sure that he wanted Lucy to be brought to Paris. But here was a chance to show his strength. He had it in his power to withhold something that was needed desperately. Besides, it would be satisfying to have a woman with him that he could manage. The French were too difficult. He couldn't get anywhere with them.

"Very well," he said. "Bring Lucy here and I will do what you wish."

"You see?" Henry's raised eyebrows said to the Queen.

That evening the Prince was changed when he appeared at the fete given in the Palais Royal. He wore a fairly presentable costume and his dark curls were combed and arranged properly. His French was fluent and he danced expertly.

92

Jermyn whispered to the Queen. "You see?" he said.

"Yes, I see," she answered, "but what I see is that his behavior was stubborn, selfish and disobedient! He is perfectly competent."

"There, there," Jermyn said soothingly. "Let's not lose any ground," he muttered.

The entertainment was in a large mirrored hall that evening. It was brilliantly lighted by crystal chandeliers and the candlelight reflected, again and again, the sparkle of diamonds on the costumes of the guests. At one end of the mammoth room was a simulated throne covered by a cloth of gold. At the other end was a stage upon which an Italian comedy was to be acted.

The party began officially with the entrance of the young King of France. Following him was Mademoiselle de Montpensier in all the finery suitable to the richest heiress in the kingdom. Her gown was sprinkled with hundreds of diamonds, and at the crest of her high coiffure there was an elaborate ornament of pearls from which sprouted three feathers, one of each of her favorite colors: white, black and rose. She enjoyed the gasp of admiration when she entered; she tossed her head arrogantly.

Following Mademoiselle was His Highness, Prince Charles. From the moment he entered the room it was evident that he wasn't going to let his shabbiness embarrass him. He was devoted to his cousin and even outdid the French courtiers in gallantry.

Louis refused to mount the honorary throne out of courtesy to his royal English cousin. Charles, equally polite, also refused and suggested that they seat Mademoiselle upon it.

She was enchanted. A throne was what she craved! She looked at her dark cousin. Maybe he wasn't so stupid after all. Perhaps this was a hint of a future proposal? She had a faraway look in her eyes as she calculated the possibility. Perhaps, if she could do no better—! She shrugged her haughty shoulders and threw herself into the enjoyment of the symbolic opportunity of having two royal cousins at her feet.

The evening ended with a grand ball. Even Henrietta had to agree, before it was over, that her son was a huge success.

The next night and the next Charles exceeded himself in charm and vivacity and he seemed to be having a wonderful time. But after the surprise of the first evening Mademoiselle responded to his advances with indifference. She let it be known that in her opinion her boorish English cousin had practically no prospect of succeeding to a throne. More than that, she was so bored with him that the change in him was of no interest to her. Besides, she had received word that the Empress of Austria was dying and the Emperor was definitely in the market for a bride. Charles appeared quite gauche in her eyes in comparison with this new opportunity.

Charles took her coolness in his stride. The French court watched him redouble his attentions to Mademoiselle with amusement. He was underfoot constantly, they said. "He assumes," said one French gentleman, "an experience in matters of the heart which he does not possess."

Then, when Mademoiselle continued to rebuff him, Charles transferred his attentions to Mademoiselle's best friend, the Duchesse de Châtillon. The gossips cheered. The young Prince wasn't completely stupid. A little competition and a little jealousy is good in a budding romance, they said. Only Mademoiselle was unimpressed.

Henrietta remonstrated with Jermyn. He answered that there was nothing to worry about. The Prince had selected a lady for this maneuver who was an exceptionally safe choice, he said. The Duchess was famous for her beauty and charm and she had, in fact, some of the noblest gentlemen in France for her lovers. Now, she made it clear that she had renounced all amours because she was madly in love with her new husband that she had eloped to marry. Her ardor for him had not cooled; she needed no one else!

Henrietta was not satisfied. She expressed her displeasure in no uncertain terms. "But it is all to good purpose," he insisted. "Mademoiselle is not a simple girl who can be won easily."

At Easter time the situation had not improved. It appeared to the experts that the Prince was overdoing his strategy. He snubbed Mademoiselle unmercifully and she was too vain to take much of that. One evening at a ball, given in the Palais Royal, she appeared to relent a little. She spoke pleasantly to Charles and asked him to dance with Mademoiselle de Guise upon whom she was conferring favors at the moment. Instead of complying with this conciliatory request, Charles led out Mademoiselle de Guerchi, who everyone knew was Mademoiselle de Montpensier's only rival in beauty and popularity. Worse than that, Charles did not ask his cousin to dance with him during the entire evening.

That was the end as far as Mademoiselle was concerned. She had given him his last chance. With a toss of her head and petulant movements that made the silk of her elegant gown swish and crackle, she announced for all to hear that she cared not one whit what her unpleasant and rude cousin did.

Henrietta was furious. "This stupid, bungling behavior has gone far enough," she cried with vexation.

Jermyn couldn't help showing that he was puzzled. "One cannot hurry the making of love," he said uncertainly. "Give him time."

"There is little time to give!" cried Henrietta. "We must have the help of France. We need money, money,

money! While my son enjoys himself being coy in an affair of the heart, his father lies a prisoner and in danger of being tried for treason!"

"Patience, dear Queen," said Jermyn. "Everything takes time. Even the events in England are moving slowly."

"At least," said Henrietta, "Charles has accomplished one thing. It is obvious that he is growing in favor in the French court."

"Yes," said Jermyn, a crafty smile playing upon his lips. "At least he has discovered that victories in affairs of the heart achieve the respect of the French nobles and make him popular with them."

Henrietta looked at him angrily. What was this evasive man about to propose now?

"We must find a suitable wife for him. When this is done we will have achieved our object. If it can be done before Lucy is brought here it will be the best solution of all."

Henrietta looked at him in alarm. "But it must be Mademoiselle de Montpensier," she said.

"Not necessarily. It may have been impossible from the beginning. Maybe the Prince is wiser than we. It has been obvious from the beginning that Mademoiselle was never very interested. At first the thought of being the future Queen of England amused her, but the prospect of being an empress is even more attractive."

He paused as he saw Henrietta's stricken expression. She knew that he was referring to the dwindling possibility of the Stuarts ever regaining their throne.

"Mademoiselle is too vain to overlook the continued rudeness of His Highness," Jermyn went on. "She has remarked publicly that she dislikes him intensely and will have nothing more to do with him. We will be imprudent if we do not accept this attitude and look elsewhere."

"What—" Henrietta started to say.

Henry pretended that he didn't hear her, because he couldn't be guilty of interrupting.

"We must be realistic," he said. "If it is not Mademoiselle, we must find another, and as quickly as possible."

"Yes," Henrietta said acidly. "We must be realistic. It is only His Highness who can do as he pleases."

"He is young," said Jermyn, "and has much to learn about responsibility." He said this instead of what crossed his mind—that poverty and exile were two things that royal brats find hard to understand.

He looked down self-pityingly at his frayed clothes. Then, glancing at the Queen's shabbiness, he said gently, "There is some talk among the French nobles that they will send aid to His Majesty. They are giving a ball at Fontainebleau to pledge their devotion."

"We need cannons," snapped Henrietta, "not dancing and sweet words of brotherly love!"

That same day Jermyn received a letter from Edward Hyde warning him that his agents had discovered that the Parliament was sending an ambassador to France with the demand that they surrender Prince Charles to them. The real reason for his letter was that he knew that Lucy was being brought to St. Germain. He wanted to remind Jermyn, in no uncertain terms, that an unworthy alliance of any kind was dangerous to the royal cause.

Jermyn replied that there was no danger of a secret alliance between the Prince and Lucy Walter. The Prince, he wrote, was at that very moment courting his cousin, Mademoiselle de Montpensier.

Hyde wasn't fooled. He knew that Justus Walter was already on the way to St. Germain and that Lord Glamorgan, with John Barlow and Lucy Walter in his party, was preparing to take ship for France. There was nothing that he could do now, he thought as he read

Jermyn's letter, but the time would come when they would call on him again. He would wait.

In London Justus Walter couldn't help being aware that he was under surveillance by spies, both Cromwell's and Hyde's. It was no wonder that he refused to talk with the messenger who came to him from Prince Charles until he had examined the man's credentials. It was late at night when he unbarred his door and let the man in. Even then he kept him standing while he sat at his desk and read the letter which Charles had written requesting him to come to St. Germain-en-laye "to meet his sister there." His lip curled disdainfully when he read the Prince's declared intention of marrying Lucy.

"Yes," he said to himself, "that's what I would expect from His dissembling Highness! But I don't believe him."

His first reaction was to refuse to go but he had a premonition that Lucy was caught in a trap; that she was a pawn in some international intrigue. He must give the matter serious thought, he said to himself, because his conscience would not let him abandon her even though she had deserted him.

Curtly, he told the messenger that he could remain for the night and that he would be given an answer in the morning. All night Justus struggled to come to a decision. He didn't wish to interrupt his studies and he was furious with Lucy; but at daybreak he told the messenger that he would go.

"You must remain hidden," he told the man sternly, "until I can obtain a pass to make the trip to the Continent. I do not wish to be embarrassed, politically, by your presence here. If you make one false move," he said with anger smoldering in his voice, "I will change my mind about going to France with you."

When they were on board ship, at last, Justus stood watching the turbulent water of the Channel. His thoughts were almost as angry as the stormy sea. If it had been any other man than the Prince who had compromised his sister, he would have sought him out long ago, and run him through with a sword. But, there were two reasons, he told himself, why he couldn't follow his inclination for revenge. Killing the Prince would be an act of treason and besides that, Lucy might not wish him to interfere in her affairs. He would withhold decision about what to do until he had seen her at St. Germain.

All these things were still going through his mind when they went ashore at Fécamp. They were met by a royal coach that took them to St. Germain-en-laye, and when they got there Justus was taken at once to the quarters prepared for him. In a short time the Prince came to him instead of summoning him to his presence. Justus seethed with resentment when he responded politely to Charles' greeting of welcome and he cringed when Charles slapped him familiarly on the back.

"She's coming, Justus," Charles said. "Lucy is on the way."

But in spite of his cordiality Justus realized that His Highness didn't intend to reveal any of his plans to him. He said only that Justus was to go with Thomas Gerrard to meet Glamorgan's ship and escort Lucy to St. Germain. Having acquiesced to this point Justus knew that he had no choice but to obey. He got into the coach and went with the courtier.

The air was mild and sweet with the fragrance of blossoms on the fruit trees in the orchards of the valley across the Seine and the cobbles in the courtyard of the old palace were warm with sunshine when an advance rider rode in to announce that Lucy's carriage was at the turn of the road a short distance away. Charles, with several of his attendants, went down into the courtyard, at once, to wait for her. He wore a brown velvet costume and his heavy black hair lay in stiff lovelocks on the lace collar that covered his shoulders.

When the carriage came to a stop in the courtyard Justus opened the door from the inside, sprang to the ground and, brushing aside the footman's help, gave Lucy his hand as she slowly descended the steps. Her clothing was covered with dust, and she swayed a bit as she stood with her small figure enveloped in a full-length cloak. Her black curly hair had been blown by the wind and her lips quivered as if she were about to cry.

The Prince did not wait for her to be brought to him but ran to her and enfolded her in his arms, lifted her off the ground and whirled around happily. Then, he kissed her eyes, her throat, her mouth. "Two years," he said, "and six months and you are lovelier than ever!"

Thomas Gerrard and the others watched the Prince and then looked at each other in amusement. They were a little ashamed of His Royal Highness. He used no restraint. His conduct was not only undignified, it was ridiculous. Henrietta watched from a tower room window. Her hands were clenched and tears were trickling down her cheeks.

Justus ground his teeth in anger. He had a wild desire to kick somebody—the Prince or his amused courtiers. And Lucy—he would like to slap her eager little face. The little fool! She was like a fly walking into a spider's web.

The Prince paid no attention to any of them. He led Lucy to a bench and held her in his arms as he talked to her, and she murmured answers. Then, to the surprise of all those who watched, she closed her eyes and fell into a faint.

It was almost a week before she recovered from what the Queen's physician diagnosed as a "fainting spell" brought on by fatigue. "The girl is indeed lovely," Jermyn said to the Queen. "Especially for a Welsh woman," he added.

"Yes," said Henrietta, "she is beautiful, but she must

have little stamina, or a weak heart, to faint so easily."

Jermyn shrugged. "It will be easier to get rid of her, then."

He looked sidewise at Henrietta. Did she have a romantic hope that the girl would have enough character to defend herself? Very likely. The Queen's scruples and romantic ideas were often exasperating. It took much of his energy to counteract them.

"The girl took the news of the deception of the unfrocked clergyman very well," he said, lowering his voice so only the Queen would hear.

"And the Prince?" asked Henrietta, also in a low voice.

"His Highness is eager for another ceremony," he said. He grinned but checked his ironic mirth when he saw that the Queen was not taking the matter as lightly as he.

"And the girl, does she insist?"

"No," said Jermyn, "she is completely trusting!" There was a sneer in his voice. "And of course she accepts the explanation that no ceremony can be performed during Lent."

"What then?" asked Henrietta.

"His Highness says that he wishes to marry her on the eighth day after Easter, the Monday after Low Sunday, which is the twentieth of April."

He paused but Henrietta was silent. He went on. "If we can divert him from his purpose until Rogation Sunday then we can convince him that marriage is prohibited until Trinity Sunday, the sixth of June. We can count on that, I think."

"And how, my master intriguer, can you divert that stubborn boy for so many weeks?"

"By subterfuge," he said. "With Hamilton's emissaries on the way from Edinburgh we may not need the support of the French court—!"

"Nor fear a marriage with the girl?"

"Exactly," said Jermyn with a crafty smile. "We can keep him busy during the day. And as for the nights—" Lord Jermyn snickered.

Henrietta looked away from him. There was a faraway expression in her eyes as if she could not bear to listen to him.

"One need only to observe His Highness to know that the girl means little to him except as a plaything," said Jermyn. "It is only romantic conscience that keeps him insisting on the marriage ceremony. He does not really wish it."

Henrietta turned pale.

"The ceremony means nothing to him," he said. "He will be easily influenced when he is tired of the girl."

Jermyn checked his words. "Your Majesty—you are ill."

She turned away from him. It was very difficult to accept what Jermyn was saying about her son even though she knew it was true. "No," she said. "It will pass."

Henry remained silent. He had gone too far; the Queen was offended. Well, it didn't matter. It was good that she was beginning to understand her son.

The Prince did seem content to let the days slip by. Lent came and went. So did Low Sunday and the days that followed when there could have been a wedding according to the rules of the English Church. Jermyn's plan seemed to be working. During the day Charles was required to work on details of the plans for uprisings in Scotland, Ireland and England. They were insignificant details where little attention or wisdom was required but this made no difference to Charles. He was like an animal on a treadmill. He did the work only to get through with it so that he could be left alone with Lucy.

Justus seethed with rage for it was evident to him that she denied Charles nothing. She paid no attention to the lectures which he tried to give her.

Henrietta was devastated by what she had permitted to happen; she stormed at Jermyn to put a stop to it. Jermyn smiled indulgently and diverted her attention to some urgent piece of business.

"The plan is working," he congratulated himself. "Her Majesty should have known that it would be a sordid business!"

Spring advanced. The sun was bright. The terraced gardens, descending from the Palace to the winding Seine, were a profusion of color: daffodils, irises and wild roses were in full bloom.

Every day Justus stood on the Pavillion of Henry IV and watched Charles and Lucy strolling along the gravelled paths between the parterres, broderies and carreaux. He could scarcely contain his anger when the Prince would reach out his long arms and try to embrace Lucy. She would dodge and run away, and he would go after her. Down the labyrinth of paths they went until Charles caught her and covered her face, her neck, her arms with kisses.

To make matters worse Justus saw that Henry Jermyn also watched with a cylinder from a window in the tower room of the Queen's apartments. This convinced him that, as he suspected, his sister was trapped in an intrigue. He knew, however, that for the moment he was powerless to help her, mostly because she wouldn't let him.

Inside the palace, Jermyn would raise his eyebrows at the erotic play in the garden, smile cynically and then move the cylinder to scan the straight, tree-lined road in the direction of Paris. He was watching for the messengers from Scotland. When he was satisfied that they were not on the road he would lower the glass and return to work with Henrietta at her desk. She was trying to use the dissatisfaction that was growing everywhere in Britain to stir up uprisings. The people of England were weary of war, exhausted by taxation and irritated by the suppression of all accustomed amusements. The decrees of Cromwell's tyrannical government were proving to them that they had exchanged an absolute monarchy for military despotism. Henrietta and Jermyn had been quick to take advantage of the change in public opinion. Their chief difficulty was that the Royalists were so scattered and disorganized that it was difficult to establish a definite policy or even a common enthusiasm. They were all in favor of the King but in varying degrees.

It was ironical that the greatest hope for the monarchy now lay in Scotland, where the trouble had started in the first place, but even there the Royalists were divided into factions. There was one party, led by the Marquis of Montrose, that was unconditionally monarchist, and another formed by the Presbyterians who declared themselves for the King but were sharply divided into factions among themselves. The party led by the Marquis of Argyle held firmly to the Presbyterian Covenant but those under the Duke of Hamilton professed a Presbyterianism which was opposed to the tyranny of the Scottish Kirk.

It seemed quite possible that if Prince Charles went to Scotland, as he was about to be invited to do, there might be an army provided for him which would be supported by one, or all, of the factions. More than that, there was hope that the English Royalists would join an army that came over the border commanded by the Prince. That army would march to London, liberate the King, and put him back on the throne. At least that was the dream at St. Germain-en-laye but the Queen and Jermyn knew that success depended, in a large measure, upon the Prince's ability to unify the Royalists.

They played a wily game, Henrietta and Henry Jermyn. Quietly they encouraged the Scots and at the same time they were inciting the Irish Catholics to rise in favor of the King. Neither the King nor Prince Charles were informed about these activities.

All plans rested upon the arrival of the emissaries from Scotland, who would bring the invitation for the Prince to join, and eventually assume command of the Duke of Hamilton's army; at least that's the impression the Scots gave Jermyn in their correspondence. It was not until the first of May that Lord Jermyn took up his cylinder and saw horsemen approaching on the road from Paris. They pulled up at the chateau, dismounted, and demanded entrance. There was no mistaking it. It was the commission from Scotland.

Henrietta and Jermyn waited for them in the formal reception room of her apartment. If Mytens' portrait of her husband, hanging on the wall above her head, pricked her conscience because of her Irish plans, Henrietta kept it to herself. She sent an attendant to summon the Prince to the conference.

Charles came at once and his tall athletic figure was imposing, his manner gracious. He acknowledged the homage of the emissaries with royal dignity and listened quietly to their invitation to command Hamilton's army. His eyes snapped with enthusiasm as they described the hopes for an invasion of England. The Scots exchanged satisfied glances among themselves. Here was a worthy leader, they silently agreed. He seemed to be all that they had hoped for.

Henrietta smiled and waited for the Prince's words of acceptance—words that Jermyn had prepared for him and which had been given to him just before he entered the conference chamber. Her face froze when he did not make the prepared speech.

He said, "I will give you an answer at sundown." He bowed to his mother and left the apartment.

Henrietta sat in dazed astonishment but Jermyn guessed what was happening. He went immediately to the tower room of the Queen's apartment, took up the cylinder and went to the window. As he expected, he saw Charles walking to where Lucy waited for him in the Palace Garden. There was no gay, erotic play this time, but an earnest conversation. The young couple walked arm in arm to a bench, remote from the windows of the palace, where Jermyn could not see them. He went back to the dismayed Queen. There was nothing anyone could do but wait for sundown.

The sun went down; the candles were lit; the Queen and Lord Jermyn waited in the conference room; the Scots joined them. They all had to make conversation for a long time while they waited for the Prince. Henrietta could scarcely contain her anger and Jermyn watched with apprehension. Charles had not consulted either of them; all day they had worried about what he would reply.

At last he came.

"I will accept the invitation of my Lord Duke of Hamilton with one condition," Charles said without preliminaries.

"And that condition, Highness?" broke in Jermyn. It was a desperate attempt to communicate to Charles that he must accept the invitation without reservation.

Charles didn't pay any attention to him.

"I will go on the condition that my Anglican chaplains go with me," he said.

Henrietta's lips parted in stunned surprise; Lord Jermyn let out his breath with a snort of disgust. The Scots stared at the Prince in astonishment. They carried explicit instructions that if the Prince refused to embrace Presbyterianism they were to break off negotiations. They had been told to approach the subject delicately with evasive answers and half promises that could be broken easily. Most of all they were to avoid a definite allusion to the subject one way or the other. Once in Scotland they could bend His Highness the way they wanted him.

Charles precipitated the whole thing by going to the heart of the matter in a way that left no avenue for reopening the negotiations. He had made the one stipulation that they could not meet, or even discuss.

Early the next morning the party of Scottish Commissioners rode out through the palace gate over the moat and on to the tree-lined road to Paris. They never looked back. They would return to the Duke of Hamilton in Scotland and report failure. The Prince would not be the commander of the army which Hamilton was mustering.

"What made him do it?" Henrietta asked Jermyn sharply.

"This cannot be tolerated," Jermyn answered. "If the girl presumes to influence His Highness in political affairs we shall have to get rid of her at once!"

Henrietta stared at him. Had he failed in this very important matter upon which he had assured her that he had everything under control? Had Jermyn ruined their hopes because of his plan to bring Lucy Walter to St. Germain?

Henry tried to convince her that the incident was of no importance but she knew by the dismayed look in his small bright eyes that he was more pessimistic than he cared to admit.

Could the girl be clever enough, he wondered, to have advised the Prince to do exactly what His Majesty, the King, would have wished his son to do? Angrily he wondered if she also had been clever enough to use her power over the lust of the Prince to demand marriage. He twisted the points of his moustache and worried. Had she been clever enough to guess what was going on? Were his carefully laid plans being upset by a chit of a girl? He could scarcely believe it.

Rogation days came and went and also Ascension Thursday. Not only the days forbidden for weddings passed but the intervening days as well.

Justus fumed with impatience. He demanded, almost rudely, that Charles give him an explanation about why he had been asked to leave his studies and come to St. Germain. Charles smiled enigmatically and turned his back without answering. Worse than that, Lucy met his questions with silence. When he taunted her with the fact that she was neither wife nor mistress she said nothing. Perhaps, Justus thought bitterly, she had ceased to care and his presence was unwanted. He wished that he hadn't come. The only thing that kept him from leaving St. Germain at once, was that it was evident that the delay was intentional. Though his sister refused to confide in him he still could not desert her when he sensed that she was the victim of intrigue. He must wait until he understood it, himself. He suspected, now, that they planned to use him to get rid of Lucy when they were through with her. He decided that he wouldn't drift along indefinitely. He wouldn't let Trinity Sunday pass without taking action.

Trinity Sunday was bright and sunny. The Queen and all her household attended Mass in the chapel dedicated to St. Louis on the ground floor of the chateau. Charles, Lucy, Justus, and a handful of the Prince's attendants went to the top floor where Henrietta had grudgingly permitted a small room to be adapted to the Anglican services. Dr. Earle, the chaplain appointed to serve the Prince in his exile, was in charge.

When the service was over the Prince and Lucy wandered out through the courtyard to the gardens. Justus and Thomas Gerrard would have followed but Charles told them sharply that they were not wanted. Thomas Gerrard snorted and Justus turned red with anger. He had to restrain himself from striking Gerrard.

"It is not his fault," he reminded himself.

They watched Charles and Lucy wander hand in hand out of the palace grounds and go off toward the town which was almost ready for Corpus Christi. Banners were hung above the crooked streets and large linen sheets with bunches of flowers pinned on them hung upon the walls of many of the houses. Temporary shrines had been erected in honor of the procession of the *Féte Dieu* at the crossroads.

Justus watched Lucy and Charles until they were out of sight and then turned on his heel and went to his apartments. He decided that later in the day he would talk to his sister. This was the day of decision! He kept glancing out a window which overlooked the courtyard hoping to see them coming back. Noontime had passed when he heard the clatter of the water gate being opened, the bridge being lowered and when he looked out he saw a party of horsemen ride into the courtyard and dismount. They were English cavaliers. They went at once to the Queen's apartments, and in a quarter of an hour he saw some of the Queen's attendants go out on a search of the gardens. They must be looking for the Prince, Justus thought.

Another hour passed and Charles and Lucy still had not been found. Henry Jermyn came to Justus' apartments.

"Where is His Highness?" he asked sharply.

"I don't know," Justus snapped back.

"Well, go find him," Jermyn commanded shortly. "No one else has succeeded."

Justus was so angry that he could only glare at Jermyn and go out to the gardens without answering. He left the grounds and went in the direction that Charles and Lucy had taken.

"The time has come to talk to that girl," he said to himself as he hurried along. "I shall settle the matter and get back to London at once."

He strode through the village, elbowing his way through the crowds gathered in the streets. The festive mood irritated him and he scarcely looked at the decorations; he talked to himself all the time, memorizing

109

the lecture that he would give Lucy when he was alone with her.

The town had only one main street and he walked the length of it and was a little way out in the open country on the other side before he found them. They were sitting under a tree holding hands. Charles was sprawled out full length and he was chewing a long straw that he had plucked from a field. Lucy sat by him on the grass and her large eyes, of that strange violet-black color that always made Justus catch his breath when he looked into them, were fixed upon Charles.

"They look like a pair of country bumpkins," he said to himself.

"Lord Jermyn sent me to tell you that you are to come to the Queen's apartments at once, Your Highness," he said.

Justus spoke with such irritation that he reproached himself for not addressing the Prince with more respect. Then he thought, "If His Highness doesn't care a fig for protocol, nor the dignity of his office, why should I?"

The Prince looked up at him indolently.

"What is my Lord Jermyn all stirred up about now?" he drawled.

"I don't know, Your Highness," Justus said. "It's some urgent official business." To himself he added, "How should I know, I'm not even informed about my own sister's affairs."

Charles jumped to his feet. "Thank you, Justus. I will go at once. Take care of Lucy, please." He hurried off toward the village; his long stride soon took him out of their sight.

Justus thought that this was the evidence that he needed to prove that what he had suspected was true. Even now the Prince was taking it for granted that he could hand Lucy over to him. He had been summoned to take care of Lucy—when needed!

"Come with me," he said shortly. She took his arm

and they started to walk back through the village. As they passed the church he led her into the churchyard which was deserted.

"Lucy, I want to talk to you," he said sternly.

"Again, Justus?" She smiled at him.

Lucy was no longer wan and pale. Her smooth skin had a rosy hue and there was a small dimple on one side of her provocative little mouth. She was lovelier than she had ever been, Justus thought, letting his love for his sister swamp his wish to be severe with her. The shadows under her eyes had deepened but the wistful expression had changed to one that was mischievous, even worldly, Justus thought. He should take that into consideration—that Lucy might have changed. She might not be as innocent as she used to be.

"Lucy," Justus began, "why did you come to France?"

"Because my husband sent for me," she answered. Her voice was low and full of happiness.

Justus made a gesture of exasperation. Could it be possible that Lucy was such a fool that she didn't know the fact that she was neither wife nor mistress? Didn't she know that the whims of princes are changeable? Couldn't she see the conniving of the Queen and Lord Jermyn? He decided not to spare her feelings but to be ruthless in the hope that he would shock her into her senses.

"You have no husband," he said abruptly.

She sighed and dropped her eyes.

"Don't you remember what happened in Barnstaple?" he asked. "You have been told exactly what your status is with the Prince. Promises! Promises! Promises! I have been informed that you refused point-blank to be the Prince's mistress, in which case you could be provided for. You demanded marriage and a fake one was performed. Can't you see what is happening? We have been here since March and nothing is changed.

111

For some reason you were brought here to be a royal plaything. When the Prince is convinced that casting you aside is to his advantage he will be ruthless. You'll be pushed aside like a broken toy! Can't you see that?"

She didn't answer him. She wasn't at all disturbed by his words, he thought.

"If it's true that His Highness intends to marry you, why all the delay? Why the promises and excuses? First, it was Lent—then the Prince was too busy—doing nothing particularly important, it seems to me—then it was Rogation. But now, my girl, it's Trinity Sunday. What's the excuse now? I intend to settle this matter today and get back to London."

Lucy laughed. "Justus, I love you when you are protecting my honor. You get so angry and become so unlike yourself."

Roughly, Justus took her by the shoulders and shook her. "Promises—you made a promise yourself, my fine lady—and one which you haven't kept—you promised me that you would have nothing to do with Charles Stuart unless he married you. I told you that you should, at least, demand an allowance of money and be content with being his mistress. Remember?"

Lucy pulled away from him. Her eyes flashed with anger. "I believed that I was wed in Barnstaple," she said.

"Well, you weren't," he snapped.

"Dear brother," she said, "don't fret. I am to be married to Charles in the chapel of Richard Browne's house in Paris, maybe on Corpus Christi. You are to come, of course. But for the present it must be kept secret. Otherwise they may try to prevent it, the Queen and Henry Jermyn."

Justus drew in his breath in surprise. As usual, Lucy was ahead of him. He sighed with relief. Maybe she wasn't a fool after all. She knew of the opposition! He looked at her in admiration. Was she ambitious? If so, she must be playing for very high stakes. He would not permit himself to be completely mollified.

He burst out, "Secrecy, secrecy—why all the secrecy? I have spent considerable time, interrupted my work to see that you are properly wed or to help you get out of the snares that have been laid for you. You have not chosen to respect me enough to tell me of your plans. Is this ceremony to be an honest one? Can we believe it?"

"Justus, dear Justus, I am sorry if I have given you the impression that I don't appreciate the loving concern you have for me. I took it for granted that you understood that I love you, no matter what happens."

"Oh, yes, I do, but I have been beside myself with worry. You don't know how evil the nobility can be when they decide to destroy an innocent person to further some intrigue!"

"Justus, you sound like Father!" she teased him. Then sobering, she added, "Justus, even you will be convinced, and pleased, by the ceremony. The plans were made only today, otherwise you would have been told. I have had no opportunity to tell you. You will see that my faith in His Highness is not foolish. You'll see."

Justus was worried in spite of what she said. There was no answer to what she revealed about the plans but he wouldn't be satisfied until the very last word of the wedding ceremony was spoken and he saw the wedding certificate, signed by a clergyman that he recognized. Even then there might be trickery. Even that might be part of a design to use Lucy in an intrigue.

"Dear Justus, I know how you worry but you can trust Charles. He loves me dearly." She smiled.

Justus reflected that he trusted Charles not at all. He had all the makings of a libertine: immature, sensual, self-indulged. From the serene, confident look in her eyes Justus knew that the point had been reached beyond which he could not influence her. She would tolerate no further criticism. He could do nothing more for the moment. He might as well keep still.

"I will tell you something else," said Lucy. "Something that will not be a secret long," she added blushing.

Justus looked at her in alarm. He already had suspected what she was about to tell him and she read his thoughts.

"Yes, I'm to be wed next Thursday and next spring I shall bear His Highness a child—perhaps a son who will one day be King of England."

"Dear God!" Justus burst out. "Is there no end to your delusions?" He threw up his hands in a gesture of despair. Lucy only laughed at him.

Henry Jermyn waited impatiently in the chateau. He already knew that Charles was making plans to marry Lucy but one of his secret agents, Dr. Stephen Goffe, had just brought news that could be very useful in preventing it. During one of his visits to The Hague, Goffe had come upon the information that part of the Parliament's summer fleet had mutinied and sailed for Holland. The sailors were demanding that James, Duke of York, their "rightful Admiral", as they called him because the honorary title belonged to His Highness by tradition, "take his place at their head and command them." The opportunity was about to be lost because the King's naval commanders were quarreling among themselves—jockeying for good positions. There was real danger that the turncoat sailors would lose their enthusiasm unless something was done at once.

"What do you suggest?" Jermyn asked Goffe.

"I would recommend that Prince Charles go at once and save the situation. The rogues would be flattered to have an admiral who is even higher than the Duke of York." He smiled at Jermyn. Both knew that, later, the honorary title which he craved might pass easily to Henry Jermyn.

"An immediate expedition to keep the men busy

would be a good thing, wouldn't it?" Henry asked Goffe.

"Indeed, yes. And I took the liberty while I was in Holland to persuade the Stadholder to provision the ships that are riding at anchor in his harbor."

"Splendid!"

Henrietta, of course, approved of anything that would further the royal interests and she readily agreed to the plan. Privately, she said to Jermyn while they waited for Charles to be found, "Is this the opportunity we have been waiting for to separate Charles from that girl?"

"It could be," Jermyn agreed. It couldn't be better! An exciting expedition would make Charles completely forget Lucy. He might even be willing to abandon her altogether. Jermyn assured himself that he wouldn't waste any time correcting the blunder he had made with the girl. He would get rid of her! The one question that remained was whether Charles would take his responsibility seriously and if he were competent to be a naval commander.

As they expected, when they told him about the plan Charles was overjoyed at the prospect of an exciting expedition. For three days, Jermyn kept him so busy with maps and plans that he thought that Charles was completely diverted from his idea of marrying Lucy. On the fourth day he knew that he had failed. It was reported to him that Charles had sent Thomas Gerrard to Paris to make arrangements for a wedding in the Anglican Chapel in the house of the English Resident, Sir Richard Browne. The chapel was maintained by John Cosin for the benefit of the members of the exiled English court that lived in Paris.

Early on the morning of Corpus Christi Jermyn went to the tower room of the Queen's apartments and looked out. He saw two carriages waiting in the courtyard below. Soon, Charles, Lucy, Justus and Dr. Earle came out of the palace and got into the first one; Edward Prodgers, Lord Newburgh and Thomas Gerrard entered the second one. They went out the water gate with several horsemen following, rumbled over the drawbridge and took the road to Paris.

Jermyn dispatched a man to follow the party but the fellow got no farther than where the road turned over the hill. His horse threw a shoe and unseated him. The mare went off at a gallop and the man had to limp back to the chateau to report his failure. Jermyn had a better idea anyway. He bribed one of Charles' servants to catch up with the party with some forgotten article. He was to join the Prince's people and remain with them the whole time they were in Paris and report back to Jermyn.

The coaches were approaching the outskirts of Paris when the servant caught up with them and joined the horsemen at the rear of the party. The coaches were moving at a snail's pace because the way was jammed with every type of conveyance filled with people going to the city for Corpus Christi. The narrow streets were full of crowds travelling on foot and the people had to stand back against the walls of the houses to let the two carriages go through.

Sir Richard's house was the only one that wasn't decorated with either flowers or tapestries. The street in front was the only spot not covered with rose petals in honor of the procession of the *Féte Dieu*. The Resident and his wife were at the door to kiss the hand of the Prince of Wales and to welcome Lucy. Their daughter, Mary, was there, too, and she took Lucy to her bedchamber to prepare for the ceremony.

"Last year on Corpus Christi Day," she said, "I was married to John Evelyn in the chapel. He is in London now on business. Have you heard of him?"

Lucy had indeed heard of John Evelyn. There was much gossip about him at St. Germain. It was said that he was double-dealing; he negotiated with Cromwell on the one hand and with the Royalists on the other in the hope of keeping his property intact. But Mary shouldn't be held responsible for her husband's duplicity, Lucy reminded herself. She smiled as a servant brushed her hair and bathed her face with lotions. Then she took Mary's arm and they went to the chapel.

There were four well-known clergymen present: John Cosin, Henry Glenham, Thomas Fuller and George Morley. All of them would be bishops in the English Church when the affairs of the kingdom were settled. Thomas Fuller read the ceremony from the Prayer Book. The light, reflecting from a small window behind him, made his fine brown hair a halo around his cherubic face. He beamed at the young couple and he half-rocked back and forth on heels and toes as his musical voice chanted the words.

"Dearly beloved, we are gathered together here in the sight of God and in the face of this company—." He didn't need to consult the book; he knew the words perfectly; he spoke them lovingly and poetically.

No one could have been other than convinced that this was a genuine ceremony. It was an impressive occasion and even Justus had to admit that it would have been a clod of a man who didn't feel that they were in the Presence of God. Sir Richard Browne's face was a mask but the eyes of his wife and daughter were misty with tears; James Livingstone, the Viscount Newburgh, stood as if in a trance; only Edward Prodgers seemed unmoved. He shifted from one foot to the other and let his small, closely set eyes dart about the room as if he were eager for the ceremony to end. He coughed slightly and did not bow his head when Thomas Fuller spoke the final words:

"God the Father, God the Son, God the Holy
Ghost, bless, preserve and keep you, the Lord

mercifully with his favor look upon you and fill you with spiritual benediction and grace; that ye may so live together in this life that in the world to come ye may have life everlasting. Amen."

It was over. The company drank to the health of the bride and groom but the gaiety was a little forced. They all knew that they had been accomplices in a bold and rebellious act. They could expect little reward from the Prince and political disaster could catch up with all of them. Some, at least, had the consolation of knowing that the evil of the mock wedding had been corrected; they all breathed a sigh of relief when the party got into their coaches and started back to St. Germain-en-laye.

In less than a week the Prince and his retinue would go back over the same rough road on their way to the eleven ships that were riding at anchor in the water at Helvoetsluys, waiting for the Prince to command them. The Prince had a problem. What could be done about Lucy while he was gone? His mother and Henry Jermyn had become increasingly cold to her. They made it obvious that she was no longer welcome in the Queen's court; there seemed to be nothing that Charles could do but take her with him to the Low Countries.

The morning of the departure was hot and humid when Charles took Lucy with him to bid his mother farewell. Henrietta received them where she sat at breakfast. The clothing of her servers was threadbare but their etiquette was perfect. They fell to their knees when they offered her plates of food; she was gracious but she scarcely touched what they offered her. It was more a ceremony than a meal. Henry Jermyn stood in back of the Queen's chair, watched every movement of the servers and checked everything that was placed before her.

The lines of suffering on Henrietta's face were accentuated in the morning light and the half-lowered lids of her deep-set eyes were swollen. She greeted Lucy and allowed her to kiss her hand but she didn't smile. She knew about the trip to Paris; she accepted defeat and the reality of the marriage in silence.

Charles spoke in an unnaturally high voice when he asked his mother's blessing upon the expedition that he was about to undertake. She gave it gravely, only half including Lucy with her outstretched hand. Then she told them goodbye and signified with her hand that they were dismissed. Charles blurted out what he had been trying to bring himself to say. "Mam," he said, "my people have come to me for money for the trip to Holland—and I have none!"

Henrietta raised her eyes to Jermyn. He responded with a slight lifting of the eyebrows and an imperceptible shake of his head. They both knew that the Queen had no money at all. She had sent every cent of her pension to her husband in England.

"The last of my jewels have been sold and the money spent to be used in the uprisings on land that will accompany your expedition at sea." She lifted a small cup from which she had drunk her morning ale. "This is all the gold that I have left," she said.

So the party had to set off without funds but before they left Charles took Justus aside and gave him the marriage certificate signed and witnessed by the four clergymen. "Put it in a safe place," he said. "Now you know why I asked you to come to St. Germain." He grinned at Justus' confusion. "You are to look after Lucy on this trip," he said, "—and whenever else that it becomes necessary."

That confirmed the suspicion that he was supposed to be available to take care of Lucy any time that it pleased His Majesty, Justus thought angrily. "Otherwise," he muttered, "I can rot with boredom while they ignore me!" For the moment he wouldn't hesitate to take advantage of the offer for him to make Lucy comfortable. He began loading Lucy's carriage with supplies. There was no money but the chateau's store rooms were wide open to his looting. He helped himself to the finest wines in Louis XIV's cellar and the best of cheeses and baskets of fresh fruit. There were so many purloined luxuries that there was scarcely room for the woman servant who was to care for Lucy.

Justus mounted a horse to ride by the side of her coach but the Prince was in a carriage far ahead with a large body of horsemen behind him. He was so busy with his secretary and military advisors that he didn't notice the arrangements made by Lucy's brother. He didn't even speak to her before they started off. "The honeymoon is over," Justus muttered. But worse than that—what was going to happen to his foolish sister when Charles realized that he had recklessly handicapped himself with a marriage which was, to say the least, a political catastrophe?

Charles' spirits were dampened by his mother's coldness but it was more because he was annoyed that she couldn't raise any money to support this important expedition than anything else.

Lucy was shocked by the Prince's attitude toward his mother. Charles had paid no attention to what she had said about having pawned the very last of her jewels and that all she had left was the little gold cup. Didn't he care that she was desolate and almost destitute—that she was dependent upon the King of France for the very food she ate?

The Queen knew that the faithful Henry Jermyn was concerned entirely with her welfare but she looked at him sadly and resolved that never again would she trust him implicitly in serious matters. She would make all the important decisions herself from now on. When she was alone in her bedchamber she sobbed brokenheartedly because of his deception and the incompetence that had brought about this new disaster. Most of all she blamed herself for having made a despicable decision. She should have left the girl with her relatives! What was going to happen to Lucy? She was afraid that Charles would desert her sooner or later.

But she could not let that enter into her decisions. She must be a Queen even before she was a mother, much less worry about one of her subjects.

4

Lucy was a little astonished at Charles' attitude toward his sister, Mary, too. He told Lucy that he felt sure that Mary would help them, and she had plenty of money! She had been married to the rich William of Orange for seven years and he still gave her everything she wanted including the support of her relatives, he said with a sneer. William was the Stadholder now, and he not only provided a home for Mary's aunt, the exiled Queen of Bohemia, but all of her children.

"I think she must be a wonderful person to do all that," Lucy said.

"Oh, she does it because she's homesick. She can't get along with the Dutch people."

"Why?"

"They think she's haughty, and she is, a little, but what they don't know is that she holds her head high because someone once told her that if she does that her receding chin wouldn't be so noticeable."

"Does she have black hair, like you?"

"No, she's blond and buxom," Charles said making a describing motion with his hands indicating that Mary had a large bust.

"Then she must look a little like the Dutch women."

"Well, yes, but there it ends. The Dutch burghers and their wives think she's a haughty foreigner and they detest her."

"That's too bad," Lucy said, "she must be very lonesome."

"I guess she is," Charles said grudgingly, "and I suppose that's the reason she fills her letters with stuff about how much she misses her family."

"Oh," Lucy said, "I think that's very nice."

"I don't," Charles said shortly. "I think her letters are maudlin."

It was not all Mary's fault that she was unpopular with the Dutch. The main reason was that they believed that William had married the Stuart princess because the House of Orange had royal ambitions and they were fiercely protective of their democracy.

Lady Stanhope, the lady-in-waiting that had come from England with Mary to serve as her companion, was of little help. She enjoyed the prosperous Dutch society and with her husband, Lord Heenvleet, who had been one of the Dutch ambassadors to England, was part of the cosmopolitan clique of diplomats who lived at The Hague. Mary couldn't cope with either the Dutch or the international society and the more she failed the more she poured her heart out in her letters to her family telling them that she longed, more than anything else, to see one of them.

William knew that, of course, and it was the main reason that he had agreed to provision the fleet, that had mutinied, for Charles. Actually, he didn't think that a naval expedition would have any effect upon the course of events in England.

He smiled when he saw that when he told her that her brother was on the way and that they would see him before he went on the expedition she was hysterically happy and when it was near the time for Charles to land on the Dutch coast he took her to their mansion in Brielle so that she could see Charles sooner.

He smiled again when he saw her flush with excitement at the news that Charles' ship had anchored. She answered him absently when he spoke to her and he knew that she was thinking of the coach with the arms of the House of Orange on the doors clattering through the crooked, cobbled streets past the orphanage and St. Catherine's Church, bringing the Prince to her. When they heard the coach stop in the courtyard William took her arm and led her outside.

Mary's face was flushed with happiness when she saw Charles step out of the carriage. She hadn't seen him since her wedding when he was still a boy dressed in white satin with his black hair curling on his square shoulders. But she turned pale with jealousy when she saw that Charles was followed out of the coach by a beautiful young girl and a young man, both of them with curly black hair; they resembled each other so much they must be twins. Who were these people that were intimate enough with her brother to ride with him in his coach? Who could they be?

Charles exchanged formal greetings with William and then turned to Mary and embraced her.

"Brother," she said formally, "I am overjoyed to see you." Then, unable to restrain her anxious curiosity any longer, she looked around his shoulder at Lucy and hissed into his ear, "Do you dare to have the intention of presenting us with your mistress?"

"No, she's my wife."

Lucy saw that Mary drew back into her defensive stance of hauteur that Charles had so accurately described. "You are jesting," she said.

"No, it's true. We were married by Thomas Fuller in John Cosin's chapel in Paris on Corpus Christi. Of course it was done secretly," he said, and added threateningly, "and you will keep it secret, too."

"With the knowledge and approval of Her Majesty, our mother?" Mary was close to tears.

"Of course not," Charles answered glibly. Then, disregarding Mary's distress he added carelessly, "Isn't she beautiful?"

This added fuel to Mary's jealousy. She glared at Charles, at Lucy, at Justus, at anyone else that her eyes turned upon.

William's pleasant face clouded and he frowned slightly as he watched. He was trying to understand his wife's agitation. He thought that the reason for her fury might be that she was thinking of the possibility of a commoner becoming the Queen of England. The idea amused him. It was a good omen for the House of Orange, he thought. Even if he had no definite ambition toward the elevation of his House, it was pleasant to toy with the idea. He looked at Lucy appraisingly and then glanced sidewise at Mary. Lucy's petite darkness didn't appeal to him!

"Mrs. Barlow," Charles said loudly with a bow toward Lucy, "and her brother, Justus Walter."

Mary replied formally but her acknowledgment was frigid.

Then, the next day she seemed to have changed her mind. She was anxious to hear the news about the court at St. Germain. "How is my beloved mother?" she asked Lucy, the tone of her voice grudgingly conciliatory.

Since Lucy didn't know anything about the state of the health of Queen Henrietta she murmured something polite and noncommittal. Mary didn't notice because she was bursting with questions about the court at St. Germain. If she had had even an inkling of how her mother felt about Lucy she wouldn't have warmed up as much as she did but since she didn't she decided to be hospitable.

Later, she told Charles, "Lucy is welcome to stay with us until you come back from the expedition."

"Thank you, sister," Charles said but there was more

contempt than gratitude in his voice. Mary's overeagerness was gauche, he thought, and it bored him.

At sunrise, a few days later, the fleet manned by mutineers, provisioned by the Stadholder and led by Prince Charles' flagship, went out to open sea through the harbor at Helvoetsluys where vessels from all over the world were riding at anchor. The expanse of sand on the shore was salmon colored and the lowlands beyond were luminous in the early morning light.

Justus watched his royal brother-in-law standing at the prow of his ship with mixed feelings of admiration and dislike. His Highness had a way with him, he thought, and he was a different man when he was away from his mother. He was a good sailor and never irritable as he usually was at St. Germain; he was in his element with the men and the sea.

But Justus had no enthusiasm for the expedition in which he was involved. It was incredible that the small fleet had been put to sea before a complete plan had been decided upon! The result was that when the ships were in the open waters of the English Channel the commanders began to argue about the point of attack. Admiral Batten thought that they should sail straight to Scotland. Some of the others pressed for the relief of Colchester, which was besieged by Fairfax. Prince Rupert insisted that the fleet go at once to the Isle of Wight where the King was imprisoned. Rupert pointed out that, as they knew, Colonel Legg had come aboard directly from His Majesty to urge the commanders to follow that plan. The sailors that had mutinied demanded that they be heard, too. When their request was granted they demanded that the fleet of merchantmen near the mouth of the Thames be captured and the prize money distributed among them.

Justus could see that the only possible advantage to that tactical maneuver would be that ships sunk in the midway would prevent the Parliamentary fleet from getting out to engage them; he was disgusted when he heard the Prince give the command to block the mouth of the Thames. The Prince chose to ingratiate himself with his common sailors rather than carry out the plan ordered by the King! Thank God, Justus thought, he had no obligation to sacrifice himself to royal inefficiency. More than that, he had no intention of abandoning himself to royal pleasure or mercy as his sister had done. So, when the ships stood close in, he took a dory, rowed himself to shore and returned to London.

The uprisings on land, which had been organized by the Queen to supplement the naval expedition, were ignited; but Cromwell was ready for them. The Royalists were defeated everywhere. The Welsh, the Irish, the English were all outmaneuvered and destroyed. Cromwell knew that the best leaders and the greatest strength of his enemy lay in Scotland; he concentrated his forces there. Very few of the defeated soldiers escaped alive and if they were not slaughtered they were captured and sold as slaves to the planters of Virginia and the Barbadoes. At the same time, if they were not sunk in the harbor most of the ships of the Prince's fleet were disabled. He managed to salvage a few that were still afloat and they were taken back to Helvoetsluys.

When they anchored the Prince said he was ill and his attendants saw that Charles was a very sick man. They carried him to his sister's house and the next day it was evident that he had smallpox.

"My God," said his blunt physician, Dr. Fraizer, "what next? It is like the tribulations of Job! I don't think that he has the pox in a dangerous form; he is strong and vigorous but who can tell? There may be a turn for the worse. Those who wish to avoid the contagion should leave the palace at once."

William was away from home but he sent word that

his wife was to move to their palace at Teyling immediately, and Charles told Lucy to go with her.

"No," she said, "I won't go."

"Perhaps, dear lady," Dr. Fraizer said, "you have had the pox?" He couldn't believe that she would be willing to risk the scarring of her alabaster complexion.

"No," she said, "I have not had smallpox though I did have something like it. Once the milkmaids in my grandmother's dairy at Brockhill in Broadclyst, had the cowpox. I had it, too."

Dr. Fraizer covered his mouth with his hand, pretending to cough. The Prince's lady of pleasure boasted that she had had the cowpox! Was the little fool so stupid that she didn't know that it was imprudent to admit that she had been the victim of a disease common to the low-born? Besides, she was expecting a child. If she took the disease she might die or lose the child. Well, he thought, who cared? Let her stay.

Lucy wouldn't change her mind; she took care of Charles all through his illness. By Advent he was fully recovered and Mary returned from Teyling to begin making elaborate preparations for Christmas. She was determined to make the holiday season a happy one for the Stuart refugees including her brother and Lucy.

Elizabeth Stuart, the exiled Queen of Bohemia, and her children had been guests of William of Orange for a long time. As the years passed her political and military defeats in her own country diminished her status and increased her poverty until she had become almost entirely dependent upon the Stadholder. Still, she was pleasant and gay and it seemed that she was determined to show her gratitude in the only way that she had left—by being a charming and helpful guest. She never complained and she did everything she could to raise the spirits of William's household. She was always available to make herself useful to Mary and she kept the wives of the Dutch burghers at bay by diplomatic actions and soothing words.

Every afternoon she rode out of the palace courtyard in one of the Stadholder's carriages and she usually took one or more of her beautiful daughters with her. Their driver maneuvered his cumbersome vehicle between the lime trees on the Voorhout in the game of seeing and being seen. Elizabeth smiled and nodded to the people they passed and they smiled and nodded back to her. She played the game that Mary didn't know how to play and in this way she was of great help to William.

John Maurice of Nassau, the Governor of Brazil, and William Frederick, the Fresian Stadholder, owned the most magnificent houses on the Binnenhof and they competed with each other in the giving of elegant and entertaining parties. Elizabeth made herself the favorite of both of them; no party was considered a complete success unless she was there.

One evening, toward the end of the holiday season, an affair which was expected to be the most magnificent of all was in full swing in the mansion of John Maurice. Hundreds of candles burned in the Mauritshuis, and the light shone out of the windows upon the Vyver and shimmered across the water; the painted ceilings and marble chimney pieces glowed. All the top-ranking diplomats and all the royal refugees were present. Dozens of servants scurried about carrying trays of pastries, rare wines and delicacies.

Elizabeth Stuart, as usual, was the focus of attention with her cheerfulness and charm. She sat with Lucy at her side and some of the wives of the international diplomats, especially those who were not of the highest social rank, whispered that they thought that Elizabeth was allowing her good nature to carry her too far. Democracy was all right for the Dutch but hobnobbing with the lady of pleasure of the exiled Prince of England was an insult to everyone!

Count Maurice held up his hand for silence and announced that he had planned a surprise for them. He had imported a troupe of Indians from Brazil who would perform a war dance. He nodded to his majordomo and the door was opened for the Indians to rush in. They gave such a blood-curdling realistic performance that one after another the ladies shrieked and screamed with fright; some even fainted! The old dowager, Princess Amelie, summoned the Count to her and, with an imperious gesture of her hand, reprimanded him. She told him in no uncertain terms that she considered the entertainment a display of bad taste. It was positively barbaric, she said indignantly.

Count Maurice was offended by this rebuke but he signalled his majordomo to stop the performance at once; the musicians were called in for madrigal singing and the ladies quieted down. Then it was time for dancing. Prince Charles danced first with his sister, Mary, and then with his cousin, Sophie, the most beautiful of Elizabeth's daughters. After that, he took out a different lady each time as sarabands, chaconnes, and musettes followed one another.

Lucy could not dance; she was short of breath because of her pregnancy and her heart beat very fast even as she sat demurely between the Dowager Princess Amelie and Elizabeth Stuart. She was as delicate and exquisitely fragile as a figure of china in contrast to the robust Dutch women whirling and perspiring in the great ballroom. Her black hair was decorated with pearls borrowed from the Princess Mary and the white satin of her gown made her skin glow like polished marble. Her shadowed, violet eyes were mysterious and she never took them off her husband. He never once looked at her as he went whirling by with one lady after another.

Aerssens, the eldest son of the Seigneur of Somelsdyck, and Henrietta, the third daughter of Elizabeth, were dancing a jig with the whole company clapping hands when two grim-faced gentlemen entered the ballroom and demanded that they be taken to the English Resident at once. The music stopped, the jiggers stood still and everyone stared at the dusty men carrying dispatch cases. They were couriers from England!

Count Maurice frowned at this new interruption and Sir William Boswell, the English Resident, came at once. With an apologetic nod he took the messengers out of the room as quickly as possible. The Count signalled for the music to begin again and Aerssens and Henrietta started to jig. They were interrupted again because Dr. Stewart came into the room and told Prince Charles that his Council requested that he come to them immediately. Everyone was aware that something terrible had happened. An ominous hush fell upon the room and when Count Maurice tried again to revive his party it was impossible. The guests began to leave and all of the remaining plans for the entertainment were cancelled.

It was not until the winter sun was throwing its first morning rays across the water of the Vyver that Charles came to Lucy. She was waiting for him in her bedchamber in the house in the Old Court, which had been given to the Prince by the Stadholder. She cried out in alarm when she saw his face. His swarthy complexion was ashen grey, harsh lines framed his large mouth and his jaw was set grimly. She ran to him but he put her aside and sank into a chair at a writing table and put his face in his hands.

"Sir," Lucy cried, "what has happened?" When he did not answer, she said softly, "Charles, my love, what is it?"

"His Majesty is about to be sentenced to death by the Parliament," he said dully.

Lucy stared at him as he sprang to his feet and began pacing the floor.

"If I could only do something," he cried out, "but I am helpless. I must stay here and go to balls and smile at statesmen that I detest. I must grovel for money, for armaments, for men. I must beg from those who would be only too glad to help if they thought that our cause would be victorious. If only I could do something to defend my father, but there is nothing, nothing! I must stand by and see him slaughtered!"

"Is nothing being done?" Lucy said.

"Ah!" said Charles, "of course. The night was spent in writing letters to Cromwell, to Fairfax, Warwick, Pembroke, the two speakers of the House—all of them! Pleas! Pleas, mind you, not commands. Humble pleas to spare the King's life. It were far better that he had died in battle than to suffer this humiliation."

"What will the letters accomplish?"

"Nothing." Despair made him drop his face into his hands again. Then he looked up at her. "The Parliamentary envoy, Strickland, probably has couriers on the way already to put the devils on their guard against any good impression that might be made by our letters. There are still gentlemen in England who will flinch at the prospect of making a martyr of their King."

Early the next morning Charles went with Sir William Boswell and his brother-in-law, William, to the States General. All morning they made impassioned pleas for help and Charles begged them to intercede for his father. They looked at him in stony silence. They had their own interests to think about.

That night there were no festivities on the Binnenhof and no myriad of lights shone on the waters of the Vyver. The brilliant international society was shocked to the core. The diplomatic representatives of many countries didn't stir from their houses. All of them were terrified at the thought of what was happening. The warnings which Queen Henrietta had included in her letters begging for aid from their governments, all monarchies, were being recalled as each diplomat considered what might happen in his own country if the King of England was executed by his own people. It would set a bad example.

It was almost midnight when Charles, not having slept since he received the news of his father's peril, sank exhausted into Lucy's arms.

She looked at him anxiously. "You are not encouraged by what was done today?"

"No," said Charles, "it is too late for anything. He is doomed."

At that moment, across the Channel, Princess Elizabeth, still held hostage with Henry, was trying to write a letter. She held the pen in her hand but after writing the date, January 22, 1649, her throat contracted with fear. Why had her father been moved to St. James Palace by his captors? Why had he sent her a message, secretly, that she must write a letter to the House of Commons asking permission to go to her sister, the Princess of Orange, at once? She was to take Henry if she could, but if she could not, she was to go herself, at once, and leave her brother behind.

Elizabeth was small for a thirteen-year-old. Her hair was burnished gold and her fair complexion was often flushed with fever. Her eyes were serious and she had an air of intelligent responsibility. Books had been her consolation; she was said to be a scholar at an age when most young girls are just beginning their formal education. She spoke several languages fluently and she read Latin and Greek.

A year had passed since she had seen her father. The last time was just before his captors moved him to Carisbrook Castle on the Isle of Wight. She had gone to Hampton Court with James and Henry to see him. The King had found the opportunity while they were there to whisper in her ear that he wished James to escape.

He had commissioned Colonel Bamfylde to make the plans and carry them out and she was to cooperate with the Colonel in every way that he asked her to.

James had been stranded in Oxford when the King surrendered. None of the noblemen had the presence of mind to take him with them or didn't want the responsibility when they escaped themselves. The young Prince didn't know what to do but remain there with his attendants until his resources were exhausted. The attendants were forced, then, to give him up into the custody of the Parliament. He was taken to join Elizabeth and Henry where they were being held in St. James Palace. It was a ferociously hot summer and the plague was raging in London; but the Parliament had left them there in the sweltering heat.

Lady Dorset had remained with them and cared for them as if they were her own children. She fought a constant battle not only for their comfort but for their very necessities. The privations they suffered were too much for her. She fell ill and died. Immediately, what was left of their royal attendants were removed from their posts and replaced by strangers who detested them because they were the King's children. They gave them as little care as possible and they treated them with no respect at all. It became so bad that Elizabeth had written secretly to the House of Lords and implored their help. It must have been a convincing letter because they appointed a committee to investigate the condition of the royal children. The report was so pathetic that the House of Lords found the courage to overrule the House of Commons. The former attendants of the children were restored to them, and the Earl of Northumberland was asked to succeed Lady Dorset.

The Earl consented to assume the responsibility with two stipulations: he must be permitted to treat Henry, James and Elizabeth with the respect due to the children of the King, and if, in spite of his vigilance, one or more of them escaped, he would not be held accountable.

The first thing that the Earl did when he took charge was to explain to Elizabeth that, though he loved the King dearly as a friend and as his sovereign, his principles caused him to adhere to the Parliament. She must remember that. She did remember and it relieved her of any sense of guilt when she carried out the plans to help James escape. The Earl moved the children to Sion House, his country residence not far from London. This was a relief in the summer because it was cool but in the winter it was miserably cold; Elizabeth came down with influenza. After that she was never free of a severe cough and her face was flushed. Soon after they moved to Sion, Colonel Bamfylde found a way to see her and they worked out a plan which was to be put into action at once.

Every evening the three children played a game of hide-and-seek in the rambling old mansion. Elizabeth and James would hide and Henry tried to find them. At first they made it easy for him, but each night they chose places which were more difficult than the last; and each night it took him longer to find them. One evening it took him over an hour and Henry was crying and his attendants annoyed.

"You are cruel to your brother," they reprimanded Elizabeth and James.

That is just what they wanted them to think!

Then, one day, Elizabeth and James saw a Dutch skiff cruising up and down the Thames and they discovered that its dory was anchored near Sion landing. They felt sure that it must be the one that Colonel Bamfylde had told them would be sent for James, and they agreed that it was time for him to go that very evening.

The game began as usual. Elizabeth hid first and let Henry find her. She and James pretended that they were quarrelling with Henry and talked loudly to him so the servants would be aware of the game. The little boy jumped up and down with glee when he found his sister so quickly.

"Now, James," Henry shouted, "it's your turn. I will find you as easily as I found Elizabeth. Go on and hide—you'll see."

Elizabeth said then, "James, I have a most dreadful headache." She coughed and put her hand to her head. "I wish to go to bed. Will you play with Henry for a while, alone, until His Grace comes to attend you to bed?"

"Yes," said James gruffly, "but I won't make it easy."

"That's all right," said Henry. "I'll find you anyway."

"No, you won't," said James.

A handkerchief was tied over Henry's eyes and while he counted to a hundred James went to the servants' hall and asked the head gardener to give him the key to one of the garden gates.

"I wish to hide in your cottage," James told him.

The gardener was flattered by what he thought was condescension by the Duke of York. He gave the key to him at once.

James skipped out into the garden, unlocked the gate, opened it, went through it and locked it behind him. Underneath a shrub, close to the wall, he found the maidservant's clothes that Elizabeth had hidden for him. He went into the gardener's cottage and changed into them. Then he went down to the bank of the Thames, untied the dory and rowed himself out to the Dutch skiff.

Back in the house, Henry looked for his brother. He hunted and hunted. Two hours passed, and the attendants were angry because Henry was crying piteously; but he would not give up the search.

At nine o'clock the Earl came to attend the two

Princes at their retiring. He sensed at once that something unusual was afoot; he questioned the servants. The gardener had to tell him that James was hiding in his cottage. Henry ran at once to the garden gate with the Earl and the gardener right behind him.

"It's locked," he said and cried even louder. He was frightened because he thought that something terrible had happened to James.

The gate was forced open; the Earl ran with the gardener to his cottage and found it empty. They discovered James' clothing in the bedchamber. They knew that without a doubt he had escaped. The household was aroused, and the people were dispersed in all directions to search for the Prince.

Elizabeth lay in her bed behind the curtains, paralyzed with fear because she could hear the baying of the hounds that were set free to track down her brother.

Next morning, her attendants told her that her brother had escaped. The dogs had followed the scent down to the water's edge, and there it was lost.

"Was there a dory tied there?" asked Elizabeth.

"No," they said. "No sign of a boat."

She sighed with relief. James had escaped and, without accident, would soon be safely at The Hague with Mary.

Now, Elizabeth thought, as she looked down at the paper upon which she had begun the letter to the House of Commons, it is my time to go. If they do not give their permission, I shall try to find a way to escape and take Henry with me. She sealed the letter and gave it to a servant to deliver it.

Almost a week passed, and Elizabeth had received no answer. Then early one morning the Earl came to her. She wondered if he had found out about the letter and if he would punish her for sending it. He had a strange expression as if he were trying to smile but finding it impossible. After a few moments he swallowed hard and gently told her that His Majesty, her father, had been given the death sentence and would be executed immediately.

Elizabeth fainted. The Earl summond her servants and told them to put her to bed and to call him when she recovered, but she did not respond to their efforts to revive her. She lay in a stupor and no one could rouse her. The Earl sent for Dr. Mayerne, but they couldn't find him until the next day. When he came the physician found her pulse faint but he said that he didn't think that she was dying.

"I think that she's conscious," he went out and told the Earl. "I believe that she doesn't want to talk to you."

The Earl went in to Elizabeth and told her attendants to leave the room. After they had gone he said to her sternly, "Your Highness, open your eyes and look at me."

She turned her head, opened her eyes and looked at him. Dr. Mayerne had been right. She was conscious and she was willing to listen to him now. There was horror in her eyes for she expected to hear that her father was dead.

"You have great courage," he said to her. "You proved it when you helped James escape. It provoked my admiration." His voice shook with emotion. "You have something to do now which will be much more difficult but I think that you will wish to do it. His Majesty," he said gently, "wishes to see you and Henry once more."

"I can't," she whispered. Her breath came out in a little sob. "I have no strength." She coughed weakly.

"God will give it to you," he said firmly. "You must go."

After a moment she nodded. "I will try," she said, almost inaudibly.

The Earl opened the door and asked Dr. Mayerne,

waiting outside, to come in. The physician gave Elizabeth a stimulant and when it began to take effect he said that she could be dressed by her attendants.

"Carry her to the coach," the Earl ordered gruffly. "We shall be waiting for her."

They left the room and when Elizabeth was dressed she was carried out to where Henry was already seated in the coach with the two men. They were taken to St. James Palace and Elizabeth was lifted out and carried in to the King's apartments.

When they were at the door of the King's chamber she said, "Put me down, I will walk."

She took Henry's hand and led him in to their father. When she saw him she caught her breath in a little sob. His hair was white and he was shabbily dressed. They knelt before him and asked his blessing. Elizabeth burst into tears and then lapsed into hysterical weeping but Henry stared silently at his father.

The King took Elizabeth by the hand and lifted her from her knees. He put his arms around her and whispered in her ear that she must calm herself because he wanted her to listen carefully to what he was going to say to her.

"Henry is too young to understand," he said.

She caught her breath convulsively.

"I have not much to say," he said, "nor much time to say it, but I cannot say it to any other and I fear to leave it in writing because of the cruelty of my captors. They might not give it to you."

She sobbed convulsively but nodded that she was listening.

"I do not wish you to grieve and torment thyself," he said. "It will be a glorious death that I shall die, being for the laws and liberties of this land for maintaining the true Protestant religion."

Elizabeth's sobs ceased, but the tears flowed down her cheeks as she listened.

"Forgive our enemies," he said. "I have forgiven them and I pray that God will forgive them also. Forgive them," he said again, "but do not trust them. They have been false to those who gave them power."

He sat silent for a moment. Henry watched him with terrified eyes.

"Tell your mother," the King continued, "that my thoughts have never strayed from her and that my love will be the same to the last."

He turned to Henry, took him by the hand and set him on his knee.

"Henry," he said, "sweetheart, now they will cut off thy father's head."

Henry stared at him.

"Mark well what I say, child," the King said sternly. "They will cut off my head and perhaps try to make thee a king; but you must not be a king so long as your brothers, Charles and James, do live; for they will cut off your brothers' heads when they catch them and cut off thy head, too, at last. Therefore, I charge you not be made a king by them."

Henry said solemnly, "I will be torn to pieces first."

The King smiled.

"I enjoin both of you to remember," he said, "that when I am taken away your obedience will be due to the Prince of Wales, to whom, with my blessing, you must pay all dutiful submission."

They nodded.

"Elizabeth," he went on, "never permit yourself to be engaged in marriage without your mother's express consent."

With a sob, Elizabeth answered, "I promise, sir."

"Love your mother," he said to both of them, "and obey her in all things except religion. Never permit anyone to cause you to change from the true Protestant religion."

"Never, sir," Henry said. He stared curiously at his father.

Elizabeth was weeping again and could not reply. She nodded that she understood.

The King put Henry down and went to his jewel cabinet. He divided what was in it between the children. Then, as if he thought it best not to prolong the visit he gave them his blessing and almost peremptorily commanded that they be removed.

A violent sob came out of Elizabeth. The King had turned to leave the chamber but he turned back and took her in his arms and kissed her wet cheeks. She fell limp in his arms. The stimulant had worn off and reality was more than she could bear.

The King summoned Dr. Mayerne, and Elizabeth was taken from him and carried from his presence. Henry followed in a daze, looking back over his shoulder at his father.

Elizabeth was revived by Dr. Mayerne's medication and again the two children were put into a coach, with the Earl and the Doctor, to begin the trip back to Sion House. Elizabeth sat silently with her eyes closed and she was very pale. When they passed Whitehall it is doubtful that she even heard the sounds of the hammering and nailing that were going on at the second-floor level of the palace where it jutted out at Holbein's Gate. Certainly, she did not see it for she never opened her eyes. Henry looked out curiously at the icebound Thames and the very long icicles hanging from a platform that was being constructed for the King's execution.

St. James Park was bleak and cold in the smoky fog of late January. The hawthorn trees stood bare and thorny in patches of muddy earth and remnants of dirty snow, and the Queen's rose garden in the courtyard of the palace was an untended thicket of brambles. There were no linnets in the leafless trees of the Royal Mulberry Gardens, and the bells in the church towers were silent.

St. James Palace was stark and unfriendly. The ancient sooty walls and massive iron gates had survived generations of royal tragedies. It was a matter of indifference to the dreary old building that a King would soon depart, never to return. There had been many before him and there would be many after him.

At Whitehall, everything was ready for the execution. A cheap coffin had been placed at one side of the platform of the scaffold that had been hastily constructed at the second-story level. In the center was a block where two headsmen stood waiting, holding their axes at their sides. They were swathed from head to toe in butchers' garb and they were disguised by masks, wigs, and false beards.

Early in the morning a company of foot soldiers were lined up on both sides of the street all the way between St. James and Whitehall. Immediately men and women with frightened faces began to gather behind them, and they jostled each other to get a view of the King when his guards took him from one palace to the other.

About ten o'clock in the morning loud angry drums began to beat and roll, and a guard of halberdiers appeared at the main door of St. James with the King. Many of the people fell to their knees when they saw him and prayed for him. But the beating of the drums was a prearranged signal for the foot soldiers to push all the people, who were close to the entrance, out into the square away from the prisoner. They were handled so roughly that many of those who were on their knees could not get up in time, and they were trampled underfoot.

Bishop Juxon walked at the King's right side and Colonel Tomlinson was on the left. Mr. Herbert was a step behind. Following was a party of soldiers. The King's face was impassive, haughty even, but his heavy-lidded eyes were sorrowful. His hair was completely white, and he looked much older than his forty-nine years.

Many of the foot soldiers whispered, "God bless you, Your Majesty," when he passed, but most of the officers spat at him and cried, "Justice!"

The King and his escort reached Whitehall without incident and went in the main entrance. Charles walked through the corridors with unfaltering steps. He went up the stairs to the Green Room, which was a Cabinet lying behind the King's bedchamber in the royal apartment. He was told that he would have to wait there because arrangements had not been completed. Midday came and still they waited. Outside, the headsmen stood ready with their axes. Dinner was prepared and brought to the King. He refused to take anything but a small manchet and a glass of claret.

The truth was that Cromwell had been unable to find any officers who were willing to sign an order for the King's execution.

An hour passed and a Puritan divine named Peters took the opportunity of the delay to insist that he had a right to talk to the King, because Cromwell had made him the chaplain of the Palace. He had tried to preach a sermon to the King on the previous Sunday, and enraged because he was evicted from the King's chamber, he had pronounced a curse upon him. He quoted the prophet, Isaiah, and his condemnation of the King of Babylon:

> All the kings of the nations have all of them slept in glory, every one in his own house. But thou art cast out of thy grave, as an unprofitable branch defiled, and wrapped up among them that were slain by the sword, and art gone down to the bottom of the pit, as a rotten carcass.

"This," the man said later, "I did intend to preach upon before the poor wretch but the poor wretch would not hear me."

Now, as the King waited for his execution, he tried to intrude upon him again, bringing an assistant with him, but he was not permitted to enter the room. When His Majesty heard the commotion he sent a message to them: "Tell them plainly that those who have so often causelessly prayed against me shall not pray with me in this agony. They may, if they please, and I'll thank them for it, pray for me."

Another hour passed and still not one of the officers would obey Cromwell's command to draw up a warrant for the King's execution.

In fact, Cromwell had already found it necessary to purge the Parliament before he could bring about the execution of the King. The opposition had opened negotiations with His Majesty and was quietly proceeding in the direction of restoring him to the throne. Cromwell knew that he had to put a stop to that. He sent Colonel Pride and a force of soldiers to stand guard before the Houses of Parliament, and one morning early in December they had refused to allow any of the members of the opposition to go in for the day's session. Most of these men resisted this interference, and they were arrested. What was left of the legislative body after Pride's Purge was called the Rump, and its members were dependent upon the army for their seats.

This Rump had rushed through a resolution to the effect that it was treason for the King to levy war against the Parliament, followed by another which gave the force of law to any measure enacted by the Commons without the consent of the House of Lords. They erected a High Court of Justice and asked one hundred and thirty-five men to serve on it. Only sixty-eight were willing.

It was this court, erected and justified by the acts fabricated by the Rump, that tried the King and passed judgment upon him that he was guilty of treason. His Majesty had denied that they even had the right to try him, much less pass judgment upon him. Nevertheless, they sentenced him to die.

But when the time came for the execution, none of the military officers would sign the death warrant. Finally Cromwell went into a rage, demanded a pen and signed the warrant himself. Then he ordered Colonel Hacker to fetch the King and present him on the scaffold.

The colonel appeared at the door of the Cabinet and said gruffly, "The time has come."

Immediately Bishop Juxon and Mr. Herbert fell to their knees before the King, and he gave them his hand to kiss. For Mr. Herbert, this was farewell. He had begged leave to remain inside during the execution for it was more than he could bear. He had been given permission to do so until the time came for him to attend the King's body.

It was the Bishop's duty to attend the King through the whole ordeal. Of course it was one of his regular duties to comfort the dying, but he was an old man and very fond of Charles. He was overcome with grief and was unable to rise. Tenderly, the King bent down and assisted him. Then he turned and signalled calmly for Colonel Hacker to lead the way.

The King and the Bishop went through the second-story window to the platform, followed by a company of officers. The King had a piece of paper in his hand upon which he had jotted down some words which he hoped he might be allowed to say to his people, but they took it away from him.

The people could not see him because a black cloth had been draped around the railing of the platform.

More than that, rank upon rank of soldiers stood between them and the base of the scaffold.

The people could not hear him say, "I pray God, with Saint Stephen, that this not be laid to their charge—I have delivered my conscience. Pray God that you do take those courses that are for the good of the kingdom and your own salvation."

They could not hear the last word he said to Bishop Juxon, "Remember—." He was not allowed to finish, because the headsman's axe swung up into the air, and down.

The first blow was mercifully successful, and the King's head was held up by one of the ghoulish executioners for the people to see. An agonized moan convulsed the crowds and swept over them like a wave. They seemed to understand, all at once, that they were being deprived not only of their sovereign but their freedom as well.

Minutes later, before they could riot, they were driven ahead of the squadrons of Cromwell's military machine like cattle driven to their slaughter. They were herded in the direction of Charing Cross and only a few escaped to go through the gate toward Westminster. The King was dead and his heir was in exile. The people were at the mercy of a dictator who called himself "Protector."

Immediately after the execution the Rump hastily passed an act which forbade the proclamation of a successor to the throne. The Royalists, of course, paid no attention to that. They selected Dr. Stephen Goffe to go at once to the Prince of Wales, who was still at The Hague. They instructed him to carry the news of the King's death to the Queen at St. Germain-en-laye, but to let nothing else delay him. The sooner there was a proclaimed King, the better!

Goffe went aboard a small vessel at Harwich and crossed the Channel in a rough sea. The storm was so vicious that it was some time before they could make a landing on the coast of France. Without rest or even taking the time to find a coach, Goffe mounted a horse and rode to St. Germain. There he found that the Queen was still in Paris, and he decided not to go there but to ride at once to Calais. The duty of informing the Queen could be left to her own attendants, he decided. Her son was of more importance now.

The weather was going from bad to worse. As he went toward the port Goffe found the wind increasing each kilometer of the way and when at last he looked out over the water he saw that it was a tempest. All vessels were tied up to wait out the storm.

He went to one tavern after the other, that were frequented by sailing captains, trying to find one of them adventurous enough to put his ship into the dangerous water for a trip to Holland.

At last he heard of a small fishing smack that had been unable to outrun the storm and had floundered into port. The captain had lost his catch, and because of that disaster he had no money for repairs. Dr. Goffe sought him out at once. He found a ruddy-faced Hollander consoling himself over a mug of gin.

"How much do you need for repairs?" Goffe asked him.

"Five thousand livres," the fellow said, taking a big swallow of gin and observing the questioner as he did so. He set down the mug and a crafty smile passed over his lips. He was dealing with aristocracy, that was clear to him!

"If the repairs can be made immediately, and you will agree to take me to Brielle regardless of the weather, I will pay it," Goffe said.

"Now?" asked the captain.

"Now," said Goffe.

The Dutchman looked at him suspiciously. "What's the hurry?" he wanted to know.

"Before God," Goffe said, "there is nothing illegal about this trip. I carry an urgent message to William of Orange." It was an inspiration to use the Stadholder's name!

"What if the vessel is damaged or lost on the trip?"

"You will be paid in full," said Goffe.

"In addition to the five thousand livres?"

"Yes."

"And what security?"

Goffe hesitated. Five thousand livres was almost exactly the amount he had in his saddle bag. He had nothing else of value except a ring with one large, perfect diamond in it, that was his own. The gem sparkled in the candlelight as he held out his hand and pointed to it. It had special memories. The beheaded King had given it to him as a reward for a piece of scholarly work that he had written. He pulled it off and laid it before the captain.

"Done," said the fellow, and engulfed the beautiful ring in his huge rough hand.

It took twenty-four hours to make the repairs and the captain tried, without success, to delay the work. After it was done he tried to postpone the trip because the weather got worse and worse. Goffe was vigilant and he persisted in the carrying out of the agreement. At last he challenged the captain on the grounds of courage, and this resulted in the shipping of the anchor when there was a lull in the storm; and they got under way at once. They were able to make it to Brielle before the wind started up again. The harbor was full. There was scarcely room for them to drop anchor amid the hundreds of craft that were tied up and waiting.

"Yonder is the Stadholder's yacht," grunted the captain.

"Ah," said Goffe. "Can you put me aboard?"

The captain nodded. He bawled an order for a dory to be lowered. Goffe held out his hand for the ring. A cunning and sly expression crossed the man's face but prudence overruled temptation. It would not be wise to incur the wrath of William of Orange. He handed over the security to his passenger and watched him curiously as the dory was rowed away. He had made a staggering profit because the repairs had not cost a fraction of five thousand livres.

William was aboard his yacht because he, too, had been caught by the storm. He was surprised to see Dr. Goffe, and he took him to the drawing room of the craft and listened with horror to what was reported to him. His pleasant blond face contorted with grief as he heard the details of the King's execution. When Goffe finished William sat in silence but his eyes went to the sword hanging on the wall that Charles had given him for a wedding present.

Finally he said, "I will inform my wife, who is by chance in Brielle at this moment. You must go at once to The Hague to proclaim—His Majesty, Charles II."

Dr. Goffe reached The Hague late that same day. He asked for Dr. Stewart. When he came and heard the news the chaplain turned pale.

"What is the best way to tell His Highness—I mean, His Majesty?" Goffe's voice broke with emotion.

"He is fully informed of the King's desperate situation," Dr. Stewart said. "He is prepared, and there is no easy way."

Goffe had himself announced in the antechamber where Charles was in conversation with Sir William Boswell. Everyone else turned and stared apprehensively at the messenger. Charles, too, sensed that this was no ordinary carrier of news, but he did not turn away from Sir William.

"Pray continue what you were saying," he said. His eyes had a faraway look in them but he assumed the attitude of listening until Sir William finished his sentence. Then he turned to Goffe, asked about his health and if he had a comfortable crossing. This gave away his pathetic pretense of calmness, for everyone knew about the vicious weather on the Channel.

Stephen Goffe, a master of many languages, had been chosen for this delicate mission because of his suavity and his ability and tact in expressing himself. But now he looked into the eyes of the nineteen-year-old son of the beheaded King and did not know how to begin. An ominous silence fell over the entire company. They listened anxiously for what they suspected they were about to hear.

Finally Goffe forced some preparatory words through his trembling lips. They came out in a mumble. Unable to speak the words that he had prepared he fell on one knee and kissed Charles' hand. With tears streaming down his cheeks he said in an unnaturally loud voice, "Your Majesty."

Charles withdrew his hand abruptly. He looked around the room at the members of his exiled court. They were paralyzed. Some had tears in their eyes, others stared at him with compressed lips. Not one of them was able to step forward and ease the situation. Charles tried to speak to them but no words came. Finally he turned abruptly and walked toward his bedchamber.

Dr. Stewart would have gone with him but he was stopped by Lucy. She put her hand on his forearm and shook her head. Charles took Lucy's hand and led her into the chamber with him, and the door closed behind them.

The noblemen in the room looked at each other in consternation. What must they do about this woman who had the King under her spell? Most of them thought she was a lady of pleasure—a high-class prostitute—not even a mistress. And she was pregnant! There were rumors, of course, that Charles had married her secretly, but none of them believed it. They could not believe that Charles would give them a Queen who was only a simple little commoner.

Most of these gentlemen had large estates and formerly great wealth. They had grown old and beaten and penniless in the service of the King. Now the future of their families depended upon the efforts of this young man. Would he be up to the courage and boldness that would be necessary to bring about a restoration of the monarchy?

Fearfully they waited, each absorbed in his own thoughts. They stared at the door behind which their King sought consolation from a woman. At last the door opened and Charles came out alone. That was a good sign, the waiting noblemen indicated to each other by quick glances.

Charles turned to Robert Long, his secretary. "Summon my council at once—also, the Lords of—." He hesitated, and then went on, "my father's privy council, who are here at the present time."

Everyone breathed easier. They laid aside their doubts in a flurry of activity. They had a King—a young, vigorous King, they hoped.

"Long live Charles II!" was repeated over and over in the great houses on the Binnenhof where the entertainments were resumed. It became the fashion to use it as a greeting shouted from the coaches of the international set when they took their afternoon rides on the Voorhout between the rows of lime trees.

5

Justus had become a respected man of the law, and when one of his clients told him that he needed an agent to represent him at The Hague he decided to go himself because he had heard of Goffe's mission to the Continent. Lucy was in jeopardy when she was secretly married to a penniless Prince with little hope of being anything else, he thought, but now that her husband was Charles II—and she was pregnant—! If it were anyone else but his sister he would think the situation comic—a plot worthy of a boisterous play—but with Lucy involved it was anything but funny; ludicrous but not funny!

He boarded a ship almost immediately and when he reached The Hague he had no trouble finding Lucy in the mansion provided by the Stadholder. She was glad to see him. It was as if times were normal, he thought, and she married to a prosperous business man with nothing to be concerned about but the joy of the coming baby and a happy visit from her beloved twin brother.

"Justus, you are just in time. Tomorrow I am going to Rotterdam to stay with Anne Harvey until after my baby is born. You know that the Harveys escaped England after the fall of Bridgwater and Henry is a successful merchant now." Justus wondered if it was her idea to go there, or Charles', but he was grateful that she would be under the protection of the Harveys.

He had the old feeling of panic and fear that came over him whenever he had a premonition that Lucy was in danger. What if she should die in childbirth? She looked horribly unwell. He averted his eyes so that she would not see his concern. Then he looked at her again and said earnestly, "Lucy, are you all right?"

"Of course I'm all right. Women always look frightful when they are pregnant. Why do you ask?"

Why, indeed! Anger welled up in him because of his frustration. As usual, Lucy didn't seem to know that she was in danger. He took her small hand in his and said, "Lucy, will you promise to send for me if you need me?"

"Certainly, I promise, Justus. I know that you love me and that you would come if I need you. But I can't foresee any reason why I shall find it necessary to interrupt your work, again. But I promise."

He wondered if he should stay in Holland until after the baby was born but decided that he wouldn't risk having her tell him that he wasn't wanted. He completed his business and went back to London. He didn't even wait to "kiss the King's hand." Let Lucy explain why he didn't!

The King's execution was more than Queen Henrietta could bear. She had held on to the false hope that it wouldn't happen; she was not prepared when it did. She went into a state of shock and sat hour after hour in silence while her attendants waited, not knowing what to do. Then, one morning she appeared dressed in deep mourning. "I shall never wear anything else," she said to them. "I shall go into retirement—Mère Madeleine took care of me when I was a child—she will take care of me now." She ordered a sedan chair and told them to carry her to the Carmelite Convent in the Faubourg Saint-Jacques. Helplessly they watched her go. "God have mercy on her," Father Cyprien, her confessor, exclaimed. "Please give the Reverend Mother the Grace to straighten her out."

Two weeks passed before she returned. "Mère Madeleine wouldn't let me stay," she explained. "It seems that I must return and take up my cross!" She smiled at the penniless people of her little court; they had no money and no place to go. Somehow she must take care of them. She summoned Henry Jermyn, "Let's get to work," she said. The letter writing began again, in the interest, now, of restoring the monarchy in the person of her son. At first, most of the letters were addressed to Charles. She asked him to come to Paris. There was no answer. Then she sent commands that he come. They were ignored. At last she sent Henry Jermyn, himself. He returned almost immediately.

"The woman, Lucy Barlow, gave birth to a child," he said abruptly.

Grimly, Henrietta waited for details.

"They took her to Rotterdam to a house belonging to Henry Harvey—of Bridgwater Castle—Harvey's wife, Anne, escaped from England and is living there. She has an interest in Lucy because she is a friend of the girl's mother, they told me."

"Oh!" was all that Henrietta said.

"It was a boy," Henry said. "They have named him James—the mother almost died—seems she has a bad heart." Henry spoke hurriedly to get it over. "Too bad she didn't," he muttered.

"Henry!" Henrietta remonstrated and then stopped. Her face hardened. She might as well admit that she wished the same thing. Why be a hypocrite!

"His Majesty is at The Hague," Henry went on, "but Mrs. Barlow is still with Mrs. Harvey. The child was put out to nurse at Schiedam."

"Perhaps Charles hasn't answered my letters or obeyed my commands to come to me because he didn't receive them!"

"No, he received them."

"Why has he not obeyed?"

"He won't come."

"Why?"

Henry Jermyn studied her thoughtfully, twisting the points of his moustache. No need to soften the information. She would have to accept the estrangement of her son.

"He hasn't received an invitation from France to establish his exiled court here."

"I know that," Henrietta said. She glared at him as if he were to blame. Her black eyes, in their hollow sockets, flashed anger.

"His Majesty doesn't wish to become your pensioner again."

Henrietta clasped and unclasped her hands in anguish. "He would rather be dependent upon strangers?"

"Yes," Jermyn said. "It would seem so."

"Dear God!" she whispered. "That stubborn, ungrateful boy!"

"It is difficult to wait, especially when one is nineteen, anxious to make decisions and get into action," Henry said gently while he thought, "He thinks that he can do everything by himself!"

Henrietta sighed. It was not Jermyn's way to soothe her wounded feelings with empty words. It was often with such a prelude that he presented his boldest, most effective advice. He was being roundabout again. She waited silently for him to go on. She would listen but she would be wary. She would not let him mislead her again.

"Day by day," Jermyn said slowly, "his little court will become more desperate, more hungry, more threadbare. Then, when he can bear it no longer, he will come."

"What is he waiting for?" snapped Henrietta. "What does he think can happen?"

"His Majesty knows as well as we do," said Jermyn, "that there are plans everywhere to resist the dictator."

"Does he not know, also, that it is I who have these uprisings under my direction?"

Jermyn shrugged his thin shoulders. "Youth," he said contemptuously, "does not use reason in such matters. They follow the command of their passions."

"What is he waiting for? Why does he not come here to assist us?"

"He is waiting for word from Ormonde in Ireland."

"I see," said Henrietta. "Then he knows that Rupert arrived safely at Kinsale with what is left of the fleet?"

"Yes."

"Is he informed about Scotland?"

"Yes, by Edward Hyde."

Henrietta scowled. That man again! "And what did Hyde have to say to His Majesty? Did he advise him not to come to me?"

"I don't know," said Jermyn, "but he warned him."

"Warned him?"

"Yes," said Jermyn. "When a party of representatives from the Marquis of Argyle presented His Majesty with another invitation to come to Scotland so they could crown him their King, Hyde warned him."

"Of what?"

"He warned him that the proclamation carried by Argyle's commissioners was so strangely worded that, though the words acknowledged that he was their King, it was clear that they intended that he should be subject to their demands in all parts of the government."

"Hm," she murmured, considering this new development.

"I was told that Hyde pointed out that the commissioners bowed their bodies and made low reverences but that they spoke more like ambassadors from a free state to an ally then as subjects to their lawful sovereign."

"Hyde's legal mind!"

"True," said Jermyn, "but he is usually correct!"

"And how does my willful, ungrateful son respond to this advice?"

"He is waiting for word from the Marquis of Ormonde in Ireland," Jermyn said again.

"That won't do him any good," Henrietta said wearily. "Ormonde is finished."

New life was everywhere in the low countries when Lucy left Anne Harvey and came to the mansion in the Old Court at The Hague. Tulips were in full bloom; the lime trees on both sides of the Lange Voorhout were a fragrant fairyland of pink and white buds bursting from delicate leaves; thousands of bees were filling the air with humming music. She was thinner and the shadows under her mysterious eyes had deepened; her alabaster skin was a bluish hue. She was very weak, and she spent many hours reclining upon a couch in the garden.

Charles spent most of his time brooding upon his problems. As the days passed while Lucy was in Rotterdam he conferred frequently with his Council and the nobles began to hope that he would be able to live up to the difficult role of an exiled and penniless King. The royal cause was not completely lost forever; there were competent men both in England and on the Continent who were secretly working for the restoration of the monarchy—perhaps at the death of Oliver Cromwell. They were banded together in a secret organization known as *The Sealed Knot*. Nothing could give them more hope than a King of personal integrity who would give the movement a focus of inspiration.

At the moment, the most crucial problem was Lucy Barlow. The King seemed unable to make up his mind about her. On the one hand he was unwilling to get rid of her but on the other he didn't seem to want to accept the responsibility for the difficult situation that she posed. He had left her—deserted her almost—with

Mrs. Harvey. But when Mrs. Harvey wrote to him that Lucy was able to travel he sent for her and commanded that the infant be left with the nurses at Schiedam. Then, after she arrived, he spent more and more time with her each day, and the nobles began to worry again.

One day, Lucy waited all morning in the garden for him while he was in a conference with his councilors. When he came at midday she saw that something terrible had happened. He was scowling and his eyes were filled with despair. There was a new crisis! Royal espionage agents had reported that an envoy, Dr. Dorislaus, was on the way to effect a reciprocal alliance between Cromwell's government and the States General. Without a doubt Holland would be required to withdraw its support of Charles Stuart, now referred to in England as the Pretender. William would be forced to refuse asylum to Charles. During the meeting very bad news was brought in.

Charles didn't tell Lucy about it immediately. He sat down on a bench near Lucy's couch and wearily rested his elbows on his knees. He stayed that way for a long time, lost in thought. Then he sighed and said, "Once more I know that it is more difficult to cope with a brash and misguided friend than an enemy!"

"How so?" Lucy asked softly when he did not go on.

"Dorislaus was murdered last night," he said abruptly.

Dr. Dorislaus! Cromwell's envoy and agent, sent to make the reciprocal alliance—murdered!

Lucy, like all the Royalists, detested Dorislaus because he had been the advocate of the army commanded by Essex, and he had been active in the High Court which had condemned the King to die. She had seen him only once, but, now, she shuddered as she remembered the coldness of his flabby face. He had a large nose, crooked and bent from an old injury, and it gave him a diabolic appearance. In death, she thought, he must be even more repulsive. She couldn't be sorry that he was dead.

"By whom?" she asked indifferently.

"Walter Whitford was the leader," Charles said dully, "and he escaped."

"What happened?"

"Twelve masked men entered the White Swan Inn where Dorislaus was dining, and one of them, probably Whitford, slashed Dorislaus with his sword and then one at a time they all passed their swords through him."

"Oh," gasped Lucy.

"And as they did so they shouted, 'thus dies one of the King's judges.'"

"He got what he deserved!" Lucy said.

"Lucy! Don't you understand that those words identify the murderers—and that the terrorists were men from my court?"

"Would anyone think otherwise?" she asked with a shrug of her shoulders.

He sat in thought before he spoke again. "It means that we must leave Holland at once, before we are asked to go."

"Oh!" She hadn't thought about that!

"No matter how much sympathy there is for me here the Stadholder will not dare to overlook this outrage against an emissary from a foreign government."

"Will you go to Ireland?" she asked.

"I don't know where to go. There is still no word from Ormonde, and Louis hasn't invited me to come back to France."

But they did go to France—uninvited—there was no place else to go. The infant, James, was brought from Schiedam with his nurses to join the exiles retreating from Holland.

Lucy rode in a carriage with Lady Cornwallis and it was followed by another one carrying the baby, his nurses and the paraphernalia necessary for his care.

Charles rode on a horse beside them. There was a frown on his dark face, and his jaw jutted out angrily. Following them were sixty other vehicles filled with noblemen, and behind them came as many courtiers as could find horses to ride on. Straggling along at the end were a hundred or more ragged retainers on foot. They could find no other way to travel and they couldn't afford to be left behind. They tried to maintain a semblance of elegance which gave them a bizarre appearance, as if they were part of a carnival or a circus. Somehow, they all got to Antwerp where they spent the night.

The next day the cavalcade took the road toward Paris and moved on. Nowhere were they welcome. They stopped in as few places as possible, and when they reached Paris, they weren't permitted to pause even for rest. They straggled on toward St. Germain-en-laye.

The time had come which Jermyn predicted. Charles was returning to his mother because he had no place else to go. He sent no word to her but her agents kept her informed of his movements; she knew that his arrival was imminent. Angrily she confided to Jermyn, when she knew he was on the way, that she was tempted to refuse him entrance into her chateau.

"Perhaps, Your Majesty," he said, "we should confer upon the matter."

"Yes," she sighed, "I suppose we must." She rose and walked toward the door leading to the gardens. The courtyard steamed in the hot sun. It had been built to receive the sun's rays at all times; it was terrible in summer, especially now, when there was an unusual heat wave.

Jermyn wiped his brow as he followed the Queen from the chateau out onto the Pavillion and down to the gardens. He turned his face toward the river, hoping to feel a stray breeze. Henrietta made no concession to the heat; she wore her black mourning clothes, summer and winter. She sat down upon a stone bench and motioned Jermyn to be seated also. Henry was delighted. It was too hot to remain standing. He selected a large flat rock that was on the ground close to the bench where Henrietta sat. Even now, he would not be so informal as to take a chair beside her. He was almost at her feet.

"Has the King changed much?" Henrietta asked wistfully.

Jermyn smiled. He couldn't tell her just how much His Majesty had deteriorated. "A little older," he said. When the expression on Henrietta's face warned him that she was in no mood for pleasantries he added, "He is much concerned with his new responsibilities."

"That's quite a change," she said bitterly. "Has the woman that he calls his wife much influence upon him?"

Jermyn hesitated. "Yes and no," he said.

"Don't be devious," Henrietta answered from habit.

He smiled cynically. "He runs to her for comfort."

Henrietta frowned. "I was afraid of that," she said. "But does she influence him?"

"I don't know." And that was the literal truth, he thought, and neither did anyone else.

"I shall find out," Henrietta said, "and I will not tolerate his rebellion any longer. Have they left Antwerp?"

Henry nodded. "Yes," he said, but he did not describe the pitiful state that they were reported to be in. The Queen would find out soon enough. They decided that special apartments would be prepared for Charles, Lucy, their personal attendants as well as the infant and his nurses, but that was all. Henrietta said that she would not assume the expense of sheltering the King's whole court. They would have to fend for themselves.

That same afternoon Charles and the first party of exiles arrived. They straggled in and after Jermyn determined that it was composed of the King and his principal retainers he ordered the gates closed. Those few were taken in and assigned to apartments.

Henrietta did not hurry to meet her son. She allowed several hours to pass before she sent an attendant to request that he present himself to her.

It was the first time that Henrietta had seen Charles since the execution of his father; she tried to put the thought aside but tears ran down her cheeks, and she sobbed a bit when he stood before her. He looked at her almost coldly, and this reminded her that she must control her feelings. She was treating with the King now, and it would be the best thing for him, and for everyone else, if she were stern with him. If he acted like a child he was not ready to be treated as a sovereign, she thought irritably.

"You are acquainted with the political situation?" She spoke as coldly as possible in order to avoid weeping again.

Jermyn watched her with a questioning look. He hoped that she wouldn't lose control and go into a rage!

"Indeed I am, Mam," Charles replied. He smiled good-naturedly. "Well enough to know that I have nowhere to lay my head."

Henrietta was shocked by this remark. Was the boy never going to take his desperate situation seriously and make plans?

"You know of our planned uprisings?" She put an emphasis upon the word "our."

"Yes," Charles said.

"You know of the plans in Scotland?"

"Yes," he said. "And I also know that I must sign their Covenant, and turn Presbyterian, to benefit by them."

Henrietta frowned. "What do you plan to do?" she asked bluntly.

"My effects are on the coast waiting to be put on ships bound for Ireland," he said.

"And you have done this without consulting me?"

Charles didn't answer.

"Why did you send my messengers back without answers to my letters?"

Charles stared at the frayed lace on the sleeve of his coat. He didn't answer nor even raise his eyes to look at her.

"Why did you not take my advice about the members appointed to your council? The choice of Edward Hyde as your Chancellor—!"

Charles grinned. "You and Hyde are still enemies, eh?"

When Henrietta saw that he was not only unwilling to cooperate but was actually impudent, her heart was heavy. It couldn't be true that her son was estranging himself from her; that he was going to act without asking her advice—after all she had gone through—after all the plans that she had laid so carefully.

At last Charles raised his eyes. Mother and son looked steadily at each other. One was the gaunt, prematurely aged Queen Mother who had survived almost unbelievable trials and suffering and the other was her large, healthy and sensual son who was yet to undergo the testing of his mettle. The smouldering in Henrietta's eyes warned Jermyn that she was becoming angrier and angrier. He cleared his throat noisily. The warning came too late.

"My son, you must listen to reason," Henrietta said. "Our situation is beyond critical. It is desperate! You must contract a suitable marriage at once. It is our only hope."

"Madame," replied King Charles, "I have a wife." He bowed formally and left the room.

Jermyn took a step toward Henrietta. She was motionless, almost as she had been when she was told about her husband's death. Slowly a flush of anger crept over her pale face.

163

"Stupid!" she burst out. "Why are the young so arrogantly stupid and unwilling to profit by the experience of their elders?"

She was silent for a moment and then went on with her voice full of sad bitterness, "I shall suffer no further for him. I am alone now. I must look after my own welfare."

"Indeed, yes!" Jermyn answered. That was what he had hoped she would say.

"He will find," said Henrietta, "that he is not welcome in France when he is antagonistic to me."

"Yes," Henry said, "the French nobles, even now, are cool to him; his party was not allowed to stop in Paris."

"If he presumes to think that Louis will be friendly he has much to learn about politics," she said.

"There is no doubt about that. France, as well as Holland, will pursue whatever course will bring the most profit to them. Mazarin is no fool. He will never give the slightest favor to the exiled King when he can see that the republic in England is growing steadily in power!"

Henrietta turned pale, but she was getting used to the fact that she could do nothing about what was going on in England, mostly because her son would not let her.

Charles' bravado sustained him until he was alone with Lucy. Then confusion engulfed him. He had assumed that his mother would be transformed into a subject, and do his bidding. Instead, she had brought up that old subject of making a suitable marriage. It unsettled him. His mother was not loyal to him! She didn't face facts, he thought. She knew that he had a wife and that he had been married by an Anglican clergyman. He stared at Lucy as if he saw her in a new light, too. The thought crossed his mind then—could his mother be right? He rejected it. He had not made a mistake!

He was King, now. He could do what he pleased! Frantically his thoughts thrashed about trying to find someone, somewhere, who would take him in and accept Lucy. He had it—the Island of Jersey!

"I should not have left there," he said to Lucy. "I should not have let my mother persuade me to leave there." He stopped and his thoughts elaborated upon that idea. "You see how she treats me now. I should have stayed in Jersey!" He had forgotten that he was tactfully asked to leave!

Lucy was astonished at his childishness. She remained silent for a few moments before she said quietly, "And do we go there again?"

"Yes. I shall dispatch a messenger to Sir George at once, and command him to prepare for our arrival."

"What will we do in Jersey?"

"We will wait for word from Ireland."

Lucy studied Charles. She was disappointed and she was worried. Did it never occur to him that he might benefit by allowing his mother to guide him for a while, because he knew so little about public affairs? It was not an unusual procedure. Louis XIV in France was guided by his mother, the Regent.

"They told me," Charles said in a voice full of self-pity, "that there was great rejoicing in Jersey when the news reached there that I had been proclaimed King. The garrison fired a salvo of artillery."

"Well, why shouldn't they?"

"They should, it's the custom, but as far as I know it's one of the few garrisons that did!"

She saw that Charles was avoiding the issue. He would neither accept his mother's guidance nor take a positive course himself. He wanted to run to Jersey, or anywhere else for that matter, where he could live in the old style and not have to take the responsibility for his new existence. She felt that she was helpless to do anything; she must go along with him for she had no place else to go, except the Harveys—and she had imposed on them enough.

Sir George Carteret rose to the occasion. He sent the King's messenger back with a letter expressing willingness not only to play the host but to assume the duties of the King's Chancellor of the Exchequer, also. He was willing to pay for the provisioning of Elizabeth Castle and for the fitting out of a small flotilla of ships to carry the King's whole court to Jersey. He had also obtained a promise from the local gentry that they would raise funds to help provide the living expenses of the King while he was with them. The people all over the island, he said, had expressed their willingness to quarter the King's courtiers because there would not be enough room in the castle.

"You see?" Charles said to Lucy.

Lucy did see, and more than he knew.

The caravan set out again, and this time the Queen didn't even grant her son an audience to bid farewell.

At Cotainville they found the promised ships waiting for them. Among them was the King's own pinnace that had been left in Jersey. Sir George had fitted it with two swivels and armed the crew with carbine, pistol and cutlass. Charles went aboard at once, and made the trip to Jersey before the news leaked out where he was going. The next day Lucy, Lady Cornwallis and the infant with his nurses, went aboard a second ship which had been especially outfitted for their comfort. The rest of the ships would wait in the harbor and carry the other courtiers across as fast as they arrived.

The King took up his residence in Elizabeth Castle and in less than twenty-four hours he had placidly resumed the life which he had lived there before, as the Prince of Wales, only now it was in the manner of a King. He basked in the change of his fortunes.

Mademoiselle Carteret had married her curate and she had a child who bore a marked resemblance to

Charles, but no one was tactless enough to mention it when she appeared at the castle to help her father entertain His Majesty. Lucy didn't know about the King's affair with the Governor's daughter and only Marguerite's husband, the local curate, seemed uncomfortable.

The King told Sir George that the new clothes which must be made for him, at once, were to be the purple of deep mourning, but they could be of the simplest cloth and design. No embroidery was to adorn his doublet or hose; he would wear only a silver star on his cloak. The scarf, he said, which he would wear across his chest, and a garter were to be of the same color. The new carriages which he would need, of course, were to be painted black. His servants were to be liveried in black with no embroideries. His wife was to have everything that befitted a Queen. Sir George saw to it that all of these requests were satisfied and what was even better, he paid the bill!

In October, when the Governor gently reminded him, Charles remembered that he was supposed to be there waiting to hear from the military activities of the Marquis of Ormonde in Ireland. Hastily he ordered Henry Seymour to go to Ireland and find out why no word had been received. Charles told him that he was not to come back without a complete report of what was happening in the field: he wanted to know where battles were being fought in the interest of his restoration and their outcome.

While Seymour was gone the festivities continued. Hunting expeditions were planned for the King and once every fortnight he was rowed over to St. Helier to attend church. An elaborate pageant went into preparation for Christmas. No expense was spared and it almost rivaled those which Queen Henrietta had provided in the old days at Whitehall. Charles accepted everything, as a matter of course, as his due. At last, Governor Carteret reached the end of his resources and was beginning to go into debt but no one, least of all Charles, paid any attention to that. The New Year was celebrated and Seymour still had not returned.

Then a Scottish Commissioner, named Winram, arrived with an invitation for Charles to go to Scotland and be crowned their King. It was from Archibald Campbell, the Marquis of Argyle, who led the Covenanters, and who was a deadly enemy of the Marquis of Montrose. He sent word that it was now or never. This was the first and the last offer that Charles Stuart would receive from him. Winram had been instructed to wait twenty-four hours for the King's reply and no longer.

That night the island was engulfed in a bad storm; the wind howled ominously around the rocks of Elizabeth Castle; but the Scottish Commissioner sent word that he intended to leave anyway at the appointed time. Charles decided to give an emphatic "no" to the invitation, because he knew in his heart that the Marquis of Ormonde in Ireland and the Marquis of Montrose in Scotland were his true friends.

Then, before he could tell Winram formally, a boat crashed on the rocks below the castle, and Henry Seymour was pulled out of the water. He had been in such a hurry to get back with his message to the King that he hadn't waited out the storm and nearly lost his life. He told his rescuers that the King's Lord-Lieutenant of Ireland, the Marquis of Ormonde, had given him an urgent report for His Majesty; he had a water-soaked letter to prove it. He was dressed in dry clothing, fortified with brandy, and taken at once to the King.

Cromwell, Seymour said, had swept victoriously southward covering Ireland with blood. At Drogheda, he had set up siege guns, battered down the walls, stormed the city and put the whole garrison to the sword. Townspeople were hung in their own doorways when they resisted pillage and rape. As if that were not enough, there was plague and famine everywhere.

"Why didn't you come back sooner?" the King asked.

"Because Ormonde didn't give up hope of a strong consolidation of the Irish until Owen O'Neil died just at the moment when he was ready to sign." Seymour didn't need to explain to the King that without O'Neil the Irish support disintegrated.

"What rotten luck!" Charles said.

"Ormonde knew," Seymour concluded, "that without O'Neil there was no further hope of an alliance and that he had to concede that he and his men were dependent upon the mercy of the Irish population."

Ormonde's letter supplementing this report was brief. It ended on a tragic note: "Our wants, having occasioned disorder, and that disorder the spoil of the country, and that spoil the flight of the country from us as from an enemy."

Seymour sneezed while the King read the letter. To cover his embarrassment he said, "There is still an army of five thousand foot soldiers and thirteen hundred cavalry who are loyal to Your Majesty." He realized, at once, that he should not have volunteered this information because the King's face brightened. He added hastily, "but there is no way to maintain them. They are starving!" He sneezed again.

The King dismissed him and summoned his council for a conference.

Charles sat with his eyes closed as the councilors talked and did not listen to what they said; he was mulling over his disappointment in Ormonde. The Marquis had succeeded in uniting the Protestant and Catholic Royalists, and at the time of the King's execution he had secured almost all of Ireland with the exception of Dublin. It had been so very promising! That was it. It was too promising. Cromwell decided to command the army himself when it went into Ireland to engage Ormonde. Ormonde was no match for him, Charles thought. Ormonde had failed!

Charles opened his eyes and listened to what the councilors were saying. Montrose in Scotland was worse off than Ormonde in Ireland. He had taken the worst beating of all from Cromwell at the time of the King's ill-fated naval expedition. The Marquis of Argyle and his Covenanters had made the most of the misfortunes of Montrose and they were now in control in Scotland.

It was Argyle's representative who was waiting for him to accept an invitation to come to Scotland and be crowned their King! What other choice did he have, now? He could retire to Holland and live as a private citizen, begging pensions from the King of Spain or of France or anyone else that he could fasten a claim upon. He had seen it done, but he couldn't stand such humiliation! He wouldn't do it.

Abruptly he dismissed his councilors and left the chamber without explanation. His swarthy face was flushed and his eyes gleamed with fanatic brightness when he went to Lucy. His jaw protruded in the ugly way that she knew so well.

"Ormonde and Montrose have failed," he said. "I shall sign the Scottish Covenant and cast my lot with Argyle."

Lucy looked at him with horror. He spoke of his two most loyal and competent noblemen with contempt. "Failed," he said. Did he have no appreciation of the sacrifices they had made because they were loyal to him?

"God forbid," she said. "Never do such a thing!"

Charles glared at her and he looked almost like a madman, she thought.

"It would be better to die," Lucy said stoutly, "than to live discredited, and" she added almost in a whisper to herself, "ungrateful."

He wasn't listening to her. "I would sell my soul to the devil for an army. I will invade England and fight

Cromwell. I can butcher men as easily as he. You'll see."

"Charles, my love," Lucy said, but this time her words did not work the soothing miracle that they usually did.

"I will acquiesce to Argyle. I will sign anything. I must have an army and I will command it myself!"

Lucy pled with him. She sobbed and wept. She reminded him of the martyr's death of his father. Nothing could make him listen. Abruptly he left her and went to Sir George Carteret.

"My Lord," Charles said, "with gratitude for all you have done for my poor family, we are now about to leave you."

Sir George would have been more than justified if he had sighed with relief that the great burden was about to be lifted from him. Instead, he fell upon one knee and with tears in his eyes, kissed the King's hand. "Your Majesty," he said, "it is with grief that I realize that I have nothing more to give. And yet, I have not done enough," he said, and it was evident that he was sincere and not resorting to flattery.

"Enough that it will not be forgotten," said Charles, "if it please God to restore me to my kingdom. You will be rewarded for what you have done."

The members of the King's exiled court were informed that the King was leaving. They had no choice but to follow him back across the Channel; the days of luxury were over; with the King gone the people of the island would no longer feed and house his retainers much less dress them and entertain them.

Once more there was the problem of what to do with Lucy and the infant. Charles knew that they would be less welcome at the French Court in Paris than in Jersey. Communications with The Hague had broken down but there was little hope that the situation had improved there. It was quite unlikely that William would receive

171

them again. And even if he did, Charles thought petulantly, his flighty sister could have changed her mind about Lucy. Mary always did what Mam told her to do. He knew that he ought to be grateful to Mary; but that only made him dislike her all the more.

His mother's letters had continued to be formal. There was only a slightly conciliatory tone in them, as if she were saying that she was willing to renew their relationship if he would do his part. He told himself that he had no desire to see her for any reason. He had not recovered from her rebukes. He wouldn't tolerate the sarcastic note in the remarks in her letter about his having found shelter after she turned him out! In a few hours he changed his mind. He would have to have his mother's help. In order not to risk the humiliation of being refused permission to visit her at St. Germain he sent a messenger with a letter asking if she would be willing to have a conference with him so that he could acquaint her with his plans. He proposed the city of Beauvais which lay at the foot of the wooded hills on the left bank of the Therain in Picardy.

Henrietta answered at once. She agreed to the meeting in formal and cold words. She would go to a house in Beauvais, she said, near the Cathedral of St. Pierre to wait for him. Between the lines it was perfectly clear that she had no illusions about her son's attitude toward her. She knew that he wished to see her because he found it necessary to ask her to do something for him.

"Henry," she said to Lord Jermyn one day while they were waiting for the King at Beauvais, "I shall encourage His Majesty to sign the Scottish Covenant." She paused. "That is," she added, "if he asks me."

"We find it advisable for the Scottish Kirk to triumph over the Anglican?" He stopped. He must be careful about his sarcasm. The Queen never permitted any discussion of her thoughts about her husband's religion. She didn't answer him.

172

Charles rode into Beauvais and pulled up in front of the house near the Cathedral of St. Pierre. He didn't dismount until the coach in which Lucy rode, followed by that of her son and his nurses, drew up and stopped. He had decided to take them with him when he had the interview with his mother.

James was almost a year old. He was plump and red-cheeked and his large dark eyes and black curly hair gave him a startling resemblance to his father. Deep dimples appeared, disappeared and reappeared as his moods changed. When he saw Henrietta he jumped up and down in his nurse's arms, broke into dimpled smiles and held out his arms to her. The forlorn and lonesome Queen could not resist such a display of affection from her grandson. She readily agreed to take care of the child while Charles was in Scotland; it took longer for her to accept her grandson's mother. She looked at Lucy coldly but at last held out her hand to be kissed.

"You are welcome to stay with my court at St. Germain," she said reluctantly.

Charles breathed a sigh of relief. He would be free of the women! He had what he wanted so there was nothing more to discuss with his mother. The next day he escorted Henrietta and Lucy into the carriage that had been borrowed for the trip, and a lady-in-waiting joined them. A second coach, borrowed from the Stadholder, was used for the infant and his nurses. Jermyn and the Queen's other gentlemen attendants followed on horseback.

The Queen, as was her custom now, was dressed in shabby black, unrelieved by lace or color, but there was a plain gold crucifix suspended from a chain about her neck. She was gaunt and pale and her eyes were tragic.

Lucy, in contrast, wore a cloak edged with sable, a parting gift from Sir George Carteret. She wore it casually; in Jersey she had learned to be a woman of fashion. She used cosmetics too, now, and her hair was arranged stiffly into a formal coiffure. Jermyn muttered that it must have taken a hairdresser half the morning to construct it. He wondered if the girl thought that she could keep up that elegant mode while she was dependent upon her impoverished mother-in-law. If so, she was about to receive a surprise! He looked down at his own shabby costume and thin-soled, scratched boots. Her Majesty provided enough to cover one's nakedness, he thought with a grin. That was about all that she would concede was necessary when it came to dispensing funds for clothing!

The Queen did not turn her head as the carriage started on its way back to Paris but Lucy leaned out of the window and watched the King mount his horse and join his courtiers and councilors. He set off in the direction of Breda to meet the Scottish Commissioners and he didn't look back at all.

6

Charles ordered a stop for the night at Ghent. A courier was sent ahead to apply to the burghers for hospitality. Back came a surly reply!

"There are good inns in Ghent," was the answer. They made it clear that the Pretender was not welcome in Holland. Charles smothered his anger and took the party to the Golden Apple, where they sat down to dinner in one of the public rooms. He was biting into a huge joint of beef when the landlord came to him and timidly said that the magistrates of the town wished to be received. Savagely Charles finished biting off the meat and chewed haughtily and slowly while the landlord waited. After he swallowed he said coldly, "No—tell them to begone."

The landlord backed off nervously clutching his apron. Soon, he was back again and spoke to Charles in a quavering voice. "Your Majesty, the magistrates request that you accept the customary pipe of Rhenish, usually offered to foreign princes—or—." He was shaking so that he stopped speaking.

"Or what?" snapped Charles.

"Or—a money equivalent."

Charles jerked his head up and looked at the landlord. The man gasped and his mouth dropped open.

"Tell them to send in their filthy Rhenish," Charles said. His jaw protruded and his dark face flushed. "So

175

we are not only treated as unwanted guests—we are called beggars."

The Rhenish was raw and strong and the cavaliers, used to fine wines, poured it down their throats and then vented their anger upon the landlord's furniture; the next morning the inn was in a shambles. A young and pretty maid brought breakfast to the King. Under the mug was a bill for 1800 guelders. Two hundred was itemized as "salt, vinegar, and butter."

"Afraid to come himself, was he?" Charles shouted. "He sends me the bill for his filthy furniture as 'salt and vinegar,' and baits it with a toothsome wench to make me forget the insults of last night. Ha! 'Od's fish—what does he think I am!"

He pinched the blushing girl on the arm and slapped her familiarly on the buttocks. "Get on with you—I've no time for you now."

Charles ordered that the bill be paid even though it left them penniless. "Could we but swear in Walloon and Dutch they'd hear how we devote them to the devil," he said as he pulled himself up on his horse. " 'Od's blood—what a headache," he said. "That filthy Rhenish was not fit to drink!"

The party rode on and at last reached Breda. The Commissioners from Scotland arrived the next Saturday, and on the following Tuesday the King received them in a bedchamber audience. They would crown him their King in Scotland, they said, but he would have to sign the Covenant, establishing Presbyterianism in all of his realm. He must also abandon Ormonde in Ireland and Montrose in Scotland.

Charles signed the first draft of the treaty but his hand shook as he did it. It was not easy to sign the death warrant of two friends. But, there was always the chance that they could escape the sword by their own efforts, he assured himself. It was the signing that humiliated him.

"To be a King," Charles remarked to George Villiers, "one must first learn to be a Judas to one's friends when necessary."

"No matter," Villiers said gaily, "I can look out for myself now that you've warned me! Let us drown our sorrows in wining and womening!"

George was still one of Charles' favorite companions. When he first heard about Charles' having secretly married Lucy he couldn't believe it. Now, he constantly encouraged the King to commit adultery. Naive women are easy to deceive, the mischievous young Duke said, and Lucy probably wouldn't believe it if someone told her. She probably believed that Charles would never be "unfaithful" to her, he sneered.

Charles was only too glad to follow Villiers' example as an outlet for his pent-up anger. The signing of the Covenant seemed to set him off; night after night they found ways to evade the Scots and didn't go to bed until the sun came up. The Covenanters made a note of his behavior and resolved to reform him when he landed in Scotland and before they crowned him. The sober members of the King's own followers were shocked, too.

"What's come over the laddie?" moaned Lauderdale to Lord Wilmot, two of the older noblemen that Charles had chosen to go with him to Scotland. "I've never seen him like this."

"Reaction," said Wilmot.

"To what?"

"To doing what he knows he shouldn't do; he's sold his birthright for a mess of pottage."

"Poor laddie," said Lauderdale. "I don't like it, I don't like it!" He was a Scot, and he spluttered and rolled his "r's" as he spoke.

The consciences of some of the ruthless Scottish Commissioners began to prick them, too, because of what they were doing to the desperate young King. One of them, Jaffrey by name, wrote in his diary that he thought that they had sinfully entangled not only themselves but the nation and the poor young man that they had made swear to their Covenant even though they knew that he hated it in his heart. He had to sign it, they knew, because it was the only terms that they would accept upon which they would permit him to rule over them which was his inherited right to begin with. He had sinfully complied with what they had sinfully pressed upon him. In doing it he was not so loyal to his principles as his father, but it seemed that his need, and the Scottish Commissioners' guilt, was all the greater.

And still another, Arthur Livingstone, wrote in his journal, "It seems to have been the guilt, not of the commissioners only, but of the whole state—yes, of the Kirk."

Archibald Campbell, the Marquis of Argyle, had not believed that the young King would walk into the trap he had set for him. When he heard that His Majesty had accepted all of the conditions laid down, the nostrils of his large hooked nose dilated slightly. "Wonder what the Pretender thought," Argyle said, "when he heard that we've caught Montrose!" He drew his mouth into a cruel line and his eyes narrowed as he gave orders for Montrose to be tortured and executed.

Charles bit his lip to keep from crying out when they told him. He said nothing, either, when they took him aboard the vessel they had brought with them from Scotland nor when they insisted on reducing the number in Charles' court with the explanation that there was not room for all of them.

It was a slow voyage but they finally landed in the small port of Garmouth, and Charles was taken by the Bog of Gicht and Strathbogie to Aberdeen. There they told him that they had executed Montrose, and they pointed to his hand that they had cut off and nailed to a beam of the bridge that they were crossing. Charles gritted his teeth and was silent because he wouldn't give them the satisfaction of showing emotion. He even made conversation by commenting that in some ways the scenery reminded him of places in England. A snort of disgust was all that he got from his escort.

When they thought that he had had enough of the rigors of Aberdeen they took him to St. Andrew's where he was received with great pomp and given the keys to the city. But he had to pay for the honor by listening to two-hour sermons on the Scots' idea of the duties of Kings.

From St. Andrew's he was taken to Falkland where he was treated quite well but most of his personal retainers were sent back to France on one pretext or another and Scottish attendants were substituted. The real reason was that a surveillance by spies was begun. He was prevented from talking freely with his friends; there was no time to play cards and certainly there was no opportunity for dancing. He had to listen to six sermons a day and in the evenings. He was invited, now and then, to play a game of golf but always with a party of Scots who were more like a special guard, to keep him from escaping, than companions.

Charles had landed in Scotland in early summer full of enthusiasm, anxious to be crowned King, and eager to command an army but the Scots postponed the coronation week after week believing that they were indoctrinating him into their way of thinking. They had succeeded only in making him silently stubborn. He was glassy-eyed with boredom from listening to so many sermons when a messenger arrived from England. The Scots intercepted him and took his dispatches. All they told Charles was that "Her Highness, the Princess Elizabeth, is dead."

Since they wouldn't give Charles or any of his English attendants any more information about his sister, Lauderdale went to the courtyard and waylaid the messenger as he was getting ready to mount his horse and leave.

"How and where did Her Highness die?" he asked the man. "At Carrisbrook," the courier said, and then hastily spurred his horse because he saw the Scots giving him black looks. He had already been threatened by ther wicked two-edged claymores and he wanted to get away.

"Carrisbrook?" gasped Charles in horror when Lauderdale told him what the messenger had said. "Did those devils send my delicate sister to that pesthole, that damp ruin that is unfit to live in and where they kept my father?"

"Yes," said Lauderdale. "It was probably her lungs," he said.

"Was Henry with her?" asked Charles.

"I don't know," said Lauderdale, his florid face turning crimson as he saw the King's grief, "but that's where it was. It was true that the Parliament commanded that Her Highness and the Duke be taken there after—." He could not finish the sentence and it ended in a splutter.

"I know," said Charles. "You mean after they murdered my father."

Lauderdale was unable to think of a reply.

"Is Henry still there?" Charles tried again.

"I don't know," said Lauderdale, "I couldn't find out."

" 'Od's blood!" Charles almost shrieked. " 'Od's blood—what fiends they are!"

The resentment had to come out some way. Denied everything but golf, Charles resorted to more flirtations with the Scottish ladies. One lady, in particular, made herself especially available to His Majesty; Charles took full advantage of her willingness. When Lauderdale scolded him like a father, Charles laughed at his courtier's blunt, awkward attempts to admonish him. After one evening's carousal Buckingham said with a snicker,

"At least, my liege, draw the curtains next time. Half the filthy Scots had their noses pressed against the window to get a better view!"

"Let them look," said Charles sourly. "Maybe they'll learn something!"

It had been the custom for centuries that Scotland crowned her kings in Holyroodhouse Abbey close to Edinburgh Castle. But the castle, on its solitary rock, had proved to be less impregnable than they thought; and it had been taken, and was still held, by Cromwell's forces. So when they decided to delay the coronation of Charles no longer, and to go through with it after the Christmas holidays, they selected the small church at Scone.

The walls of the little church were hung with tapestries and that was all that the Scots would supply in the way of embellishment for the occasion. Even the anointing was omitted because the Covenanters declared that the rite was superstitious and Romish. It was a true coronation nevertheless. The Scottish ministers stared silently at the dark King throughout the ceremony. Later they spoke among themselves and agreed that he had behaved "very seriously and devoutly and that there was no doubt of his ingenuity and sincerity."

They didn't know that he gritted his teeth and blocked out hearing the interminable sermons in which were enumerated the "sins" of the royal family. The idolatry of his mother and the need for the King's personal reformation were the favorite topics. The only sin that he felt any guilt about, Charles told himself firmly as he tried not to listen, was the signing of their bloody Covenant. He was so sick of his bargain that he was ready to give up the plans for raising an army. Furthermore, reports brought from General Massey, who had been sent down into England to incite the English to rise and support the King, were discouraging. There was grumbling that the King of the Scots was bringing the

Bluebonnets over the border again, to conquer England.

Somehow, Charles thought, the English must be convinced that this was not true, and that he had permitted the Scots to crown him because it was their heritage and his, and because he must have an army to command. But if they wouldn't support him in his effort to liberate the whole kingdom he would have to abandon the invasion.

If the invasion plans were abandoned and he became a private citizen, it would not be so bad, Charles was beginning to think. There were ways to raise money. He had no lust for power, he told himself, and if his subjects did not appreciate him, why should he worry? He could go back to The Hague. He would follow the example of his Aunt Elizabeth; he could be as charming as she. William of Orange wouldn't abandon him when he was a private citizen. He would be welcome if he weren't a dangerous subject!

Before he could act upon this decision another English courier came with the news that William had died of the smallpox. Worse than that, after his funeral the Republican party gained the upper hand; the states refused to elect his son, born to Mary a short time after his death, to succeed him as Stadholder. Each state was planning to administer its own affairs and though Friesland and Groningen chose a friend of William's, William Frederick of Nassau, to be Stadholder, the army was left without a commander-in-chief. The House of Orange, which had been the chief support of the Stuarts, was definitely on the decline.

Now Mary was in trouble, Charles thought resentfully. She was worse off than he. She could be of no help to him now. Who else would support him if he became a private citizen? No one. He had no choice but to continue with the Scots and their invasion plans.

By this time the Scots had replaced almost all of Charles' personal attendants. Lauderdale, especially, had to go because he had been bold enough to intercept the courier who carried the news of Elizabeth's death. He did manage to stay with relatives in another part of Scotland and planned to join the King's army when it mobilized.

Only George Villiers succeeded in staying with the Scots' approval. He was more sly than they were! He convinced them that he would use his great influence with the King on their behalf. The King's councilors could have told them that any influence the Duke had upon his Majesty was viciously immoral.

Even Dr. Fraizer was replaced by Dr. Cunningham; Charles detested him. One day when Charles and Buckingham set out for a game of golf, followed, as usual, by a party of Scots to watch them, Charles amused himself by starting a conversation which would strain the Scots' hearing.

"One good reason," Charles said, "for remaining in good health is that fellow, Cunningham. He looks more like a butcher than a physician."

"A typical Scot," sneered Buckingham in a low voice.

The Scots followed the King so closely that they had to stand back each time he took a swing at the ball. Sometimes when they did this Charles took the opportunity of amusing himself by making uncomplimentary remarks about them to Buckingham.

"There is no limit to some men's ambitions," he said as he made a powerful drive with the Scots standing back, and the ball rose slowly to its highest point and then sailed straight ahead.

"No truer word was ever spoken, sire," Buckingham answered as he made his next shot.

"Argyle has proposed that I marry his daughter," Charles said and loudly enough for the Scots to hear.

"I thought the man was mad," said Buckingham under his breath. "That proves it."

"Not necessarily," Charles muttered, making a good iron shot. "He is merely overshooting the green."

Buckingham chuckled, and the eavesdropping Scots looked puzzled.

"I shall send Captain Titus to St. Germain," the King said loudly, as he swung his club. The Scots had to stand back as he added, "to ask Her Majesty's permission." He winked at Buckingham and the Scots strained to hear what he would say next.

As they watched the ball in its flight, Charles said, again, loudly, "I shall inform Her Majesty of the power and merit of Argyle and explain the advantages to both England and Scotland if I contract a Presbyterian marriage." He stopped and looked at Buckingham with a blank expression but his eyes twinkled. "Besides," he said, "Argyle's daughter is a bonnie lass."

Buckingham guffawed and the Scots scowled with rage.

"It stands to reason that if His Lordship wishes his daughter to be at my side on the throne of England he'll have to give me an army of Scots to put me there!"

Next day Titus was dispatched to France. It was a bleak day late in January; he did not get back until the month of May.

When he did arrive the letter he carried made it evident that the Queen and Henry Jermyn had guessed Charles' intention correctly. They replied in a way that would not offend Argyle. It might even flatter him a little. Henrietta explained gracefully that there was no objection to either Argyle or his daughter and a marriage of the King with one of his subjects was possible. However, she thought it would be prudent to postpone her sanction, and even the negotiations, until a later date. She felt sure that the Marquis would agree with her that such an alliance, at the moment of a planned invasion of England, could be an occasion for objections both in Scotland and England.

Captain Titus carried another letter to the King from Henry Jermyn. Charles was preoccupied as he read it. He read it a second time and frowned as he did so.

"Bad news, sire?"

"No more than usual."

Buckingham assumed the attitude of a beagle, paws in air, waiting for a reward from his master.

At last, to satisfy him, Charles tossed him a morsel. "Mrs. Barlow," he said "has given birth to a child. Father Cyprien de Gamache baptized the infant and they named her Mary."

"When?" asked Buckingham.

"The child was conceived—" Charles began, "she was born—" and then he stopped. Didn't he have enough trouble on his hands without explaining everything to George. It was none of his business. Of course it was his child. Knowing Lucy there was no doubt in his mind about that. It probably happened that last night before he left her with his mother, he thought with a grin.

Jermyn wrote that the Queen was destitute. The King of France had been petitioned for the favor of an increased pension but, so far, it had not been granted. The Queen, he said, was unable to support Mrs. Barlow any longer, much less another child.

The King shrugged his shoulders. Lucy had been a burden too long. Let her fend for herself for a while!

At last the Scots gave Charles his army. It was mobilized at Stirling. Because of the importance of an engagement with the Pretender, Cromwell, himself, took command of the opposing army, and he watched the mobilizing of the King's army from across the Forth. His forces were encamped at a place where the river was fordable and he was anxious to get into battle and finish off the King. He was far from his bases and his supplies were decreasing. General Leslie, commander of the Scottish cavalry, knew this and he took up a position on the hills south of Stirling, at Torwood, and refused to be lured down to the attack in order to delay an engagement.

For two weeks nothing happened and then Cromwell decided to move. He crossed the Forth and divided the King's army and cut him off from his main source of supplies. This left Charles with three alternatives; he could risk battle with Cromwell; retreat into the western highlands; or start a march down toward England. Cromwell had left the road to the south open, as bait, and the King fell into the trap. He took a roundabout route to London and hoped that he could add English volunteers along the way. Cromwell expected that he would do this and he gave the order for his own army to take the direct way: from Newcastle they went through Yorkshire, Nottingham, Leicester and Warwickshire. Then, a hundred and twenty miles from London he ordered a halt, took up a position on the ridge along the bank of the Severn, at Worcester, and waited for the King to arrive. He had blocked the way and chosen the battleground!

From his high point a party of Cromwell's reconnaissance men watched the King ride, at the head of his retainers, through the gate of the walled city. His black hair, curling to his shoulders under a white-plumed hat, and his cloak with the Order of the George on the shoulder, gave him a romantic and jaunty air. His bearing was regal but not martial. It looked like the people from a fairy tale kingdom to the men watching on the hill.

"In God's name who does he think that he is?" sneered one of Cromwell's men, "King Arthur?" The others guffawed because that was what all of them were thinking.

Inside the town Charles set up his headquarters in a private residence at the end of a narrow street in the

Corn Market, not far from St. Martin's Gate. There, he and his generals made preparations for the battle that he knew that he must fight. The number of English recruits that they had made along the way had been disappointing because, when they crossed the border, the English people in the towns they passed through recognized General Leslie riding at the head of the cavalry. They had seen him before! He had commanded the cavalry that came over the border to fight the King and His Majesty had surrendered to him at Newark. They were not going to be tricked into aiding another Scottish invasion! The result was that Charles had to face a highly professional regular army of thirty thousand seasoned troops with only twelve thousand green Scottish volunteers.

But the King and his commanders hoped that they had a good plan; they manned Fort Royal and General Montgomery was sent to destroy Powick Bridge. It was hoped that this would keep Cromwell's forces, that were stationed on the other side of the river, from reinforcing the main body. Piscottie's Highlanders were stationed behind Montgomery and General Leslie's cavalry was assigned to Pitchcroft Field. All this was reported to Cromwell in his headquarters on the crest of Red Hill to the southeast of the town. He gave orders for a pontoon bridge to be built immediately to replace the one destroyed.

Cromwell's officers laughed at the King's flimsy preparations. "Child's play," one of them said.

Cromwell didn't join in the laughter. His thoughts were on General Leslie and the Scottish cavalry at the edge of Pitchcroft Field. He knew that matching wits with Leslie was not "child's play" and that the tactical problem in this engagement was to guess what the Scottish general would do.

The King was worried about General Leslie, too, for he sensed that something was wrong. When he left his headquarters and addressed his officers just before they mounted their horses to go to their separate posts for the battle, he watched Leslie apprehensively.

"Montgomery and Piscottie will hold Fleetwood back while we attack Cromwell at Red Hill, and—" Charles went over the plan they had agreed upon, "—General Leslie's cavalry will reinforce us!" He gave a farewell salute and his officers returned it. Then, Buckingham and Wilmot fell in, one on each side of the King, and stayed close at his side as he spurred his horse, galloped through the town and went out Sidbury Gate at the foot of Friar's Street on the southeast boundary of the town. They passed Fort Royal and reached Perry Wood where the King's main force was waiting for him. According to the plan the command of the right wing had been given to Hamilton and the left to the Earl of Derby. The King, himself, commanded the middle.

The King unsheathed his sword and holding it high shouted the order to charge, and his men followed him straight up Red Hill toward Cromwell's headquarters. The daring attack surprised the enemy but Cromwell's well-trained personal body-guard rode down immediately, straight at the King who was well out in front of his men. He cut them down, man after man, until only a few were still in the saddle. Then, the King charged the entrenchments near the top of the hill, killed the artillery men and commanded that the guns be turned on Cromwell's own tent. He had escaped a few moments before but the Royalists blew it to bits anyway. Then Hamilton and Derby brought up the wings and down below Cromwell's reserves were unable to cross over their pontoon bridge because Montgomery held them back. All was working! The time had come for reinforcement by Leslie's cavalry.

Leslie did not move.

The battle on the hill raged on. Four hours passed with the Royalists charging again and again, the King at their head. His height, his grey horse and his white-plumed hat made him a continual target but somehow he escaped. His breastplate repelled every attack. Fleetwood overcame Montgomery at the pontoon bridge. Behind Montgomery, Piscottie's foot soldiers held their ground to the last man, but after that there was nothing to stop the thousands crossing the river. Cromwell brought up his reserves; the King's reinforcements did not move. Leslie was still on Pitchcroft Field. The Royalists on the hill rallied once more; their ammunition was exhausted and they fought with swords and pikes.

Leslie still did not come to their aid.

The King turned his horse and, followed by Wilmot, Buckingham and Lauderdale, rode down through the Royalists, fighting hand to hand, to Pitchcroft Field. He shouted at Leslie, "In God's name, General, give the order to charge!"

Leslie turned his head and looked at his men. "They won't fight," he said.

The King pulled up his horse and faced the cavalry. "Brave Scots," he shouted, "strike one more blow for Charles Stuart, your King, and he will be victorious!" A negative rumble was the only answer.

Lord Wilmot leaned from his horse and spoke to Lauderdale, "My Lord," he said, "if that's the case, ride to the town and get fresh horses at the blacksmith's near Sidbury Gate for the King's escape. We'll retreat."

"—understand!" Lauderdale answered, "I'll do it." He turned his horse.

"Get men to stand ready to block the gate when the King rides through," Wilmot shouted. "If there's not time to close it, tell them to block it, if they can!"

Lauderdale did not slow down. He raised his arm as he spurred his horse to indicate that he understood what Wilmot had shouted to him.

The King pulled his horse around, away from Leslie's cavalry, to return to the action.

"Sire," Lord Wilmot implored him, "do not return—you will be killed."

Charles spurred his horse. "Follow me," he commanded. Wilmot and Buckingham fell in behind him. There was no return. They rode into a sea of retreating Royalists staggering ahead of the enemy and trying to get away from them. The King's horse reared, turned about, and ran at the head of the retreat toward the town. He could not rein him in.

"They've taken Fort Royal!" Buckingham shouted to Wilmot as they struggled to follow the King. They had to exert every ounce of their strength to keep their horses close to him and in spite of all they could do they both entered Sidbury Gate just slightly ahead of him. As they cleared the entrance a cart of ammunition overturned behind them. The way was blocked!

"Fools!" shouted Wilmot, "the King is outside!"

They dismounted and ran toward the wagon. The King was crawling through the wheels. They dragged him to one side without first helping him to his feet; the Roundheads had taken the Fort and were turning the guns upon the gate.

The enemy poured into the town, and there were so many of them that they came in over the walls or anywhere they could find a place to get in. Savage hand-to-hand fighting filled the crowded streets. Both sides slashed and bludgeoned. The dead and wounded piled up until there was no passing around them. Blood ran in the steep gutters on both sides of the narrow streets. There were few Royalists to run ahead of them but still Cromwell's men poured in.

The King walked around the dead and wounded when he could and over their backs when he couldn't. He pled with the soldiers that had dropped their swords and raised their hands in the air. He begged them to fight again; they kept their hands up. He persisted and they ran away from him. Finally he stood still. It was no use. He cried out in despair, "Kill me, then, if you will not fight! I don't want to see the end of this day!"

Lord Wilmot was following him. "No, Sire!" he cried, grasping the King's arm to get his attention. "We will get you to safety."

Talbot and Derby came running from a side street. They had fought their way through and their unsheathed swords dripped blood.

"Thank God you're safe!" Talbot shouted at the King.

"You see, Sire," Wilmot shouted, "we must save you!"

The Earl of Derby staggered, as he called out, "Everything is lost. St. Martin's Gate is the only one where the devils are not swarming in. That's the way to get His Majesty out of town."

Lauderdale's harsh spluttering voice was heard even before they saw him coming from another side street. His red hair was blowing wildly about his perspiring face.

"Get him away—get him away—" he shouted. "Douglas and Forbes have fallen and Hamilton is wounded and carried to the Commandery. Hurry! Hurry!"

He went to Wilmot and said in a lower voice, "Horses from Bagnall's are waiting at the back of the house in the Corn Market."

"Good," Wilmot answered. "Why at the back?"

"The back door opens close to the city wall, and unless they surround the house the King can get to Saint Martin's Gate—that is, if we hurry!"

A man with blood spurting from a sword-cut across his nose came running up Friar's Street from where they had just come.

"In God's name, where is His Majesty?" he shouted as soon as he was close to them.

Wilmot pointed to the King with his sword.

"They've cleared the passage at Sidbury Gate," the man said, "They know that the King came through the gate and they are looking for him."

"Who are you and where do you come from?" Wilmot demanded.

"Captain Carless from Lord Cleveland," he said. "He sent me to tell you that we will fight them off as long as possible—so His Majesty can escape. But you must hurry—we cannot hold out long! I'll report to my lord that His Majesty is still alive," he said, and without pausing for an answer he started back in the direction from which he had come.

Wilmot caught up with the King. "Sire, I implore you! Do not give up. They are laying down their lives at Sidbury Gate to give you time to escape."

With that, Charles started to walk as fast as he could and soon reached the half-timbered house of his headquarters.

"—all meet at Barbon Bridge!" Wilmot shouted as he and Lauderdale turned to follow the King.

"There is one thing that I must do," Charles muttered as he went into the house.

Wilmot followed him in but Lauderdale remained at the door, sword unsheathed. "Take him out the back way," he said.

Lauderdale answered, "Aye."

The King whistled for his little spaniel. There was no answering yelp. The dog was gone.

He made no effort to gather up his valuables, but hunted frantically for the dog—under the bed, behind the chairs. She must be hiding somewhere!

Lauderdale burst into the room. "In God's name, Sire, Colonel Corbett and his Sussex rebels are approaching. They will beat down the door. I implore you to leave before we are all killed!"

Charles started for the back door.

"Sire!" spluttered Lauderdale, "I must go first. They may have surrounded the house."

The enemy had not yet surrounded the house and Buckingham and Wilmot were waiting in the back with the horses. As the King jumped into his saddle they heard a crash. It was the front door being broken down.

"Hurry!" said Lauderdale.

Before they could spur their horses, a maidservant came running out of the scullery. "Your Majesty—she was in the street and I brought her in," was all she could get out between gulps of breath. She reached up to Charles and handed him a trembling, whining ball of fur. It was the spaniel!

"Out of the way," shouted Lauderdale and the girl jumped back into the house.

The King and his escort rode through Saint Martin's Gate and took the road to Kidderminster. Wilmot and Lauderdale were ahead, anxiously watching for signs of ambush. Buckingham rode behind the King, keeping a sharp eye out for pursuers. Charles was numbed by the collapse of his hopes. Victory had been so close that defeat was unbearable. He held the spaniel close to him under his cloak, and he closed his eyes and bowed his head. He never wanted to raise it again. Failure! Failure! Failure!

He thought of how all the monarchs of all the courts of Europe had turned their backs upon his pleas for help—of how the States General in Holland had tactfully hinted that his departure would be welcome because of the murder of Dorislaus. He thought of his father—murdered—of his mother and his little sister, Henriette, living on the charity of the King of France—of his brother, James, living on the charity of the House of Orange, Mary's in-laws, who despised her and were giving her no more favors since William's death. He thought of Henry all alone with those devils in England!

He was the head of the House of Stuart and he had failed them all. He had degraded himself for a chance to get into battle, and then he lost it and led his army to destruction! Worse than that, he realized, even though his brain was fogged with weariness, that the Commonwealth would be united now. He should have foreseen that the English would fight with Cromwell, because they thought the King was a Scottish invader! How could he have been so imprudent?

He thought of the humiliation which the Scots had heaped upon him—their insulting sermons—their threats—their treacherous promises.

"There was no other way," he repeated. A sob caught in his throat and tears of weariness and despair ran down his battlestained face into the fur of the little spaniel.

"You wicked dog," Charles murmured. "You were almost left behind."

When they reached Barbon Bridge, a mile out of Worcester, the King had regained his composure. He sat erect in the saddle with his head up. The white plume of his hat curved down over matted black hair, and his face was splattered with mud. There were torn places in his cloak, but the diamonds of the George still sparkled.

It was sunset and black rain clouds were gathering to the north. The air was sultry and a few large drops of rain splashed on their shoulders as they reached the bridge which arched a small tributary of the Severn River. Sixty mounted cavaliers waited for them at the right side of the approach to the bridge.

Lord Talbot was there. A snag was torn in the knee of his breeches, and it was stiff with dried blood. Lord Derby was there, and his face was pale and drawn with the pain of neglected wounds. William Armourer, Colonel Blague, Colonel Roscarrock, Mr. Darcy and Mr. Giffard were all there. Somehow they had all managed to find horses. They had come out through St. Martin's Gate ahead of the King, and they were waiting for him at the appointed place.

William Armourer was the first to recognize His Majesty.

"Thank God, Sire, you are here!"

To the left of the approach to the bridge, facing the cavaliers, General Leslie sat on his black horse. His narrow ruddy face was set in stubborn coldness and his thin lips were drawn into a tense line. Some distance behind him was the regiment of Scottish Cavalry. Their equipment and clothing were in perfect order and their horses were fresh.

The King rode straight to Leslie. "You have some new plan of attack, General Leslie?"

"No, Your Majesty," said the general.

"Your men are in good order—a surprise attack might bring victory." The King was too desperate to be rational.

"Retreat is your only course, Sire," Leslie said.

"That was your plan from the beginning, was it not, General?"

"Let us say, rather, that it was inevitable," Leslie barked insolently.

Buckingham's hand went to his sword but Lord Wilmot put out a restraining hand. "Stay, George. You will only make matters worse."

"Bloody bastard!" Buckingham cried, loudly enough for Leslie to hear. "He should be run through for addressing the King in that manner."

Leslie recoiled slightly and said more respectfully, "It was inevitable from the beginning."

"And that is why you would not give the order to charge?" asked the King.

"Exactly," said Leslie, "and because they would have mutinied if I had."

"Do your men know that there is a handful of men

laying down their lives back in the town to cover this shameful retreat?"

"If they do, they know also that those men are Englishmen, not Scots."

"Indeed! And are Piscottie, Hamilton, Douglas and the Earl of Rothes not your countrymen?"

"My duty from the beginning," said Leslie, his icy blue eyes traveling momentarily to where his men stood waiting, "was to guard Your Majesty's person."

The King raised his black eyebrows in surprise. The Scots had tricked him again. They had sent a nursemaid instead of an invading army!

"Thus," Leslie went on, "I have waited to escort you back to Scotland."

Charles looked to the right of the bridge at the party of ragged, exhausted, beaten cavaliers and then back to Leslie.

" 'Od's blood!" groaned Buckingham. "Let me at him!" Again Lord Wilmot restrained him.

"My regiment of horse is large enough to withstand the parties which will be sent out to capture Your Majesty. Your only chance to live is to go with me to Scotland," Leslie said.

"Then I will die in England," Charles answered, a sob in his throat.

General Leslie saluted gravely and before he turned his horse to join his men he said, "I shall take the road to Newport. If you wish my protection, you will find me in that direction."

"Scottish bastard!" Buckingham almost wept with rage. "Let's kill him!"

"No, George, the King said. Let the traitor go."

The Earl of Derby pulled his horse close to that of the King. "By your leave, Sire, it is urgent that we confer with you immediately."

The King nodded. He took the spaniel from under

his cloak and handed her to Wilmot's servant. "Let her run a bit," he said.

So with the little spaniel running about under the hooves of the horses, the King drew aside from the main body of his party and conferred with Wilmot, Buckingham, Talbot, Lauderdale and Derby. The King looked from one to the other of his nobles that had survived the battle.

"Can we rally and strike one more blow?"

"No, Sire," the Earl of Derby answered. "We are defeated. All that is left is the hope of preserving your life."

Charles looked at Lord Talbot.

"I agree, Sire. We are completely beaten," he said.

He turned to Wilmot, who nodded in agreement.

Buckingham pulled viciously at the cuff of his embroidered glove when it was his turn. "If those bloody Scots had been honest, it would not be so!"

"I will follow you, Sire, wherever you will have me go." Lauderdale's harsh voice sputtered out when the King looked at him and his wild, red hair framed a very distraught face.

"Perhaps I could ride to London in the darkness tonight," Charles said. "Perhaps I could reach there before the news of the battle. The Royalists would rise and we could control the city."

"No," Buckingham said. "It's impossible. When it's known that you have escaped, the Roundheads will begin a merciless search. There will be a price upon your head and every country bumpkin will be looking for you. You will be killed or captured if you try to go to London."

"I will go to London with you tonight if you wish, Sire," Wilmot said.

"I didn't say that I wouldn't go with him," snapped Buckingham and his face turned red with anger. "I will die for Your Majesty gladly—anywhere!"

"What would you have me to do, George—join Leslie?"

"God forbid," said the Duke. "I think we should get you to the coast and find a ship to take you to France."

"And start all over!" murmured the King.

"It can't be helped, Your Majesty," the Earl of Derby said quickly, for he knew that if it were humanly possible, that was what they must do. They must get the King to some seaport and find a ship that would take him to France. It was the only chance.

"I would rather die in battle than suffer the insults of exile again," the King said to Derby.

Of course he would, they thought. They all would. But that was not their duty. Their duty, now, was to preserve the King.

"The worst disaster that can befall us now is your death or capture," Derby answered.

"What would you have me do, Your Grace?" the King asked.

"The best thing will be to hide you for a few days," the Earl answered.

"Where?" asked Charles.

"We know of a hunting lodge belonging to the Giffards in Lord Talbot's domain that would be a safe place."

The King turned to Lord Talbot. "Would Captain Giffard be willing, under the circumstances?"

"There is no one on the Giffard estate who would not lay down his life for you, Your Majesty."

The Earl of Derby said, "I, myself, have hidden in Mr. Giffard's hunting lodge. Colonel Roscarrock and I were there after the Battle of Wigan. I can assure you that in all this part of the country it is the safest place for Your Majesty."

Charles looked around at his exhausted men. "How far is it?"

"Twenty-six miles, Sire," Lord Talbot said. "That is,

it is twenty-six miles by the main highway, but it would be better to go off the main road because Cromwell's militia will be everywhere. It is farther by the country lanes but it will be safer."

"Who knows the way?" Charles asked.

"We have Richard Walker, my scoutmaster, who can take us northward by way of Kinver Heath," Talbot said.

"Gentlemen," the King said, "I can see that this is well planned. I am in your hands."

* * *

Late in October the King stood on the deck of a coal brig, looking down at the rough water of the English Channel. Lord Wilmot was at his side.

"No one would believe what we've been through the last six weeks, eh, Wilmot?"

"No, Sire, they would not."

"Then," said Charles, "there's no reason to tell them. Cromwell's devils would hang anyone we so much as mentioned."

"The captain of this filthy barge was not fooled. He lost no time in coming to the cabin and bending the knee to Your Majesty."

"The more credit to him," said Charles, "that he was willing to make this dangerous trip before he acknowledged that he knew me."

"I am not convinced," Wilmot said. "He only promised to take us to Poole when we set out from Shoreham."

"Haven't we learned, Harry, not to question those whom we have decided to trust? We find out in good time how they can work it out."

Wilmot murmured a grudging agreement.

"We don't have long to wait," Charles said. "Here comes Captain Tattersal."

Though there was no one else on deck and they were out of earshot of any place where an eavesdropper might be hidden, Captain Tattersal gave no evidence that he thought his passengers were other than a casual nuisance to him. They were paying him to take them to Poole along with a load of coal, he had told the crew.

He looked directly at the King and said, "It will avert suspicion, Sire, if you will petition me, in front of my crew, to take you to the coast of France."

"How so?" Charles asked with an "I-told-you-so" glance at Wilmot. "You have a plan, Captain?"

"Yes," said Tattersal, his face as impassive as if he were driving a hard bargain with the owner of a cargo. "I shall put up resistance to your proposal and you must get the men on your side. I will agree, then, with reluctance."

"Excellent," said Charles. "I have become expert in playing a role to save my neck! When am I to do this?"

"Now," said the captain. "I have a crew of four men and a boy. I will bring them up on deck and pretend to be angry."

"Very well. Bring them here."

They straggled up, chronic belligerence to authority on every face. What new burden was to be put upon them now?

Charles stepped forward. "Good sirs," he said, "you have saved my friend and me from debtors' prison!"

They stared at him, and as his words permeated their dull minds, a crafty smile spread over each man's face. Mouths parted, showing broken, stained teeth or none at all.

"In France I have a treasure waiting for me, a big one! If you will persuade your captain to take us to the French coast I can collect it, and I will share it with you."

He waited but there was no immediate response. The men looked suspiciously from the King to their captain, who stood away from them with an angry expression upon his face.

"Harry," said the King, "give these good men all the money we have. Convince them that if they will take us to France we will pay them more."

Wilmot forced crocodile tears to his eyes and presented each member of the crew, including the cabin boy, with twenty shillings.

"This is all we have, sir," he said, casting a pitiful glance at the King.

"We will give them a hundred times more than that if they get us to shore," Charles said, "—and we collect our money," he added with emphasis.

The men were convinced. They turned to the captain and begged him to alter his course for France.

"No," he said. "I must deliver my coal to Poole without delay."

"It won't take long, Master," one of them whimpered. "We'll work extra hard to make a fast passage."

"In that case," he said, "I'll agree. We'll make an extra profit."

A swift passage guaranteed, the King amused himself by helping in the sailing of the vessel, but at sunset he gave the rudder to the captain.

Then he turned to Wilmot. "Go to bed, Harry. I will walk the deck for a while. I have some thinking to do."

Wilmot was only too glad to be dismissed. He went below and in no time was sound asleep.

Charles paced the deck. "I am no longer a 'hunted animal'," he thought.

For the first time in his life he was faced with something new. His conscience was rearing its head! He thought of all those who had helped him to escape after the Battle of Worcester. They had passed him along from one to the other at the risk of their lives and fortunes for six weeks. Some were tortured and killed because they would not give information. Tears came to

Charles' eyes as he thought of Francis Yates. When the pursuers found out that Yates had not only seen him but harbored him, they tempted that simple man with a reward that was a greater amount than he could save in a lifetime. He chose death rather than betray his King. Why?

He thought of the oak tree that he had been hidden in as a last resort when soldiers were beating the bushes below—while his protectors, the Penderel brothers, were calmly carrying on their duties as woodsmen as if nothing unusual concerned them. He thought of how Captain Carless, with the festered sword-wound across his nose and his cheeks bright with fever, had held him in the tree so that he would not slip off the limb. To his shame, Charles remembered that he himself had slept all through the ordeal.

He thought of Captain Woolf's father, Colonel Lane, Jane Lane and Mr. Whitgreave—his nephews standing watch in a small tower for soldiers on the road—and Father Huddleston!

The closest brush with capture that he had had was that one in Mr. Whitgreave's house, where it was the custom to shelter hunted priests. He had slept all night in Father Huddleston's bed while the priest stood watch. Then the next morning an alarm sounded because soldiers were approaching, followed by a pounding on the door that meant that the house would be searched.

Father Huddleston said to him, "Follow me," and led the way up a narrow flight of stairs to the garret. There the priest pulled open a pair of heavy folding doors which revealed a small chapel. He had scarcely fastened the doors on the inside when they heard loud voices from below. The priest opened a panel behind the altar which concealed a hiding place under the gables, a place designed to hide priests. It was large enough for one person, lying down at full length. Father Huddleston helped him crawl in and lie down. Then he fastened the panel into place and took up a position of prayer before the little altar.

Down on the first floor Mr. Whitgreave was interviewed by the leader of a party of soldiers. They asked him if he had been at the Battle of Worcester.

"No," he said. "I have been ill and confined to bed."

The soldiers had already checked with the neighbors about Mr. Whitgreave's movements and knew that this was true. Their leader listened, anyway, to all that was said and then sharply gave the order for the men to proceed on their way. They had no time to waste looking for refugee priests while Charles Stuart was still alive. The men left, after giving a stern reminder to Mr. Whitgreave and his elderly mother that all those who had information about the King, and refused to divulge it, were being put to the torture in Wolverhampton. Mr. Whitgreave was silent. Why?

When they were gone Mr. Whitgreave sighed with relief. "Do you know who that was?" he asked his mother.

"No," said the tiny grey-haired woman, "but he was a most unpleasant man!"

"That was Southall, the famous priest catcher," he said.

"Thank you, dear God," said the little old lady, making the sign of the cross.

Up in the garret, Father Huddleston had released him from his hiding place. Tears sprang to Charles' eyes as he thought of how the priest had hidden him and exposed himself. If the soldiers had reached the garret and found the priest they would have been satisfied with their prize and ended the search. A scrap of quotation blurred in Charles' mind: "—greater love hath no man than this, that he lay down his life for his friends."

At the time he had said impetuously, "Tell me about your religion."

Only a sharp intake of breath indicated how surprised Father Huddleston was to hear him say that. He smiled and suggested that they return to the study where they could have a more relaxed discussion. He led the way back down the stairs, probably praying every step of the way for the King's conversion, Charles thought wryly.

When they were comfortably seated, Father Huddleston handed him a little book entitled *A Short and Plain Way To The Faith and The Church*. Then he had read for a little while, with the priest sitting in silence.

He read more and more, and then feeling that he should break the silence, he remarked to Father Huddleston, "I have read many things provided by my tutor in theology; but I have not seen anything more plain and clear upon the subject. Can you add anything? Proceed, good Father, with your instruction."

Father Huddleston began a didactic discourse and what he said made sense, but what Charles really wanted explained to him was whether it was their Faith that inspired men to be like the Penderels and Mr. Whitgreave and Father Huddleston. At last he asked him.

The priest smiled and did not go on with the theological discussion which he hoped would supplement the teaching of Brian Duppa in the light of Roman Catholicism. He said simply, "Because they believe that in the light of eternity, it is not important what others do to us—only what we do to them."

"Hmm," Charles had thought, that makes sense of what Brian Duppa called "Love" or "Charity."

Their conversation had been interrupted by Mr. Whitgreave. A message had come from Colonel Lane. The King should be brought to him as soon as possible. The plans were laid and they were ready to take him to Bristol in disguise, where a ship had been found for him.

"God be praised," said Father Huddleston.

Charles held out the book that Father Huddleston had given him but the priest said, "You keep it, my son. You may wish to read it further."

"Thank you, Father," he said. "I will do that," and he had put the book inside of his shirt, intending to read more later.

They took him to Colonel Lane at Bentley. Then they got to the ship, and now were safely aboard with every hope of reaching France.

Thoughts of gratitude were followed by despair as Charles walked back and forth on the deck. "A dark emptiness fills my soul," he muttered. "This life is meaningless. We should grasp every pleasure that we can while there is still time. There is nothing else."

Still the memory of the people who had sacrificed themselves, or risked everything for him, persisted. Again the question presented itself—why?

The haunting memory would not let him alone. He took out Father Huddleston's little book from inside his shirt and started to read it again. He sat down on a coil of rope and tried to recapture the magic of the first reading, but he did not find it.

The priest, he thought, said the same old things that Brian Duppa and the other chaplains repeated over and over; about reincarnation, redemption and resurrection. There was no difference, and now he wondered why he had been so captivated when Father Huddleston talked to him in Mr. Whitgreave's house.

He thought of Lucy and then drifted into reminiscing about Jersey. That was the life! He was born to be a King—to live as he had lived in Jersey—that was what he wanted. Wasn't that why all those people and their families from the Penderels, the simple woodcutters, to the gentlemen, like Colonel Lane, helped him get aboard the coal brig? They hoped for a restoration of the monarchy and the improvement of their own fortunes. It was not religion!

He had played the fool—everybody's fool. It was time he grew up! Was the primary purpose of his living to be directed toward that uncertainty after death, or was it to be directed to being a King again, here—now—in this life?

This soul-searching went on all through the night, and the sun was beginning to rise when he made the decision. He would take the certainty of the enjoyment of this life and let eternity look out for itself! He walked to the side of the barge and dropped Father Huddleston's little book into the water. It floated on the waves for a distance and when it was saturated with water it sank.

He went to his cabin and lay down on the bunk but he could not sleep. Plans for the correction of "past errors" began to whirl in his brain.

He had been Lucy's fool. His mother had been right. If Lucy would not pretend that she was his mistress and keep their marriage secret, then he should rid himself of her. He should have made a proper marriage a long time ago with Mademoiselle de Montpensier; or better still, married his cousin, Sophie. Sophie appealed to him more than the haughty Mademoiselle. And Sophie would please the English people for she would give them a houseful of little Protestants. He grinned. Everyone should be pleased, except possibly his mother, and she no longer counted. Or maybe she would be pleased. She had nagged him enough about getting rid of Lucy and making a suitable marriage. He would do it!

One difficulty, he thought, was that he had married Lucy in the Church of England in Dr. Cosin's Chapel in Paris. But there were ways of getting around that! Wildly he attacked Lucy, mentally, as if she were the main obstacle to his restoration to the throne. He worked himself up to the conclusion that it was for the good of the nation that he should get rid of the vicious woman who was casting a shadow on the British throne.

Besides, he was bored with her. Even in Scotland he

had met more interesting females, and certainly more obliging ones. They had been more generous with their favors and less demanding of him. Why should he bother about Lucy?

The first thing he would do was to dissociate himself from her, repudiate her, perhaps even discredit her. Maybe if he left her to her own devices she might commit adultery. Then it would be easy to get a divorce!

He could not sleep so he went back upon the deck and saw that the sun had risen and that the shore of France was in sight. They were safe! He saw Captain Tattersal watching a vessel in the distance through his glass. When he realized that the King stood by his side he offered him the glass.

"I fear, Sire," he said, "that it is an Ostend privateer. We cannot move into shore, because we must wait for the change of tide. We are trapped if they attack us."

"Perhaps," said Charles, "it would be better for me to go ashore in the cockboat, at once. If I stay aboard we run the risk of being captured by the Dutch, or even worse, by a Spanish vessel!"

"Aye," said the captain. "This is what occurred to me. I am much relieved that you agree. We are not armed and we could do nothing against an attack."

"I understand," said Charles. "Go below and send my companion to me."

The boat was lowered, the King and Wilmot got into it and two of Tattersal's men rowed them as close to the shore as they could. They carried Charles on their shoulders to the dry land and put him down. When Wilmot waded in to shore they looked from one to the other and said, "How about the money ye promised us, Master?"

Charles laughed. "I'll have to collect it first—remember, I told you that."

The men, who had been prepared to be rough if he did not come through with money, were left in confusion. They did remember that he had said that. Stupidly, they got back into their boat and as the wind changed they were carried rapidly back to the coal brig. Charles sighed as they saw Captain Tattersal's ship turn about when the men were aboard and start back to Poole.

The adventure was over. They were safe on dry land at Fécamp. Wilmot produced money, which he had hidden, and it was sufficient to obtain horses on which they rode to Rouen. There they stopped at an inn and sent a message to the Queen. They asked her to send suitable clothing and a carriage to take them to Paris.

* * *

The hawthorns of St. James' Park had dropped their leaves. They lay in great bronze-red platters on the dusty, fading grass of Indian summer and the bare trees stood in the midst of them with orange-red fruit still clinging to their thorny boughs. It was past the middle of October. The people of London were still gossiping about what might have happened to Charles Stuart, who brought the Scots over the border to invade England. One day it was reported that he had been caught and hanged and the next the report was refuted. Someone had seen the Scottish King on the seacoast, trying to get passage across the Channel; the wrong man had been hanged.

As he went about his business, practicing law, Justus Walter listened to all the gossip with irritation. For all he cared, Charles Stuart could have been hanged on some country gibbet or died gloriously in that ghastly fiasco at Worcester. It was of more concern to him that he had not heard from Lucy since the birth of her daughter early in the year. He tried to tell himself to keep his thoughts on his own business, but he couldn't. At last he could stand it no longer. He succeeded in getting a pass under an assumed name, before Thurloe, Cromwell's Chief of Police, knew what he was doing. He crossed the Channel and made his way to Paris to find out for himself what had happened to his sister.

He took rooms near the Palais Royal and began making cautious inquiries about Mrs. Barlow. He joined the young men from the French court every afternoon when they strolled along the boulevards, through the Luxembourg Gardens and along the banks of the Seine. They displayed their finery, gossiped about other people's love affairs and bragged about their own amours. One tattler was especially eager to talk about Mrs. Barlow. "—charming, witty, beautiful, the belle of the season!" he said.

"Lord Taafe is captivated," said another, and lifted his eyes suggestively.

"My lord would have us believe that he befriends the King's lady of pleasure for love of His Majesty," said another.

This added fire to the misgivings that were already nagging Justus. He said to himself firmly that he wouldn't convict his sister on the malicious gossip of the boulevards. He would pursue his inquiry in other places. He began frequenting the drawing rooms of French ladies, who welcomed the appearance of every personable bachelor. At one soiree he interrogated a kindly grey-haired lady who seemed to be well acquainted with everyone in Paris. Justus pressed her for information about his lordship. "My Lord Taafe is in Ireland most of the time, and he has a daughter almost the age of Mrs. Barlow," she said. "Out of kindness he has loaned her his residence. Poor thing, she is destitute and with no hopes for the future now that the King has disappeared."

Justus decided that it was time to see for himself. He went to Lord Taafe's mansion and sent a servant to announce him. He had to wait for half an hour before

Lucy received him. Even then she did not invite him to her private rooms but came to him in an anteroom—as if he were a tradesman, he thought angrily. She greeted him coldly, he thought, and there was a veiled expression in her shadowed eyes. She didn't seem to be glad to see him!

Justus studied the jewels on her fingers, the ropes of pearls around her neck and strings of them twining in her black hair. He could not take his eyes off the costly gown that exposed her beautiful bosom. She invites seduction, he thought, by the scantiest concealment. Angrily he thought about where she must have got the money to pay for everything.

"Have you pawned the jewels His Majesty gave you?" he asked in the hope that she would confide in him.

"Of course," she said. "I had to, to obtain money to live on. I have also given Lord Taafe the ring, with the sealed knot, as security. He puts a high value on it, because it is a unique memento of His Majesty; and he will return it to me when I can redeem it. He didn't want me to sell it."

"Have you news of His Majesty?" Justus asked drily.

"He is dead," she said bitterly.

"Dead?" Justus exclaimed. "What makes you think so?"

"I don't 'think so,' I know it."

"How?" Justus persisted. "How did you learn of it?"

"General Leslie was captured," said Lucy, "and the King was with him. One of Leslie's men escaped and came here a week ago. He brought the information from him."

"The King, then, was captured," Justus murmured to himself. "I can't believe that he went with Leslie, after all!" This destroyed the last remnant of any good feelings that he had for His Majesty. He'd do anything to save his skin, apparently.

"The King of the Scots was not captured," said Lucy. "I did not say that. I said that he was killed!"

"How?" asked Justus. "You mean the Roundheads did not take him alive?"

"He was not killed by the soldiers but stabbed to death by a country woman, a woodsman's wife who had hidden him—and he seduced her."

"I don't believe it," said Justus.

Lucy laughed cynically, but there was a suspicion of tears in her eyes. "Strange, isn't it, dear brother, that we have changed places in our opinion of His Majesty?"

"I can't believe it," Justus repeated. "Where is this Scot who told you of this?"

"He is in the service of Lord Taafe."

"Oh," said Justus. "I see." His eyes blazed. He would have said more but they were interrupted by Lord Taafe himself.

"Ah, my dear," said the portly gentleman, "here you are." He bowed over Lucy's hand and kissed it with just a suggestion of familiarity.

Lucy smiled at the middle-aged nobleman whose hair was almost white. His manner was gentle and his eyes kind, but a blinding flash of anger arose in Justus as he watched. His thoughts ran amok. Taafe was a hypocrite! He affected a look of innocence to seduce his prey, he told himself.

"Ah," Lord Taafe said, looking keenly at Justus. "I have not met this gentleman."

"My brother, Justus Walter," Lucy said.

"I see a resemblance," Lord Taafe said.

Justus bowed and then said coldly, "There should be. We are twins, but my sister seems to forget our close relationship."

After an embarrassed silence Lord Taafe turned to Lucy. "The carriage is waiting, my dear, are you ready?"

"Yes," Lucy murmured and she averted her eyes

from Justus so she would not see the pleading in his eyes.

"We are on our way to Fontainebleau, my good sir," Lord Taafe said. "Will you join us?"

"No," said Justus. "I have business of my own to attend to."

The business was to get back on a ship and recross the Channel to England. If he stayed a lifetime, he thought, Lucy would not do him the honor of explaining further. He felt sure of that. If she were playing the fool again, he was through with her!

Lord Taafe bowed to Justus and then said to Lucy, "I will wait for you at the carriage," and he left the room.

"Justus," Lucy said with some hesitation, "Lord Taafe has been like a father to me when everyone else deserted me."

Justus snorted in derision.

"Whether you believe it or not, it is true. So far, the Queen has provided for Mary but little James and I are destitute. I can't ask anything more of the Harveys. Henry has lost everything again—and I'm afraid that it has been partly due to his protecting me. The agents of the Princess Mary have ruined his business! She believes that I am an obstacle to the restoration."

Justus stared at her. Perhaps he had been too hard on her after all. She couldn't write all this to him, of course, because it would have been intercepted by Cromwell's police. "And now?" he asked.

"My Lord wants to marry me."

"What! Will you do it?"

"Yes, if it is proven that Charles is dead. I have nowhere else to go, and I cannot take care of my son otherwise."

"What shall I do?"

"Go back to England. There is nothing you can do now, and you may cause trouble." She set her lips in the firm line that he knew so well. She kissed him on the forehead and he saw tears in her eyes, but she said firmly, "Goodbye, Justus," and turned and walked slowly out of the room.

"To go to His Lordship, I suppose," Justus muttered. He was more puzzled than angry. What could he do? For once he felt helpless. With some hesitation he went to his ship and started toward England.

During the crossing Justus looked out over the rail of the vessel at the turbulent water of the Channel and brooded. No matter what his sister did, he could never abandon her. She was like the other half of himself.

* * *

In Paris it was chilly, even for late October, and Henrietta was miserable in the Palais Royal. The walls of her apartments were damp and cold in spite of the rich heavy tapestries that covered them. She stayed close to the fire in the mammoth fireplace, because the heat did not radiate very far. Henry Jermyn, of course, was not far away. He, too, was cold. His thin nose above his greying moustache was tinged with blue, and he rubbed his wrists occasionally to encourage the circulation. He was watching the Queen. In fact, he was staring at her.

"What is it?" she said when she noticed him. "If you are wondering what I am thinking about the King being safe again, I can tell you that I never doubted that he would survive, so I can be no more than a little joyful."

"Yes," said Jermyn.

"I am wondering," she said, "how we will feed him and clothe him now that he is back after still another failure because of his incompetence and disobedience."

Henry was shocked at the Queen's coldness. He stroked the points of his moustache and cleared his throat softly.

"Come, come," Henrietta said, "none of your devious methods, Henry. I know you have something to tell me."

"It's about the woman, Lucy Walter," he said.

"What about her?" snapped Henrietta. "Is there more scandalous talk about her?"

Jermyn smiled. "There's always talk about a beautiful woman," he said. "Men hope for the worst, and women are jealous!"

Henrietta said nothing but her black eyes betrayed her displeasure.

"Mrs. Barlow has asked me, formally, to speak for her," he went on. "She proposes that her child, Mary, be placed permanently under Your Majesty's protection as a foster child."

"Mm," said the Queen, "I'm not too surprised. She has no way to maintain her."

"That is not all," said Henry. "She proposes that you will bring her up in the Faith. She hopes, she says, that you will be willing to give her the benefit of Father Cyprien's instruction." He smiled his cynical little smile while he waited for the Queen's response. They both suspected that Lucy was willing to make this offer because she could not support the child! It would almost guarantee the Queen's agreement! Henrietta made no immediate comment, but her eyes filled with tears.

Henry was silent, too. He looked at the Queen with sympathy. The Faith always came first with her, he thought. Often the battles she fought would have been easier if it did not. Now it presented her with a strange problem. Ruthlessly, she had been pursuing a course of getting rid of Lucy, but in spite of her intention she had gradually become very fond of her. The girl was incredible, Henry thought. She never failed to insert herself into the heart of a matter. He had never been able to decide whether it was because she was unbelievably clever or so innocent that she was capable of the most astounding action by sheer intuition.

Henrietta lived now upon two hopes: the restoration of the Stuarts to the throne and the conversion of one or more of her children to the Catholic Faith. Henry watched her almost with amusement. She was clasping and unclasping her hands, and the blue veins at her temple throbbed visibly. She was lost in thought and torn apart by inner conflict.

"Is it not so, Your Majesty," Henry asked softly, "that the King will make his own decision in the matter of his relationship to Mrs. Barlow?"

"Yes, yes," she said wearily, "I know."

"Then you have only to decide about the care of the child, Mary. We can make her your ward, officially, if you wish."

"Tell Mrs. Barlow that I will accept the responsibility of her daughter and she shall have the benefit of Father Cyprien's instruction. What ever comes of it will be God's Will." She sat lost in thought for a few moments and then said curtly, "I am ready to receive His Majesty."

A courier went at once.

Charles didn't look up at him when the man entered his bedchamber. His attendants were staring at him anxiously as he sat at his writing desk in the apartments that had been assigned to him in the Palais Royal. His mother had not been very glad to see him nor that he had escaped capture—or that he was still alive, he thought. She had not asked him to come to her immediately but sent Lord Jermyn to him instead. Jermyn was blunt. He said the Queen was in dire straits and could not help him financially. In fact, she could not even feed or clothe him. If he dined with the Queen, half of the cost would be charged to his account. She couldn't provide him with as much as a change of linen. My lord had put the facts baldly, Charles thought bitterly. In truth, the very shirt that he had on his back belonged to Jermyn!

Now, his mother had sent for him! Should he tell her about the thoughts which had been nagging him or keep them to himself? He could not forget the little book that Father Huddleston had given him, nor the charity of those who had helped him escape. Almost all of them were Catholics. He thought of what the priest had said to him. He had said that the Roman Catholic Church was the Church established on earth by Christ and all others were heresies. Of course there had been corruption in men—Huddleston freely admitted that—but that did not invalidate the truth of the Church. One bad monk does not spoil the monastery, he had said. Like a bad apple in the barrel, Charles thought wryly. A heresy, he had said, exaggerates or understates some article of faith, and it was men who distorted the truth. That was why the Church benefited by the purification of persecution, he said.

Why had Father Huddleston given him that book anyway? The sly thought presented itself that the answer was that the priest had given it to him, because he had asked for it. He put down the thought angrily. Was he not himself head of the Church of England? Did he not have enough troubles without being presented with the infallibility of the Roman Church? Still, that very convincing little book plainly stated that if you believed in the infallibility of the Roman Church it was a mortal sin not to embrace it. If you did not know, it would not be held against you! Why had Father Huddleston not left him in his ignorance!

He would answer his mother's summons because he had to. He would go to her, and he would tell her a thing or two. He would tell her that the Roman Church was not infallible, and remind her that he was head of the Anglican church. He got up and paced the floor.

Back and forth he strode. His spaniel followed him and at last got under his feet. He kicked her.

Remorse flooded over him. He burst into tears. It was the first time in his life that he had ever kicked one of his dogs. What was working in him that brought out such violence? He picked up the little dog and stroked her.

"Forgive me," he whispered.

He went to the Queen's apartments, then, and he looked at Jermyn haughtily. Could his mother never be without that parasite, he thought.

"I wish to see my mother alone."

"Is it a matter of state?" Henrietta asked coldly.

"No," said Charles. "It is a personal matter."

The Queen raised her eyebrows in surprise, but she looked at Jermyn and said, "Leave us alone, Henry. My son wished to speak to me."

When he had gone, shutting the door quietly behind him, Charles sat down on a stool close to Henrietta.

"Mam," he said at last, scarcely knowing what he wanted to say. It was more a question—an appeal for help.

"Wait," said the Queen. "Before you begin there is something which I must tell you."

"Mam," said Charles wearily, "must you always be a Queen—can you never be a woman and a mother?"

Henrietta drew in her breath sharply at his rudeness. "A Queen is always a Queen first and a mother second," she said reproachfully. "And it should be that way with a King. He should be a King before all else."

Charles rose as if to leave her.

"Wait, my son," she said. "I have something important to discuss with you and I am not as inhuman as you think. What I have to say comes first from your mother—though it does have a bearing upon affairs of state. We cannot escape it, you and I; we have no personal life which is independent of our royalty."

She fell silent and looked at him pleadingly, hoping that he would try to understand what she meant.

Charles studied his mother. It was true, he scarcely ever thought of her as a woman. She was old. Her hands were gnarled with rheumatism and her face bore the marks of suffering. Her large eyes in their deep sockets were kind but her mouth was stern and unrelenting. He felt like a green schoolboy in her presence. His hands and feet were too large and he felt angry—at what he didn't know!

"What is it, Mam?" he asked. "What have you to tell me?"

"It's about Lucy," she said.

"Are we to go over the same old arguments again?" he said.

"No," said Henrietta, "I must tell you that there has been too much gossip about her."

"You'll have to do better than that!" Charles said.

Henrietta's thin lips curled disdainfully. "If you persist in being infantile I cannot talk to you," she snapped.

He didn't answer.

"I have grown quite fond of Lucy," said Henrietta. "You acknowledge that my taste is not so poor after all."

At a gesture of exasperation from her he murmured, "Sorry, forgive me!"

"What I am trying to say," said Henrietta, "is that there is much gossip that Lucy is the mistress of Sir Henry de Vic—"

Charles looked at his mother in astonishment. Then he burst out laughing. How stupid and malicious can the gossips be? That old man!

"And others—Lord Taafe—" She watched Charles narrowly.

Charles broke into another roar of laughter.

"Surely," he said, "you don't believe that!"

218

"I didn't say that I believe it," said Henrietta. "I'm telling you about the gossip."

"This I can say," said Charles. "You can convince me of many things, but you can never make me believe that Lucy would commit adultery. She is foolishly, stupidly, incredibly faithful. One wonders why. I cannot be that attractive. It's quite a bore! Perhaps it is her way of holding me; to reproach me by her fidelity."

Henrietta watched her son sadly. It was worse than she had thought. He had grown coarse and worldly. His eyes were knowledgeable of lust, she thought; he has experienced many women by now. His adversities have been too much for him. He has sought forgetfulness in the arms of women!

"What I wish to discuss with you is the possibility that Lucy may be interested in the Roman Church. She has asked that Father Cyprien be allowed to give her daughter—your daughter, Mary, instruction. Do you give your permission?"

Charles was caught unaware. He had underestimated Lucy—perhaps what he had taken for naiveté was a religious cast of mind, like his mother.

His eyes smoldered with anger. His large ugly mouth drew into a line and the muscles of his jaw contracted. His jaw protruded in the symptom of rebellion which everyone had learned to dread.

Then he said, "I, too, have thought, lately, about the Faith. It is that which I wished to discuss with you."

Henrietta was astonished. "Even though any public interest you may show would jeopardize your prospects to the throne?" she asked.

"Yes," Charles almost shouted, "but I cannot. I must be a King first!" He threw her words back at her.

"Let us consider," said Henrietta softly. "Let us consider—"

"There is nothing to consider," said Charles coldly.

"I will be King, even if the devil takes my soul! An English King must be head of the State Church. Henry VIII decided that!"

Henrietta cried out in anguish. Charles rose and said, "By your leave, Madame." Abruptly, he left the room.

He passed Jermyn who was waiting outside the door.

"No need to eavesdrop any more, Jermyn," he said roughly. "Go in to the Queen. She needs you."

When Henry reached her, Henrietta was weeping—harder than she had ever wept in her life.

"My God, have mercy on me—my son is lost—and it is my fault!"

"No," Jermyn almost shouted, and for the first time in his life a passage from the New Testament came to his lips—and he didn't know where it came from. Surely, he didn't remember it consciously, "the seed fell on shallow soil," he said.

Lord Taafe was waiting for the King when he went back into his apartments.

"What do you want?" Charles snapped before Taafe could speak.

"Your Majesty," the nobleman began, "you know, I'm sure, that Mrs. Barlow has been under my protection."

"Well," Charles said with a sneer, "I hope you have enjoyed her favors, sir!"

"Your Majesty!" Taafe protested, and then stopped. He saw that it would accomplish nothing to protest his innocence.

The King glared at him.

After a moment Taafe said quietly, "At her request, Your Majesty, I have brought Mrs. Barlow, the lady Lucy, to you. She is waiting in a drawing room downstairs for you to send for her."

"No," said Charles. "Tell her that she will not be admitted—now or any other time."

Taafe was stunned. He stood uncertainly, not knowing what to do.

"Get out," Charles shouted. "Get out and take 'the lady Lucy,' as you call her, with you."

A woman, Betty Killigrew, was also waiting for the King. She was not only amused by the performance that was enacted before her, she was delighted. She watched Lord Taafe retreat from the room and then she threw back her head and laughed.

"Your Majesty," she said, "you are superb when you are angry."

Charles took her in his arms, crushed her to him and kissed her lips viciously with his big mouth. Then he drew back, without completely releasing her and waited for her reaction.

She didn't pull away nor push him back. She ran her jeweled hand up the sleeve of his velvet coat and touched his clenched jaw lightly with her index finger.

"Sire," she said, "you are magnificent!"

The King took her into his bedchamber and slammed the door in the face of his attendants. She didn't leave the palace until the sun came up.

7

"My Lord," Lucy said to Lord Taafe, "I cannot adequately express my gratitude for your protection—but now it must end."

"My dear," the kindly nobleman said, "I only wish I could do more—but I do understand." He frowned. "How will you manage?"

Tears filled Lucy's eyes. "I have an unexpected small source of income. Recently, I received a letter from my brother telling me of the death of my mother. She had a legacy from my grandmother, Elenor Gwinne, and it is now mine."

"My sympathy, Lucy, for your bereavement. I presume that your brother will manage the inheritance for you in London?"

"Yes, it is a very small legacy, my Lord, but I shall be able to live on it. Also, I have had a letter from Anne Harvey, and Henry's fortunes have improved again. They have invited me to live with my son in one of their houses in Antwerp."

"Very well, my dear, I shall take you there, at once." He was relieved that the embarrassing situation could be resolved so easily.

* * *

In his apartments in the Louvre, still living upon his mother's grudging and meager hospitality, Charles existed in a depressed state. His secretary complained that His Majesty's desk was cluttered with letters and documents that were unread or unsigned because Charles was too indolent to look at them. Week after week, month after month, Edward Hyde pled with him to get out of bed in the morning and receive ambassadors from foreign countries.

"He has to get his sleep so he will be ready for the evening's carousals," Hyde muttered.

For two years this went on: dancing, drinking and lovemaking began at noon when Charles finally got out of his bed. The corridors of the Palais Royal were filled with lewd jests and loud laughter all afternoon and far into the night. That was nothing to what went on behind the heavy draperies that covered the recessed windows, and in the King's private chambers. His Majesty was engrossed with thoughts on how to please each one, in their time, of a succession of mistresses.

The first was Betty Killigrew. She was eight years older than the King and an experienced, worldly woman; she promised to make the King forget his troubles. She had been lonesome herself, she told him; Francis Boyle, to whom she had been married for twelve years, found intellectual pursuits more attractive than domestic life. "He was a mere boy, a well-bred Eton chap," she said sarcastically. "He was unprepared to take on the responsibilities of marriage! He was rarely in London because he spent his time studying in Geneva with a tutor."

What was she supposed to do in her big house near St. Margaret's in Lothbury? Weave all day and rip out the work at night, like Penelope? Certainly not! She had opened her house to a coterie of London sophisticates in which her brother, Tom Killigrew, was the center. "Never a dull moment after that," she told the King. She forgot that she was lonesome. If things slowed down a bit she paid a visit to The Hague, she said, where her sister, Kate Killigrew, was lady-in-waiting to the Princess Mary. "Your Majesty knows about the pleasures of the international set," she said, lifting her pencil-thin eyebrows suggestively.

Indeed Charles did; he practiced them without restraint in Paris. In due time Betty presented him with a girl child. She changed her tactics, then, and charged him with the responsibility of fatherhood. That was more than he had bargained for. Besides, he was weary of her company. He realized that, after all, she was too old for him! He could see that now. There were plenty of younger and prettier women to amuse him. He promised her a pension and title for her daughter when he was restored to the throne, but he would not see her privately any more.

It was just at that time that Lord Byron came down with smallpox—and died. Since the King was free of amorous involvements, at the moment, he took over the pleasant duty of consoling the widow. Helplessly, his councilors watched the two of them squander fifteen thousand pounds, borrowed from whomever they could extract it, on the credit of her husband's estate. Eventually, Lady Byron terminated the affair; she had a baby! Another pension and another promised title; the King was free again.

"Pregnancy is an unfortunate habit of women," Buckingham consoled the King. "I suggest that Your Majesty remove to Cologne and get away from her!"

"A change of air would do me good," Charles thought. "I will follow the suggestion."

He got up bright and early the next morning and announced that going to Cologne was not all he was going to do! He was going to take his duties seriously; he was ready to entertain proposals of marriage with suitable young ladies, for example. To prove the change in his way of life he took a vigorous walk in the park. After breakfast he read and signed everything that was stacked up on his desk; in the afternoon he went for a strenuous ride on his horse.

His serious-minded Chancellor, Edward Hyde, never understood Charles' ironic remarks. He commented to one of the other councilors on the subject of the King's willingness to contract a suitable marriage, "I wonder if His Majesty has any idea of how hard it would be to convince the ambassadors of any of the governments that there is any merit in an alliance with the House of Stuart."

Charles, himself, was not deceived in the matter. He knew that he might propose marriage with any of the most important princesses that he pleased but everyone knew, especially the heads of foreign states, that he was in no position to go through with it. That evening to carry the joke further Charles made a point of paying court to his cousin, Mademoiselle de Montpensier. He tried to make love to her openly.

She found him, she told a friend the next day, most amusing in his new role. He had become quite expert in uttering sweet nothings and other practices of the little arts of *l'amour*. He amused her, she said, but she would not marry him. She was looking for more than "sweet nothings." She wanted a virile husband and a throne. Her cousin had deteriorated so much that he couldn't offer her either!

Her scornful rejection didn't embarrass Charles any more than it had previously. As he had done before, he turned his attention to Isabelle Angelique, now a widow because of the death of the Duc de Châtillon. "I'm beginning to specialize in widows," Charles remarked whimsically.

Edward Hyde sighed in exasperation and reminded His Majesty of his resolutions. To his surprise, Charles agreed and let Isabelle alone. It did seem that he intended to reform. He turned all his energies to a proposal of marriage that was being made, officially, to his cousin, Princess Sophie. How it could be made possible no one explained.

"How could I have been so blind?" Charles asked Buckingham. "Sophie is the wife for me!"

He didn't fool Buckingham, his companion in debauchery. The Duke raised his eyebrows quizzically and made no comment.

Charles pointed out that no wife that he would choose could be more popular with the English people than Sophie. "She will present us with a houseful of little Protestants," he said.

Buckingham snorted in disgust.

Besides, Charles said, Sophie's good health, gay disposition and effervescent joy would be refreshing to his jaded spirit. Immoral women were beginning to bore him!

Buckingham guffawed.

The King's suit was received favorably by his Aunt Elizabeth. She still lived upon the alms of the House of Orange and she still paid her way by being the perfect guest; but it was becoming more and more difficult to smile in the face of her adversities. She was not getting any younger and her problems were increasing. She was willing to give her daughter, Sophie, to the King of England even though he was only a "pretender."

Sophie flatly refused. She would rather die in complete poverty, she told her mother. She confided to her friends that she could take or leave thrones, jewels, and social elevation, but she could never stand life with a debauched husband.

After that failure Edward Hyde and the other councilors were desperate. Something had to be done before the King lapsed into dissolute ways again.

"It would be better," said one of them, "to persuade His Majesty to take back the Barlow woman. Where is she?"

"She has left the house of Lord Taafe," said another.

"She moved to Antwerp with her son, James, and is living in a house belonging to Henry Harvey."

"And her daughter, Mary?"

"She is in the convent of the Faubourg Saint-Jacques with Mère Madeleine."

* * *

The Queen was more relieved than anything else when she heard that Charles was moving to Cologne. She was afraid of the influence, by example, that he exerted upon her other two sons, James and Henry. She suspected that she could do little about James because he had already been drawn into the King's debauchery but Henry was still young and impressionable, and had only recently been sent to her with his tutor because the Parliament wanted to get rid of him.

Soon it became clear that there were political reasons for Charles' decision to leave Paris and go to Cologne. It was part of the maneuvering of Edward Hyde. When Cromwell made an alliance with France and waged war against Spain he arranged for Charles Stuart to sign a treaty with Don Juan of Austria, Governor of the Spanish Netherlands. There was an agreement that uprisings against Cromwell would be promoted in England and on the Continent: Charles would participate in a winter campaign of the Spanish army; Don Juan would pay him a regular allowance. Charles wrote to his mother and asked permission for his brother, James, to go with him.

Henrietta gave the permission for she knew that when the King sent for James he would go, with or without her blessing. "They are all gone, except Henry and Minette," she said sadly to Jermyn. "I have no influence over any of the others."

* * *

Cromwell defeated the Spanish and captured Dunkirk; Charles and James Stuart were in the van of the conquered army but neither was injured. Then, even though Spain's cause was ruined in Flanders the promise of financial support for the exiled English King was honored: the allowance was paid in full. Charles accepted it because he had to, and he went to Bruges and moved into a house near the Chapelle de Saint Sang. This degrading dependence threw him into a depression from which he would arouse himself only for brief periods of self-indulgence.

"The Spanish money is enough to keep me alive," Charles answered when his councilors scolded him, "but not enough to provide entertainment. I have to find my own that won't cost anything."

Four years of dissipation had left its mark upon him. His face was sallow and bloated, and there were permanent puffs under his dark eyes; often they were jaundiced. He glared at the councilors and sneered at their suggestions for wholesome recreation. "The only thing that amuses me," he said, "is the wine which the burghers are willing to buy for me at the White Swan!"

Hyde's placid face didn't betray his disgust at this remark, but the Marquis of Ormonde's voice was a little exasperated when he said, "There are the archers of the Guild at St. Sebastian."

"I can't shoot all day, every day, and all night," Charles snapped.

Ormonde hastily changed the subject. No one wished to have the King mention Catherine Pegge, who had just presented the King with a son. Charles had lost interest in her, but his councilors had no hope that this meant improvement. Out of sheer boredom he would choose another woman to share his lechery. So far, no one had appealed to him.

The tulips came up and burst into bloom; Charles scarcely noticed them as he walked along the banks of the canals. He stared absently at the swans floating on the placid waters, and then moved on through the narrow, cobbled streets. Children playing in front of their houses stopped what they were doing and watched the tall, dark, shabby exiled King of England as he passed them. He didn't speak to them because he was not aware of them; he was thinking about Lucy and his son, James.

He tried to turn his thoughts to other women but everywhere he looked he saw her face—in the water of canals—in the faces of the women he passed on the street—in the gardens, which reminded him of St. Germain-en-laye. "First love," he muttered, "one can never forget a first love—it stays with one forever!"

One day, after sitting at his writing table in gloomy silence, for a long time, he said to Edward Hyde, "Where is Mrs. Barlow?"

"In Antwerp," Hyde answered. "She has an apartment in one of the houses of Henry Harvey." Hyde may have been surprised by the question, but he was rarely caught without information.

"How can I get rid of her?"

Since Hyde didn't know that Charles had been engrossed with thoughts of her, he couldn't guess that what Charles meant was that he wanted to get rid of her memory—the memory of a fresh young girl who adored him—his "first love." It was a gesture, Charles said to himself—not even a matter of conscience—he just wanted to be free of her and he wanted to do it in the only way he knew how, the way he had freed himself from his other liaisons.

"If you would be free of her you must provide for her," Hyde said.

Charles' big mouth parted in a bitter smile. That was the way it had been done before! "Are the scandals about her true?" he asked abruptly.

Hyde bit his lip. He studied His Majesty's face for a

clue to his thoughts. What turn was the King's boredom taking now? Why this reference to Mrs. Barlow? She had given the King no trouble. In fact, she had completely ignored him. What made him think of her now? He didn't know what to say. For once, he didn't have definite information—only rumors. In the first place he had no idea how any unmarried woman in the exiled court could live without depending upon the favors of gentlemen who found her desirable. Besides, Lucy was an enigma to him. She didn't behave like the other women in her situation. He honestly didn't know whether the gossip about her was true or not. What difference did it make anyway? If the King wanted to be free of her, that was a practical matter.

"A definite amount of money guaranteed to the lady would remove the necessity for scandal, Your Majesty. I recommend that she be given an allowance which will provide a decent living for only the mother and the son. The daughter is taken care of by Her Majesty."

"Yes," Charles said and was silent for a few moments before he asked, "Is the mother a papist, too?"

"No," Hyde said. "She relinquished her daughter to the Queen's custody, but she didn't pursue the instruction with Father Cyprien herself. She remained loyal to the Church of England." Mentally he added, "Thank God."

"Tell Edward Nicholas to arrange for an allowance," Charles said. "How much will it take to be rid of her?"

"Five thousand livres is all we can manage," said Hyde.

"Not much for a lady and her son to live on," Charles said comparing the amount with what his mistresses demanded of him!

"—with the usual promise of more, if it please God to restore Your Majesty to the throne."

"Of course, of course," said Charles. "See that it is

done." So far the idea of giving Lucy an allowance only whetted his appetite for her!

Hyde never let anything go without a thorough check. He sent an agent to get information about Lucy. The man reported that she lived quietly under the protection of her mother's old friends, Henry and Anne Harvey; that she had a small legacy left to her by her mother which her brother managed for her in London. That was all the information that there was about her; everything else was rumor.

When the new allowance was paid to her by the King's agent the gossip about Lucy increased because it made it possible for her to employ a maid and a gentleman attendant, and she placed her son with a nurse-governess in the home of Mr. Claes Ghysen in Schiedam, about a mile outside of Rotterdam. She visited the little boy often, and they spent a great deal of time in the garden during the warm days of spring. For hours at a time she watched the little six-year-old playing with his pets and toys. It was so good for him to be in the country! And she had a sense of peace and well-being whenever she was with her son.

"No matter what happens," Lucy said to Anne Harvey one day, when she returned from a visit to Schiedam, "I have little James."

A flicker of anxiety crossed Anne's face, because her husband had just told her of a rumor that was circulating at The Hague, where he had been for several days on business.

The next day Henry said to Lucy, "My dear, there is something I wish to discuss with you." He ran his hand over his bald head, smoothed down the few strands of hair that remained, and considered how to begin.

"Of course, Henry. What is it?"

He indicated, with raised eyebrows, that she was to dismiss her maid. Lucy sent the girl out of the room and then looked at Henry with an expression of fear in her shadowed eyes.

"My dear child," he began, "do you have mementoes of His Majesty and your life with him?"

"Indeed, yes. I have a packet of his letters that I have tied together with a ribbon," she said lightly in an effort to cover the pain that Henry saw in the depths of her eyes.

"Anything else?"

"Yes," she said. "I have a ring that His Majesty gave me. Lord Taafe held it as security for the money that he loaned me. He returned it without requiring payment; but I am paying him anyway from the money that Justus sends me."

Henry smiled. How many women would be so meticulous about their debts to noblemen? "Is it a special ring?"

"Yes. It is fashioned of gold filigree in the form of a bow knot. At the knot is Charles' seal; he gave it to me to use in an emergency at the beginning of our relationship. I wear it in my clothing at all times. Would you like to see it?"

"Yes, my dear, I would if you wish me to see it."

She left the room to take the ring from her clothing where it was hidden and when she returned she handed the ring to Henry. He held it in his hand and examined it. "It is very beautiful," he murmured. He kept his eyes lowered and studied the ring and waited for her to speak, but she remained silent. "It must have special meaning for His Majesty," he went on. "*The Sealed Knot* is the name that he's given to a council of Royalists who are the leaders of all the groups secretly working for the King's restoration." He handed the ring back to her. "How about the marriage certificate signed by the four future bishops?" He was trying to speak as lightly as he could.

"Justus has it."

"Good. I hope that he realizes how important it is to keep it in a safe place—but I'm sure that he does. Justus has made an impressive reputation for himself in London as advocate and businessman."

"Why are you talking this way, Henry?"

He looked down at the floor and was silent for a moment before he took a letter from the portfolio that he had brought with him. "Put this with your mementoes, my dear," he said. "And the next time you have the opportunity, give everything to Justus to put in a safe place for you."

"What is this letter?"

"It fell into the hands of one of my agents quite by accident. It proves that Thomas Howard, Master of the Horse for the Princess Mary, is Cromwell's spy."

Lucy was astonished. "Why," she asked, "do you give it to me?"

"Because Howard's agents are already on the trail of it. They'll leave me alone only when they are satisfied that I don't have it. I shall try to convince them that I have destroyed it but I don't think they'll believe me."

"But why do you give it to me?" Lucy persisted. "Why don't you send it to Edward Hyde or the Marquis of Ormonde?"

"Because you may be able to make good use of it." He hesitated and then went on, "I think I should tell you something, Lucy. My agents at The Hague have reported to me that Lady Stanhope and her husband, Lord Heenvleet, have set afoot a plan to discredit you and remove young James from your custody." He paused again before he added thoughtfully, "I think that this was done at the command of the Princess Mary."

Lucy sat for a moment before she replied. "I'm not surprised by the first part of the information," she said. "The Princess Mary was my friend when I lived as her guest at The Hague, but all that has changed. I knew some time ago that Her Highness had withdrawn her protection of me. It is because I am an obstacle to Charles contracting a politically favorable marriage."

Harvey sighed with relief. Lucy was not completely ignorant of her terrible plight.

"The second piece of information," she said, and her voice was sad, "is completely new to me." Her mouth went dry and she was overcome by a feeling of helpless fear. It just couldn't be true that she might lose James!

Harvey wished that he could say something to give her comfort, but it was better that she be prepared for what was to come.

"I cannot understand why they wish to take James from me," she said. "I have remained faithful to my promise to keep the secret of our marriage. Surely His Majesty cannot know of this malicious plan to remove my dear little son from me."

"I am afraid, my dear," said Harvey, "that he does, because he has given orders for it to be done."

Tears sprang to Lucy's eyes. "I can't believe it of him," she said. "Why?"

"Because he wants him!" Harvey said contemptuously. "And when His Majesty wants something, he gets it. Now, you have something he wants—his son! That's the only reason I can give!"

It was true. Charles was in a turmoil of desire for Lucy! His advisors had convinced him that his relationship with her, at least on the terms that she insisted upon, was a political obstacle. Egged on by his sister, Mary, he substituted the wish to have his son taken from her.

At last he could stand the tension no longer. "I am going to Antwerp," he said. "Send a message to Mrs. Barlow that I wish to see her. Tell her to be prepared for a visit from me at Harvey's house. Buckingham will go with me. No one else," he said.

The councilors knew that it would accomplish nothing to try to prevent the visit. In fact, they were so desperate that they hoped that it might have some good result but they didn't see how it could!

It was a warm day late in May when Charles and Buckingham rode into Antwerp, which lay on the right bank of the Schelde. The elegance of the cathedral tower that rose four hundred feet above them dominated the broad avenue, terraced on each side by fine houses. Still, a mood of depression seemed to have settled upon the city. The King commented upon it as they rode along and Buckingham agreed. "The treaty closing the Schelde to navigation has done its work. The docks are idle."

"That must be the reason that no one is going in or coming out of the Bourse of Exchange," Charles said as they passed the big building. He chuckled. "The moneyed men of commerce will soon be as bad off as we are."

Harvey's house was on a quiet street off the main thoroughfare. It wasn't as large as the ones belonging to the merchant princes but it was impressive. The King dismounted. He hadn't come in a coach because he no longer could afford one of his own; he hadn't borrowed one because he didn't want to advertise this visit.

Lucy had had mixed feelings when she received the King's message that he was coming to see her. What did he want? She was happy in the life that she was making for herself. She had friends—good friends—and she was beginning to find herself: to know the meaning of life, to know how she wanted to live. Her marriage to Charles seemed like a dream—a nightmare maybe. How did it happen? She was swept into it without thinking very much about it; she had to admit that she regretted it. She didn't belong in the royal court by taste or temperament. She wished that he would not come to see her; she was afraid of being swept off her feet again.

235

She wished that he would stay away but she was waiting for him when he came.

Charles saw that she was more mature than she had been before the birth of her two children. Her skin was still as white as marble; the curls on her bare shoulders were intensely black by contrast. The mauve shadows underneath her eyes were darker than he remembered. Her eyes still had the surprised, hurt look of a wounded doe, he thought disdainfully. She was very thin, but her bosom, half visible in the revealing dress, was full and white.

Desire rose in him. He had denied it too long, he thought. She was more voluptuous than any woman he had ever known. At the same time she had the titillating manner of a fresh and innocent girl. It was maddening! Even her low-cut bodice seemed to be worn with casualness, he thought. Betty Killigrew and Catherine Pegge wore such gowns too—all the women did because it was high fashion—but Betty and Catherine wore them with design. Their charms were pointed up so that a man couldn't escape seeing them—or maybe so a man couldn't escape! They certainly knew how to make the most of their prey once it was caught! Their eyes had the expression of bad-tempered children that must be indulged to be kept quiet. Lucy had none of that expression. She looked at him with a sort of challenge to meet her on an equal footing. Her invitation was that of a mature woman, he supposed, desiring love as well as pleasure; Charles was afraid of that challenge. Other women didn't expect so much of him! They were satisfied with money, and titles for their children.

He thought that he saw that she was genuinely glad to see him. Her eyes sparkled, and to cover a slight embarrassment in not knowing just how to speak to him she tried to curtsy to him as she did in the old days. He lifted her to her feet by her elbows and started to say, "rise fair maiden" as he used to do, but touching her sent the blood rushing to his head. His hands travelled hungrily to her shoulders, her neck, and her bosom and at last he crushed her to him. She didn't resist when he kissed her mouth. Then, he held her at arm's length. "You are willing?" he asked. "I will take no woman against her consent."

She went limp in his arms, but it was not surrender. She said, as she had before, "I am your wife, and I love you." But did she? Yes, if loving him meant that she wished the best of everything for him—that she was ready and willing to sacrifice her own welfare for him—then she loved him—but she no longer liked him—and certainly he had no sexual attraction for her any longer. He was coarse and self-indulged. His swarthy skin was roughened by a rash, and there was a large sore on his upper lip. She almost shuddered. He was repulsive to her!

Charles let her go. His face flushed and his eyes narrowed. "If you love me you will come to me as I wish you to."

"As one of your harlots?"

"Yes—no," he stuttered in confusion for she asked the question matter-of-factly as an answer to his question, and it threw him off his guard. He was used to having women play coy and greedy games with him.

"I am your wife—legally and in the sight of God," she said completing the answer to his question.

That again! Charles sighed wearily, sat down in a convenient chair and motioned imperiously for her to sit also. "It has been explained to you over and over that it is impossible; that you can be my mistress but never my wife. The marriage performed by the Anglican clergymen is an obstacle to my restoration and must be annulled to set me free, politically."

"I have never revealed the secret of our marriage."

"That is not enough! Anyway, if you will agree to the legal proceedings for an annulment I will see that you have an allowance as long as I can squeeze a penny out of the treasury, or borrow it wherever it can be borrowed." He looked at her intently. "Lucy," he said, "I need you. It is not just passion, though God knows I have that for you, too. No woman but you can satisfy that for me—but it is something more. Some poet has said that woman can inspire something in men that only God can satisfy. I think that is part of the problem, for I am troubled in spirit as well as body! Edward Hyde tells me that you didn't go on with instruction from Father Cyprien when you gave the custody of our daughter to the Queen. You are not a Catholic then?"

She moved her head in a negative gesture and murmured, "No, I tried, but I could not. I learned my religion from Frances Vaughan and the clergymen who took refuge at Golden Grove—like Jeremy Taylor. I understand that the Roman church is also a church of God—and in many ways it is almost the same as the Anglican. It is a matter of allegiance, I think. But I belong in the Anglican church with my family."

He looked at her intently and with longing in his eyes; he didn't seem to be listening to what she said.

She saw no reason to explain further so she remained silent, and calmly waited for him to speak.

"I need you, Lucy, in every way that a man needs a woman; I have come to an important decision. First, let me explain. Perhaps it is due to my mother's influence—" He paused as the image of Father Huddleston and the others that had helped save his life at the peril of their own flashed through his mind. "I have decided to ask to be received into the Roman church—either openly or secretly, whichever is necessary."

Lucy was astonished and stared at him—she didn't really believe him; she could no longer believe anything he said.

"I have decided," he went on, "that if you will agree to a legal annulment of our Anglican marriage and ask to be received into the Catholic Faith, I will take you to Rome with me."

Was he mad—or was this just another impetuous act—more serious in the consequences—as when he insisted on marrying her at Bridgwater?

"If you will do this," he said fervently, "we can be received into the Faith by the Holy Father. I will marry you again, in Rome, and publicly acknowledge that you are my wife. I will make you my Queen—if possible. If it is not possible—if they will not accept you—when I am restored to the throne, then I will renounce it and let James be King!"

Lucy was speechless.

"It might even be an advantage. The Catholic sovereigns on the Continent and the Pope will support me if I am a Catholic. Most of the men in the *Sealed Knot* are Catholics—with their help my Catholic subjects in all three kingdoms will rise; I will be restored to the throne almost at once."

He is either daydreaming or he is trying to play a game with me! The idea is so preposterous as to be beyond belief, Lucy thought. He would not be restored to the throne if he were a Catholic openly. Everyone knew that! He would have to be a Catholic secretly, whether he married her or not. Maybe he was only proposing it so his Catholic subjects and the sovereigns on the Continent would support him. How despicable!

Still—he was obviously disturbed. What was her Christian duty? She hesitated—then she thought of Charles' mother, Queen Henrietta. Lucy had learned to love and respect her almost as much as Frances Vaughan! The Queen was deeply religious and a devout Catholic. She would know how to advise her son. She would know if he were serious. "It is not my responsibility or my duty to influence him or to do what he is demanding of me," she assured herself.

Her eyes were tragic but she answered firmly, "I

tried to become a Catholic and I must confess that I did it to gain the Queen's support—and now I'm sorry for it. Her Majesty accepted the responsibility of our daughter's care and education as I requested, without any reservations. I will never be a Catholic; I should not have tried."

Anger was slowly rising in Charles. He had never been so addressed by one of his subjects. How could she dare to talk to him like that!

Somehow, she knew that the time had come for her to clarify her position and make it clear to Charles. "I don't want to live at court under any circumstances. I know that my relationship with you was wrong from the beginning. It was first love for me and I really didn't know what I was doing—or the circumstances of the life of a royal prince. I am sorry that I caused so much trouble. I just didn't know any better. Now I know that I would be utterly miserable at court. Please, sir, I want it all to end—however it must be done. I beg of you to leave me to my own way of life."

He stared at her. His whole face was suffused with a sort of hatred and his lower jaw protruded. "Then," he burst out, "I will have other mistresses and I will marry a Catholic princess—and I want my son!"

Lucy burst into tears. "No, no, no," she protested. "You cannot have him." Her voice rose in panic. "—unless I can live in the same house with him."

"Hysterics will get you nowhere," Charles said coldly. "I mean to have him."

"Get out—get out—and from now on leave me alone. I can be happy if you will just leave me alone!" Tears came to her eyes. She hadn't intended to let him see her dislike of him!

She had never seen him as he was now—ugly with his nostrils dilated and breathing heavily as if he had a constriction in his chest. He rose slowly from his chair as if he were trying but fast losing the ability to control himself. She rose, too, and faced him. "She is disrespectful to me," he thought angrily, "and I am not only her husband but her sovereign!" His slender hands gripped her white shoulders and his nails bit into her soft flesh; she cried out in pain. That seemed to infuriate him even more.

He struck her—a glancing blow, a slap on the face, but hard enough to send her reeling against the wall.

Astonished by his violence Charles looked at her in horror, rushed out of the house, sprang into the saddle and spurred his horse and rode furiously out of the town. Buckingham tried to catch up with him but even though he rode as hard as he could he was unable to overtake Charles. The King did not want him to see that the tears were pouring down his cheeks.

8

The next day Lucy sent a note to Justus by special courier. "Dear Brother, if you still love me—in the name of God, come to me at once."

Later, that same afternoon, she got into a hired carriage and ordered her gentleman attendant to go along as groom. She had decided that she must make arrangements for a bodyguard for her son. She would go to Schiedam and see Mr. Ghysen at once. She told her man that she would break the journey at an inn which lay about halfway between Antwerp and Schiedam.

It was late afternoon when they reached the place. She went inside and told her man to help the driver make the necessary arrangements for the replacement of the horses. In a little while he came inside and asked to speak to her.

"Madame," he said, "it so happens that my elderly parents live about a mile from here. My mother is ill and I beg your permission for an hour's visit with her."

"Of course," Lucy said, "you may go, but I wish to be in Schiedam before sundown."

"Very well," he said, "I will be back."

But he didn't come back. Lucy waited for quite a while but when the sun went down she was worried. Something was wrong. What did she know about her manservant after all? He had been sent to her by a person she scarcely knew. He was probably a spy for someone!

She called the innkeeper. "Can you give me an escort, at once, and a driver for my carriage?"

"Madame," he asked in alarm, "is something wrong?"

"Yes," she said. "Hurry!"

He brought two of his own people. "They are reliable, Madame," he said.

"Hurry, hurry!" she cried to the driver as they set off.

When they reached Mr. Ghysen's house they found it in an uproar. James was gone.

The child's nurse was in hysterics. "Madame," she screamed when she saw Lucy, "a man crawled over the garden wall and took him away from me. He carried him away on a horse!"

"Which way did he go?"

"That way," the woman cried, pointing to the road leading to the coast.

"Get fresh horses," Lucy commanded. She turned to the men who had escorted her from the inn. "Will one of you go with me?"

"Yes, Madame," one of them said, "I will go with you but what has happened?"

"My son was kidnapped. We must find him at once! The coach is too slow. I will ride."

Lucy put on riding clothes loaned by Mr. Ghysen's wife, mounted a horse and they set off at once.

"Which way shall we go?" the man asked when they were on the road.

"To Maasland-Sluce," Lucy said. "I think that they'll try to take him to The Hague."

They rode all night. Several times her escort insisted that she stop for something to eat or drink or even just a few moments to rest. She protested each time but he insisted.

"You'll never make it, Madame," he said, "unless you do."

The sun was coming up when they approached the harbor.

"Where to now?" the man asked.

"To the docks," Lucy said. "Hurry!"

They could see a ship preparing to sail. As they got closer it was obvious that passengers of importance were going aboard. Lucy thought it might be the kidnapper but when they reached the dock they found that it was the Sieur Newport and the Lord Mayor of Maasland who were embarking.

Lucy dismounted and ran to them. "Please, please, please, help me!" she implored.

They turned and, seeing that she was a lady of quality, they listened to her; but she was so hysterical that they couldn't understand what she was saying.

"Her son has been abducted," the escort explained.

"Who is she?" demanded the Sieur Newport.

"I don't know," the escort said.

That didn't help any. The gentlemen thought that both Lucy and her attendant were mad. They turned their backs on them and started to go aboard the ship.

Lucy increased her pleas. She was so distraught that she wept loudly and a crowd began to gather. When the people understood what she was saying they entreated their mayor to do something about it.

"Very well," the mayor said, anxious to be on his way. "If one of you is willing to take the lady and the man to your home I will authorize a search for the child." He looked at the crowd expecting that no one would volunteer but several voices rose with offers to take them to private homes.

"Very well," the mayor said, "begin to search."

Lucy stayed in the home of the port's postmaster and several days passed before James was found. The mayor's protection, the search, and the fury of the townspeople had evidently frightened the hired thug that did the kidnapping. He didn't want to get involved with the local police! He abandoned James to strangers, who lived in an isolated house in Loosdymen, and then he vanished. These people took James to his mother when they heard about the search.

Lucy put her arms around the little boy and kissed him. "Did he harm you?" she said.

"No," he said. "He played with me, and he gave me toys and a little dog." He pointed to a puppy.

When the Harveys heard what had happened they sent Lucy's maid and one of their own menservants to her. They carried orders to take Lucy and James to a house nearby, named Boscal, which Henry owned. Several days later when Lucy felt rested she and James went back to Antwerp to the Harveys. There, she engaged an extra guard to watch over him.

In less than three weeks Justus arrived from England. He wore a rapier and dagger; his manservant was armed with dagger and pistol. When he was admitted to Harvey's house Justus told his man to stand guard outside.

Lucy came to him at once. He opened his arms, and she went into them and put her head on his shoulder and wept bitterly. Tenderly, he kissed the curls on the top of her head.

"What happened?" he asked when her sobs decreased.

"The King commanded me to surrender James to him and I have refused because he won't let me live in the same house with him."

"Why not?" Justus asked. "What reason do they give?"

"Forgive me," said Lucy. "You have had a hard journey. Take off your cloak and when you are comfortable we will talk about it. I shall tell you all that has happened."

She was about to summon a servant but Justus stopped her. "Wait," he said, "that can come later."

He swung the cloak from his shoulders and threw it on a chair, laid his hat with it, and pulled off his gloves.

"Very well," he said. "Now tell me all about it."

She told him about the abduction and that she had an extra guard for James. "I came back here," she said, "because I was afraid that you might not be able to find us if we stayed at Boscal."

"You knew that I would come as soon as I could, didn't you?"

"Yes," she said with tears in her voice. "You have never failed to help me even when I showed little gratitude."

"Well," said Justus, "I am here. What am I to do? The situation as it is can't last forever—what shall we do?"

"First of all, Henry advised me to give you all my papers," she said. "Will you keep them in a safe place?"

"Of course, but why has Harvey suggested it?"

"One of Henry's agents at The Hague got possession of a letter which proves that Tom Howard, Master of the Horse for the Princess Mary, is Cromwell's spy."

Justus whistled through his teeth. "The scoundrel!" he said.

"Henry gave it to me and advised me to put it with my other papers."

"Why did he give it to you?"

"Because he said that maybe I would find it useful in defending myself in the plans that have been set afoot."

"What about the King's command that you surrender the child? Tell me about that."

"The Princess Mary has convinced Charles that he should annul our marriage so that he can contract a political marriage that will be useful in his restoration to the throne."

"As if he could," sneered Justus.

"What do you mean?"

"It's no secret in London," Justus said with anger, "that it was proposed that Cromwell's daughter, Frances, marry the King. That would give the Protector a way of establishing a royal line in his family. He doesn't dare accept the crown himself."

"Is the proposal still being considered?" Lucy asked quietly. Had Charles lied to her about what he intended to do? Had he tried to trick her?

"No," Justus said. "The girl and her mother consented, and Lord Broghill began negotiations, but Cromwell himself stopped them!"

"Why?"

Justus hesitated before he told her, "The Protector said, 'His Majesty is so damnably debauched he would undo us all.'"

"Oh," said Lucy, "it's as bad as that."

"I am afraid that it is."

"Charles has given permission for James to be seized in any manner that it is necessary to get him from me."

"And the Princess Mary is back of this?"

"Yes, and Lady Stanhope and her husband, Lord Heenvliet."

"Do you know the names of any of the men they have employed?"

"Yes," Lucy said. "At least some of them. Arthur Slingsby, Lord Bristol's secretary, Daniel O'Neill and Ned Prodgers. Do you remember him at my wedding in Paris?"

"How could I forget!" snapped Justus.

Lucy was thoughtful for a moment and then added, "Tom Howard, of course, is married to Lady Stanhope's daughter."

"A regular den of thieves," Justus burst out. "Has Howard tried to get his letter by legal means?"

"Yes. He found out some way that Henry gave it to me, and he is suing me."

247

"Well, don't give it to him."

"I won't," Lucy said. "I am giving it to you!"

"Good! So the King is demanding James, eh?"

"He says he wants to educate him and make him a Duke when he grows up and marries."

Justus snorted. "So he says! He can't resist the thought of his son, eh? How about all the others that he has fathered? Is he interested in providing for them, too?"

Lucy's eyes filled with tears, but she said nothing.

"I think, my pet, that His Majesty still lusts after you. The boy is only an excuse!"

"He told me that he would take me back if I would consent to an annulment. He would make me his mistress and I would live at court."

"And you refused, I presume. Still the old scruples?"

"If you wish to call it that, yes," she said. "He says that he wants me back and he became very angry when I told him 'no.'" She hesitated—she had already decided that she shouldn't tell Justus the whole truth. He might decide to use the information against Charles. She just wanted to be left alone in peace. She could be quite happy with her friends and an isolated life with little James. That's what she said to herself over and over.

Justus laughed. "It's the most ironic circumstance that I have ever come across," he said. "A man asks his wife for an annulment so he can make her his mistress!"

He looked at her speculatively. He couldn't understand the problem. Why not go back to the King, he wanted to advise her, and make it easier for herself! It couldn't be a matter of scruples about not being married because she was married to him. What difference did it make that it wasn't publicly acknowledged? It was incredible that she might think she couldn't adjust to living at court with Charles. She was too intelligent and she had already demonstrated that it was possible—in Jersey and at The Hague.

What was the truth? Could it be that she was through with Charles personally? Was she using excuses to cover up her desire for freedom? Was it she and not the King who wanted to end the affair? If that's the way it was— it was quite a switch for Charles!

"Have they tried anything else since the kidnapping?"

"They have spread lies about me. It is said that I am a harlot!"

Justus turned pale. "What shall we do now?"

"Would it be possible, Justus, for you to take me home to England? Perhaps I could even go to Golden Grove and stay with Frances Vaughan."

Justus thought for a moment and then said, "Lucy, I have something to tell you." He knew that what he had to tell her would hurt her even more than the death of their mother. "When I got back to London after my last visit, I learned that Frances died just a week after our mother. When three months passed the Earl married again."

The blood drained from Lucy's face and Justus thought she was going to faint but she raised her hand to indicate that she was all right. She sat with her eyes downcast for a few minutes and said nothing.

After a little while Justus went on, "Maybe, we could go if we went right away; but we cannot go without the King's permission." He had no way of knowing what was going on! Maybe, he thought, His Majesty will be glad to get rid of her. If they acted quickly enough they might be able to take James with them.

There was a noise outside. Something was happening in the street.

"Be prepared to go if I can get His Majesty's permission." He opened the door and looked out. He saw Tom Howard weakly leaning against the wall of a house

249

across the street and a surgeon dressing a wound on his shoulder. He also saw that a policeman was taking his manservant into custody.

"That fellow," the man called out to Justus, "climbed up and tried to break into the upstairs window!" He pointed to Tom Howard.

Justus walked across the street, pulling out his dagger as he went. "Do you think, sir," he said to Howard, "that my sister is foolish enough, after your threats, to leave her papers in a bedchamber?"

"A-a!" Howard breathed, "and who are you to challenge me?"

"You know very well who I am," Justus said. "And I am here to protect my sister in any way that is necessary. I warn you!

"Wait," Justus said, turning to the policeman that was dragging the manservant away. He put a piece of silver in the officer's hand, and the prisoner was released at once. With a jerk of his head Justus indicated that the servant was to follow him into the Harveys' house. Tom Howard glared at them and continued to stare at the door of the house after it was slammed shut.

Several days later the Marquis of Ormonde came to see Lucy. "His Majesty sends his apologies," he said.

Lucy blushed, but she didn't think that it was possible that the Marquis knew what he was apologizing for; certainly, the King wouldn't apologize for not coming to see her, himself, as the Marquis implied.

"My dear," he said, "I know that His Majesty has great affection for you."

"Yes, I know."

"You do understand, I see, that he finds it necessary to give you up under circumstances that he cannot change." He hesitated and then went on. "His Majesty regrets that he gave a hasty order for your son to be kidnapped. He promises that it will not happen again!"

"I understand," she said, "that His Majesty must choose between me and his responsibilities." She paused and then added, "With all due respect to His Majesty, I believe that I have a right to make a decision about my son and me."

The Marquis looked at her with admiration and then he said, "I have been instructed to tell you that His Majesty gives permission for you to go to England with your brother. He also wishes you to carry out a mission for him."

She stared at him in surprise. Then, she said, "I will serve His Majesty in any way that I can."

"Recently, John Mordaunt came from England to Brussels. He described the plans that have been made for uprisings all over England. Everything is almost ready for His Majesty's return."

"Indeed," Lucy breathed, "that is good news."

"His Majesty wishes you to take both of your children to England and place them under the protection of the men of the *Sealed Knot*. When the uprisings occur, and he makes a landing, you and his children will already be there. Perhaps—" he hesitated before going on so as not to commit His Majesty to anything, "if all goes well everything may work out for your satisfaction and happiness."

What was the Marquis implying? Apparently Charles had not taken what she had told him seriously. He still thought it possible that she would return to him under favorable circumstances. In any event the way was open for her to return to England with both of her children. She could go with Justus!

"I believe that I understand my mission, sir," she said.

The Marquis was gratified. He was convinced that Lucy could be trusted to place the King's heir under the protection of the *Sealed Knot* and that she would not reveal the plans for the uprisings. He gave her the gift that Charles had sent her. She opened the elaborately carved wooden box and found an exquisite string of pearls in it.

She smiled and then almost laughed out loud. Once before, she thought, he sent me "one perfect pearl"— and now he has sent a whole string of them! Their relationship had changed! Or was His Majesty telling her that in his mind violence was a greater crime than tempting her to lose her virginity!

The Marquis bent over and kissed her hand and prepared to leave. He wished that His Majesty could see Lucy with the radiant smile lighting up her face.

When Lucy showed the pearls to Justus he examined them carefully. "They must be worth over fifteen hundred pounds," he said. "He is indeed anxious to get rid of you, my pet. These must be for the purpose of being sure that you have the financial means to go!"

"You have become cruelly cynical."

"What else can experience have taught me?" he answered shortly.

"Maybe the King cannot always follow his personal wishes."

"From what I hear, that's just what he does. My lords, Ormonde and Hyde, are almost out of their wits trying to get His Majesty to do a little work."

"Poor Charles," said Lucy. "He is so very lonely."

"Huh!" said Justus. His lips curled disdainfully. "Is that why he has a new wench every night?"

"Justus!" Lucy's face flushed scarlet.

"Somebody ought to tell His Majesty that flattery by predatory females is not a cure for loneliness!"

"Justus, stop—for the love of me, stop!"

"I hate him. I have always hated him! I would like to run him through with a sword."

"Justus!" Lucy was frightened. She came close to him and put her hand over his mouth. "Don't talk that way! Even saying it is treason! Someone might hear you!"

9

They made quick preparations and, taking James, set off, planning to stop only in Paris for Mary.

While they were there Justus paid a secret visit to John Cosin, one of the clergymen who had been present when Lucy and Charles were married in Paris. He left Lucy's papers, including the marriage certificate, with him. "It is safer," he told Lucy later. "No one will guess that Cosin has them. One of us, or both, may be arrested. If that happens the papers will not be found."

They boarded a ship and soon were on their way across the Channel. When they went to the Captain's table for dinner they were surprised to find Tom Howard already there. The spy was following them! He didn't rise to greet them but affected a smile that was a hypocritical smirk.

Justus went to his cabin and took a dagger from his luggage and stuck it in his belt under his coat before he went back and sat down at the table.

After dinner when the children were asleep in their berths Justus took Lucy up on deck for a walk. As they stood at the rail of the ship and looked out over the moonlit water he said to her, "Lucy, I have something to tell you."

"Yes," she said, "what is it?"

"You know," he said, "that Mother boasted of your marriage to the King, even though she could speak of it only in the family."

"Yes, I know."

"She never stopped talking about how proud she was of you. I am glad that she didn't live to know that you were abandoned."

Lucy's lips tightened but she said nothing. She had given up trying to explain to Justus that she didn't blame Charles for anything. It was mostly her fault for not knowing her own mind. She should never have married the heir to the throne if she didn't want to do what was expected of her. She wasn't abandoned—she had just let herself be buffeted about like a ship without a rudder—at the mercy of wind and waves!

"You know," Justus went on, "I have been disposing of Mother's personal effects."

"Yes," Lucy said. "I know."

"There is a memento that she asked me to give to you that I have not told you about." He pulled a locket and chain from his pocket.

"Oh," said Lucy. "It is the locket that Mother always wore."

"Does it strike you as strange that it has a miniature protrait of Thomas Byshfield inside and that Mother always wore it? Did you never realize that you and I bear a marked resemblance to him?"

"Well, why not—he's Mother's cousin. It's a family resemblance! Poor Mother—you know, don't you, Justus, that he was Mother's lover and that he abandoned her?"

"Yes," Justus said, "and I also know that he was our father!"

Lucy gasped and was silent for a long time. Justus could not see her face for she was bent over the rail, staring down at the water. "Strange," she murmured, at last, "that I never thought of that possibility. But it did strike me as strange—unnatural, almost, that I was not more moved when I heard that William Walter had fallen in battle." And that explains why he used to look

255

at me the way he did when I was a little girl, she thought. He really did dislike me—not because I was unlovable—but because I was not his child and he had to take care of me!

Justus sighed with relief. "I'm glad that you take it that way. It is the same with me. I had no love for William Walter!"

"I'm afraid that's the way I felt, too, and now I see why—he didn't love us. But we should be charitable, Justus—he did take care of us."

"Huh!" Justus exploded. "It wasn't our fault that we were denied a loving father!"

"Our parents had their problems and we have ours. After all, what counts is how we treat other people, not how we are treated."

"I don't understand you," Justus burst out. "I never did."

She smiled at him but didn't say any more.

* * *

Never had Britain had an espionage system like that set up by John Thurloe, the Lord Protector's Secretary of State. Spies watched everybody and each other. Agents among postal employees opened and made copies of every dispatch and every letter. Nothing was too insignificant to be investigated. The arrival of Lucy Walter, whom everyone knew had an intimate connection with the Pretender, Charles Stuart, caused quite a stir. It was reported to Cromwell immediately, by the head of his Secret Police, and he was agitated by the news.

The Lord Protector was so unnerved by the many plots against his life that he suspected that a cavalier lurked in every shadow, ready to spring out and stab him to death. He wore his armor indoors and out. So far, Thurloe had deciphered every code, uncovered every intrigue and apprehended every plot against Cromwell's life, but there was one thing that he had not solved and that was the membership of the *Sealed Knot*.

It was a terrorist group that would stop at nothing in the interests of the Stuart King. They were suspected of rendering aid to every uprising, plot or intrigue that was set in motion by the Royalists, and they probably did. Now, they received Lucy and housed her near the residence of her brother.

Thurloe's agents got information from Lucy's maidservant that cavalier gentlemen came to see her every day, obviously paying courtesy calls. The police followed every visitor that she named but didn't succeed in getting much information, and none of any value. But all of the spies agreed that Lucy must be, at least, an agent of the King!

Thurloe refrained from having Lucy arrested, at first, hoping that she might lead them to the members of the *Sealed Knot*. But when it was evident that he wasn't going to discover anything, he fabricated a charge and had her arrested and lodged in the Tower with the political prisoners. He decided upon this action when he discovered that the little girl, Mary, had disappeared. If the *Sealed Knot* had spirited her away the boy, James, might go next!

Thurloe reported the case in full to the Lord Protector in one of their daily conferences behind bolted doors; he had a complete report from Tom Howard, he told Cromwell. His spies had trailed Lucy's brother from the time that he left London, and Tom Howard had taken up the scent in Antwerp and followed the brother and sister back to England.

"What is the real reason for the woman's impudence in coming to England?" Cromwell asked.

Thurloe smiled. He had the Lord Protector where he wanted him. He was begging for information! He studied the man sitting behind the big desk, wearing armor.

He had seen many men, he thought, who were tracked down, caught, and tortured, but he had never seen one who was any more cravenly fearful.

"They tell me that you have seen the boy, James," Thurloe said.

"Yes," Cromwell said shortly, his florid face flushed a deeper red. "He is the son of Charles Stuart, without a doubt. I watched him sitting for a miniature portrait in Cooper's studio."

"You saw him in Cooper's studio?" Thurloe asked. He was surprised that the Lord Protector had found the courage to go to the engraver's house without a police guard. He was curious to know why he had done it.

"Yes," Cromwell said. "I wanted to see for myself. The boy and his mother came to the studio with Lord Russell's sister, Diana." He scowled. "I don't like it. She's the wife of Newport, who's mixed up in every Royalist plot." He repeated, "I don't like it."

Thurloe grinned. "Newport's in the Tower at the moment, as he has been off and on for months. He can do us no harm!"

"I don't like it," said Cromwell. "It smacks of danger."

Another of the Lord Protector's exaggerated fears, Thurloe thought. The man became more of a coward every day. Running around the streets alone without protection was certainly not a wise thing to do in any event. He was beginning to be childish! "Not unusual that Mrs. Barlow should see Lady Newport," he said soothingly. "They were friends when they were children. Mrs. Barlow lived in Covent Garden with her parents for a time."

"And the wife of Stepney—she sees her, too, you said."

"The wife of Sir John is Justiniana Van Dyck," Thurloe said. "Jan de Reyn, the painter, was her guardian! Mrs. Barlow met her in the Low Countries." What

258

a waste of time to go through these trivial details to alleviate the Protector's fears! "Do you think the mother brought the boy to London to be educated by her brother, as she says?"

"No. It seems more likely that there is a long-range plan. Do you agree?"

"Yes. The most likely is that they intend to install the child in some remote country house of one of the members of the *Sealed Knot*, preparatory to—" He sought for the proper word. He shouldn't say assassination! "—uprising."

The Lord Protector blanched with fear. "Do you know yet who any of them are?"

"None, with the exception of Richard Willis."

"Why have you not apprehended him?" snapped Cromwell.

"There is nothing to apprehend him for," said Thurloe, "not yet, but we are watching him for an opportunity—never fear!" he added to give assurance.

"Yes, yes," said Cromwell, "go on about the plot."

"Possible plot," Thurloe corrected him. "In the event that Charles Stuart makes an attempt to return to England and is destroyed—as he most certainly would be if he tried—" Thurloe added hastily.

"Yes," said Cromwell, his hands shaking.

"Then," said Thurloe, "it could be proved that the King not only married Lucy in a secret illegal marriage in Barnstaple, but a binding one in Paris and they could prove that the child was the legal heir to the throne."

"But the woman is a commoner!" said Cromwell. "Would that be tolerated?"

"Of course," said Thurloe. "She is not lowborn, you know. She is directly related to the Earl of Carberry. Her child could be made immensely popular by clever maneuvering!"

"What have you done to stop this?" Cromwell asked shortly.

"I have been gathering the personal records of the woman and destroying them," said Thurloe. "Everything—so it would be easy to discredit her. I have had the records from the church in Haverfordwest, where she was born, called in and burned. There is nothing left in England or Wales—" he hesitated.

"Everything?" asked Cromwell, sensing that somewhere the operation had not been perfect.

"I have not yet been able to obtain the papers which we think Mrs. Barlow's brother left with John Cosin in Paris—including the wedding certificate."

Cromwell's face flushed with anger and impatience. "Why has this not been done? That's the most important paper of all."

"It will be done," Thurloe said quietly, "when it can be accomplished without drawing attention to it. There is no hurry. John Cosin is trustworthy, and he is not likely to give up the papers that have been entrusted to him without a struggle. But," he added calmly, "no one lives forever. We have a servant lodged in his house for the sole purpose of discovering and seizing those papers when the right moment comes."

The Lord Protector was convinced. "Splendid work," he said. "Now, what do we do with the woman and the boy?"

"No purpose will be served in detaining them in the Tower," Thurloe said. "Neither is it to your advantage to let her go free in England."

"What, then?"

For the first time Thurloe smiled. This was the sort of thing that he found delightful—a battle of wits. He was not a violent man, and he enjoyed carrying out his missions with brains instead of bloodletting. In that way he differed from Cromwell, who preferred hanging people in their own doorways. "The woman is a great source of annoyance to Charles Stuart," he said.

"You mean she lives an immoral life?" asked Cromwell. "I thought the attempt to defame her character was unbelievable."

"Indeed, yes," Thurloe grinned. "To say that Charles Stuart would discard a woman because of her infamous reputation is unbelievable under any circumstances."

"Yes. There is no doubt that profligacy would only make a woman more interesting to him." Cromwell's thick lips beneath the large red nose, curled self-righteously.

"She is a political nuisance to him," Thurloe reminded him.

"I am waiting," Cromwell said sharply. "Proceed."

"I would suggest," Thurloe said, "that we send her back to Charles Stuart and that we make it very clear that we believe that the boy is the Pretender's heir. We'll hold the girl, Mary, when we find her, in case we need a hostage."

Cromwell was silent for a moment, thinking it over. Then he burst out laughing. "Couldn't be better," he said, "couldn't be better! We'll embarrass the Pretender by sending his imitation Queen back to him." He laughed until his face was crimson with exertion. "I'll write the order myself."

Thurloe shrugged. He was accustomed to having the Lord Protector take credit for his work. That was all right with him. It left him with less danger of vengeance from the cavaliers. Cromwell's vanity was even greater than his cowardice! He slipped a piece of paper in front of Cromwell and handed him a pen. There would be no need to question Lucy.

With a flourish, Cromwell signed the order for Lucy's release from the Tower. Then Thurloe handed him another. It was an order for Lucy's deportation back to Flanders with her son, James. There was one defect in the operation that he didn't see fit to report to Cromwell. The *Sealed Knot* did, indeed, have Mary, and they had hidden her in a remote convent in Scotland.

Justus was unable to make arrangements to follow Lucy, because Thurloe's agents watched him night and day. He couldn't get a pass, either, under his own name or a fabricated one; but some time later a secret courier got the news to him that Lucy had landed safely and that she had gone back to live in one of Henry Harvey's houses in Brussels and that she had been able to keep her son with her—at least so far! He was not told that she was penniless because Thurloe intercepted the income that Justus sent her from London and her allowance from the King was withheld after her return. The only income she had was money that she obtained on the credit of the right to the allowance and the pension promised by the King as security. Henry Harvey provided the roof over her head.

One day, when she had been in this predicament for some time, the Marquis of Ormonde came to call upon her. He had a mission to perform for the King, he said. He had been given the authority to act as sternly, and in any way that he found necessary. He chose to carry it out in his own gentle way.

He was never known to be anything but chaste in his personal life, but it was Edward Hyde, not he, who frequently berated the King to his face and complained continually to the other councilors about His Majesty's debauchery. Ormonde was incorruptibly loyal to the King though he disapproved of Charles personally.

Lucy received him in her little drawing room, and he kissed her hand with courtly manners and accepted her invitation to be seated. He went to the point at once.

"I have been sent to you by the King," he said. "His Majesty hopes that you will willingly and graciously grant his wish that you send his son, James, to him. Since the mission in England failed it is not safe for him here."

Lucy set her lips firmly. She was about to refuse, but before she could say anything, he went on.

"I beg leave to advise you in the capacity of a man who has had much experience in the realities of life. At the same time I have great sympathy for you because of your unfortunate situation."

Lucy stiffened, and he saw that she anticipated what he was going to say. He decided to state his mission quickly without trying to soften it.

"I have been commanded by His Majesty to tell you that your allowance will be permanently withheld unless you surrender the boy to him."

Lucy drew in her breath sharply, and her eyes filled with tears.

"His Majesty is not himself," Ormonde said kindly. "Exile is a hard trial for a King to bear," he added.

Lucy couldn't speak.

"Though I must obey the King's commands, I shall dare to tell you that I advise you not to make your decision on the basis of threatened poverty alone. I shall see that you are provided for out of my own resources, whatever you decide." He paused for her reply but she said nothing.

"I beg of you to consider the advantages to the child," he went on. "The King might decide to declare his legitimacy and make him the heir to the throne."

"I understand," Lucy said slowly. "I have given it much thought lately, and I realize that I cannot educate him in the manner that would prepare him for royal responsibilities. After all, James is Charles' son—and a legitimate son—which can be proved by the records of the English church and by the witness of several of His Majesty's churchmen."

"I must warn you," the Marquis said, "and I do this on my own authority, that His Majesty will, in all probability, make an official statement that he has never been married to anyone—after he makes a marriage treaty with some royal house on the Continent."

263

Lucy gasped but she said quietly, "It won't be true if he does!"

The Marquis smiled. She couldn't be "bought off" or intimidated, he thought—and he admired her for it.

"Do you really think," she said, "that James would be better off if I relinquish him?"

"Yes, I do, and with all honesty."

"Would I be able to see him sometimes?" she asked pathetically.

"I swear that I will see that you do."

"Very well," she said, "I will relinquish my son to His Majesty."

She also agreed to cooperate with plans which the Marquis would set up for a new guardianship and the education of her son. It would take a little time, he told her.

There were tears in Ormonde's eyes as he bent over her hand and told her goodbye. He didn't like the task that he had carried through successfully though he did believe sincerely that it would be better for the little boy. "You have my admiration, Madame," he said.

10

Spring came and passed into early summer. Lucy heard nothing further from Ormonde. She still had James but she didn't receive her allowance and still had to live on credit.

One evening Sir Arthur Slingsby, secretary to George Digby, the Earl of Bristol, came to her. "Madame," Slingsby said, "I have just been married, and my bride and I have taken a house in the Park. I have come to ask the favor of your taking up residence there with us."

"You come from the Marquis of Ormonde?" Lucy asked, thinking that this must be the next step in the plan that had been presented to her.

The lids of Slingsby's small eyes narrowed to slits. He didn't understand the question but saw that it could be used to advantage. "Ah, yes," he said.

She made the move to his house and almost immediately discovered that she was a prisoner. Neither she nor her son were permitted to walk in the Park without being accompanied. Still she waited, thinking that she would learn the next step for the new arrangements for her son. Her credit was exhausted. She and James were dependent upon Slingsby for the food they ate and the clothes they wore. The first week in December Lucy could stand it no longer. She went to Slingsby.

"Sir, I must have an explanation about my detention here in your house. I'm not your guest, but your prisoner."

"Ah, yes, indeed," said Slingsby, his slender face taking on the expression of a fox that is closing in upon a rabbit, "not my prisoner—but my lodger—and one who has not paid her bill for six months."

Lucy caught her breath in surprise. "I had thought that it was the wish of His Majesty that I come here to await his pleasure."

"What gave you that idea?"

"There is no doubt in my mind," Lucy said, "that you are fully aware that I am dependent upon the King's allowance and that I have not received it. Surely you know the reason for all this delay."

"Ah," said Slingsby insultingly, "His Majesty, perhaps, has lost interest. He has no inclination to pay it."

Lucy's eyes flashed with anger. Her promise to keep the secret of her marriage to the King no longer seemed binding. Surely it was only justice that if he did not fulfill his duty to her then she was relieved of her responsibility. "Then," she said angrily before she could restrain her temper, "I must resort to posting up the King's letters to prove that I am entitled to maintenance."

A sly look crossed Slingsby's cruel features. "Then, Madame, you leave me no choice but to conduct you to the prison reserved for debtors in the city of Antwerp."

Before he could touch her, Lucy ran from the room to James, playing with his dogs in the garden and took him by the hand. Slingsby followed and tried to grasp her arm. She eluded him and ran with James out into the street. Slingsby ran after her but could not catch her. She ran at top speed, pulling the boy along with her. The townspeople gaped at the sight of a lady, dressed in a silk gown, light slippers, and without a cloak, running as fast as she could over the cold paving stones in the chill December air.

At last, gasping for breath, she had to stop. She pulled James close to her side and held his hand tightly.

He was terrified and crying loudly, the tears running down his cheeks. Slingsby was right behind them.

Roughly, he caught Lucy by the arm. "Now, my fine strumpet," he said, "off you go to the city jail."

Lucy cried out, "No, no, no."

Slingsby tried to pull James from her grasp. The terrified boy screamed louder and louder and clung to her skirt so he could not be pulled away. A crowd began to gather and among them Lucy recognized Monsieur Mottet, secretary to Don Alonzo de Cardenas, the Spanish Ambassador.

"Please help me, Monsieur."

Mottet thought she was the victim of a holdup. He wrested her from Slingsby's grasp and took her and James into the Earl of Castlehaven's house, nearby. Slingsby followed them and Mottet recognized him.

"Away with you, man, until you cool off," he said to him. "You must be out of your mind."

The next morning Monsieur Mottet talked with Lucy about the incident. He spoke English with a soft Spanish accent. "Was Slingsby inebriated?" he asked.

"No, Monsieur," Lucy said. "He was sober. I think that it is part of an intrigue to kidnap my son," she said.

"A-a-a!" Mottet's soft voice expressed the greatest compassion for a mother whose son is being taken from her. "What can I do for you, my dear?"

"It will be a great favor, sir," Lucy said, "if you will write to the Marquis of Ormonde and explain what happened yesterday. I think that he's the one who should help me."

"Very well, my dear. I shall do it at once."

He walked to his writing table as he added, "My Lord Castlehaven and Monsieur Berkley, who also saw what happened, are leaving today to go to the King's court. They will describe the incident to His Majesty."

Lucy's eyes filled with tears. She couldn't bring herself to explain to Monsieur that maybe it was the King, himself, who had given Slingsby his orders. Anyway, she really didn't know.

"The townspeople," Monsieur Mottet said, "have protested to Don Alonzo about what happened to you yesterday. They have asked him to write to the King about it. My Lord Ambassador agreed with them that what was done was barbarous and most abominable, and he has written to His Majesty."

"It is very kind of them and of His Excellency," Lucy said.

Monsieur sat down, then, and wrote his own impassioned letter to the Marquis of Ormonde describing the incident. In part, he said he was so ashamed of the proceedings of Monsieur Slingsby against Mrs. Barlow and her child that he was loath to relate the particulars. He further said that the Lord Ambassador, Don Alonzo de Cardenas would write to the King, himself—but that Slingsby was telling everyone that it was the King who had ordered him to do what he did. Would His Excellency let them know the King's pleasure so that they could act accordingly?

Lord Castlehaven and Monsieur Barkley left, after kissing Lucy's hand and telling her not to worry. Mr. Mottet's letter was dispatched and Lucy and her son settled down to wait uncomfortably aware that they were unwanted guests. Slingsby was seen frequently skulking around outside the embassy and the Lord Ambassador's security guards kept him under their surveillance.

The Marquis of Ormonde replied at once. He said that he had shown Monsieur Mottet's letter to His Majesty and that the King appreciated all that Monsieur had done. His Majesty, he said, had given Sir Arthur Slingsby the commission to get the child out of the mother's possession with the purpose of advantage to both mother and child. Certainly His Majesty never intended that it be done with uproar and scandal. The

King, he wrote, would be grateful if Monsieur Mottet would speak to Lucy and bring her to a reasonable attitude about the whole affair. The King intended to have the child delivered to the custody of those whom he had appointed, without fail, even though there may have been an error committed by them in the execution of their duty.

He concluded the letter with a warning that Lucy should be made to realize that from the moment she refused again to obey the King's command neither she nor her son would be cared for, or even owned, by His Majesty. Furthermore, he said, anyone taking sides with Lucy in her mad disobedience to His Majesty's pleasure would be regarded as one who was committing an injury to the King of England.

Monsieur's mouth dropped open in astonishment when he read the warning. It was true that Charles Stuart was only "the Pretender," but there were rumors of a movement for his restoration! He had not intended to precipitate an international situation! He thought that he was only giving succor to a lady in distress. His hands shook as he carried the letter to Lucy with the intention of getting her out of the Spanish Ambassador's custody as soon as possible.

"My dear Monsieur Mottet," she said, "I have no wish to embarrass you or My Lord Castlehaven. There is really no necessity for it anyway, since I have already agreed to all that the King desires. I feel sure that somehow the Marquis of Ormonde and His Majesty have been misled."

"Indeed?" said Monsieur. "Then you are maligned, my dear. It seems to me that someone is trying to discredit you."

"Yes, Monsieur. That is true. If you are willing to help me just a little more, it would be of great service to me if you would write again to My Lord, the Marquis of Ormonde, and tell him that I am of the same mind that I was when he paid his call to me. It is only that the man, Slingsby, took the matter in his own hands and mismanaged it."

Monsieur looked at her with pity in his dark eyes. "Indeed I will," he said.

"Tell him further," she said, "that I request that the pension we agreed upon be settled upon me now. Tell him that I am willing to live in any house that the King designates, with the exception of that of Slingsby."

"That seems a reasonable request."

Lucy smiled at him. "I would be happy if Lord Castlehaven would be willing to shelter me, at least for a time, that is if His Majesty gives his permission."

The Spanish Ambassador's secretary was too gallant to abandon the lady he had rescued, even though there was some risk involved. The letter was sent to the Marquis at once.

Someone told Slingsby what was happening, and he flew into a panic. He was afraid that he would lose the King's favor because of his mistake. He wrote a letter to Ormonde also, and he attacked everybody who had anything to do with Lucy. He wrote that the Spanish Ambassador, Mr. Mottet, his secretary, and Lord Castlehaven had meddled in something that was none of their business. They had wrested a criminal from the law! He had brought a civil action against Mrs. Barlow, he explained, in which he demanded that she pay him for the board and lodging that was rightfully due him. Since she could not pay, she should have been removed from his house to the debtors' prison, but justice had been thwarted. The meddlers had given the culprit sanctuary in the Earl of Castlehaven's house.

Furthermore, Slingsby protested, Mr. Daniel O'Neill had told him at Ghent that it would be of great service to His Majesty if certain papers were taken out of Mrs. Barlow's hands. He knew that was true, because she was legally married to him. He had assumed that the

King would want to obtain the papers from her. That was why he had quartered her in his house and bided his time.

He knew that he had failed dismally so far, he said, but it was not his fault. O'Neill had not taken him into his complete confidence nor explained in what manner the mission was to be carried out. He begged for an opportunity to repair the damage, now that he knew the King's wishes in the matter. He would see to it this time that no one would interfere in the carrying out of justice. He humbly suggested that a letter be sent to His Excellency, Don Alonzo, the Spanish Ambassador, thanking him for his endeavors in compelling Lucy to submit to the King's wishes. He should be asked to consent to having her property searched. His Excellency should know that Mrs. Barlow was in possession of "suspicious" papers, and since he had been involved in her affairs through the meddling of his secretary, and no fault of his own, he would undoubtedly be only too glad to comply. He was sure that His Lordship would agree that it was imperative that he, Slingsby, be present during the search!

What the Marquis of Ormonde thought about this letter he kept to himself. He did consult His Majesty about Slingsby, and His Majesty told him to correct the situation the best he could. Slingsby had been overzealous, he said. That was all!

Ormonde, unhappy that his gentle and effective plan had been frustrated, knew that the thing to do was to get rid of Slingsby. But before he could do it another rascal saw an opportunity of insinuating himself into the affair. His name was Ned Prodgers and he called on Lucy at the Earl of Castlehaven's house and claimed that he had official authority to represent the King. He demanded that the letter revealing that Tom Howard was a spy be given to him.

This time Lucy was not fooled. She pretended to acquiesce and said that she would go to her chamber to get it. Instead, she went out of the room only to get someone to help her get rid of Prodgers. He sensed what she was doing and before he could be thrown out he walked out to the garden, where little James was playing alone. Lucy could no longer afford a nurse or guard. He seized the child and carried him out to his carriage. Lucy heard the boy's cries and ran back at once, only to see the driver of the carriage lash the horses with a whip to make them lunge forward and pull the coach rapidly out of sight.

An hour later a servant of the Earl of Castlehaven found her on the floor, unconscious.

The next day she was unable to get out of bed when William Erskine, the King's cupbearer, came to call upon her. She had to receive him in her bedchamber.

"I have been sent by the Marquis of Ormonde with His Majesty's consent," he said kindly. "They are both distressed by the cruel treatment you have received. His Majesty has asked me to serve you in any way that I can."

"What are they doing with James?" she asked weakly.

"His Majesty is appointing William Crofts of Little Saxham, Suffolk, to be his guardian; and Mr. Crofts will be created a peer of the realm. So you see, my dear," Erskine said, "His Majesty is honoring James by arrangements indicating that he is his son."

"Where will they take him?" Lucy asked.

"They will take him to Paris," he said, "set him up in a household of his own near the Queen Mother, and he will be provided with tutors and servants."

Lucy smiled faintly.

"You are pleased?" he said.

"Yes," she said.

"And now," Erskine said, "do you wish to stay here in the Earl of Castlehaven's house now that everything is arranged?"

Lucy frowned, trying to make up her mind what to do.

"His Majesty is leaving Bruge," he said. "He is establishing a residence here in Brussels. He will be pleased to see you again." He paused and looked at her with significant meaning.

Lucy was startled. Surely His Majesty did not intend to come to her again! She would get out of the way to avoid that possibility! She never wanted to see him again.

"I wish to go to Paris," she said. She didn't want to be in the same city with His Majesty!

Lucy went to Paris with William Erskine escorting her. He arranged for a royal pension to be paid to her regularly and bought an elegant little house, staffed with two servants, for her use. There was a carriage with liveried groom to attend her.

It was a pleasant arrangement and she soon found that many of her old friends were living in exile in Paris and she also made new ones. She was even received by the Queen Mother when Henrietta was there, briefly, for the social season.

Every afternoon she rode in her carriage on the boulevard and through the park along with the other fashionable expatriates. She smiled and waved as her carriage passed another one but her mind was busy with thoughts about how to make the most of her new life.

One day when her carriage was rolling swiftly past the palace of the Louvre she suddenly thought, "I am getting nowhere." What was the meaning of life, anyway? Why was she different? Why couldn't she just enjoy life the way the ladies at the court did. Certainly, Charles had given her every opportunity—she could be the leader of the social set! At last she thought of Dr. Cosin and decided to have a talk with him. Maybe he could help her.

She talked with him for an hour on her first visit—

pouring out her thoughts and disappointments. Dr. Cosin made no comment but invited her to come back for another visit soon. She went one or two afternoons every week for a month and, then, she posed the question, "Why am I different?"

By this time Dr. Cosin knew her well. And she wasn't much different from what she had been when she was married to Charles, he thought. In her personal relationships she was incredibly naive—childlike. And she was still innocent—she didn't understand the evil in the world or how to cope with it.

"Perhaps," he said, "it is a grace from God."

She stared at him not understanding.

"I have the feeling that you can't believe, or rather, that you refuse to believe that people are often cruel to each other and that they are often overcome by their lust and greed. You make excuses for them that are close to you—and sort of—" he searched for the word, "idealize them—that is, you imagine they have the ideals that you have. That you have those ideals is what I mean is a gift from God."

In his experience he knew that a child sometimes can see the hypocrisy and evil in his parent but because he is dependent upon that parent for his very life he can only tell himself that the evil does not exist—especially if he is an intelligent and sensitive child like Lucy. He had heard the gossip about the scandal of the divorce case of her parents and, as he remembered it, each of them accused the other of adultery!

Lucy simply hadn't grown up but what an incredible thing that she had captivated that incurable roué, Charles Stuart, and married him, not once but twice! She probably made excuses for the way the King had treated her! It was difficult to advise her—he couldn't just say, "grow up", for fear of offending her.

"You have made the right decision, I think," he said slowly, "not to live at court with Charles."

If she couldn't cope with the debauchery of the court it would be better to avoid it. And as to the idea that she might be a good influence on the King, it was probably too late. The King's habits were already formed. He might even be infuriated at Lucy for not being able to live the way that was all too popular in his court.

"Have I harmed Charles in some way—that is, other than being an obstacle to a political marriage?"

She must think that if she had done what Charles wanted he would not have become what he was—a man who chose to indulge his sexual appetites without restraint!

"No!" he said. "The King's moral character is his responsibility. It is not your fault. Don't worry about it. Think only what you would have done if you could—and that you have made the right decision now."

Lucy continued her visits and seemed reconciled and peaceful in her outlook on life. Dr. Cosin thought she even seemed to be losing the tendency to blame herself for what had happened. Then, one day, when she rose from her chair to leave his study, she fainted.

He summoned the servants and had her carried to his private house where his wife took charge. A physician was summoned.

"She is very ill," the doctor told them. "I think that it is her heart."

When Lucy regained consciousness Mrs. Cosin told her that she must remain with them until she was better.

"You are very kind," Lucy murmured and she felt that, at last, she was with people that understood her—and she understood them. Not since the time she lived with Frances Vaughan had she had such a feeling!

Even though Justus was a successful and prosperous member of the Temple he couldn't get a pass to go to the Continent when he tried because Thurloe's agents watched him constantly. He had been unable to pay Lucy a visit.

One day Justus went with his friend, George Fox, to Hampton Court on business. They happened to see Cromwell riding by at the head of his guards. "He looks like a dead man," Justus commented. "Of course I'm prejudiced," he added with a smile.

"It is true," said Fox, "that the Lord Protector's health is failing. The hardships of his campaigns are beginning to take their toll. He is only fifty-eight but he looks older, doesn't he?"

"Yes," said Justus. "Have you noticed that his handwriting on official documents is feeble? The signature appears to have been written by a trembling hand."

"He hasn't been the same since his daughter died— she was his favorite," said Fox.

"Elizabeth Claypole?" asked Justus.

"Yes."

"But that was last February."

"Some people, even the strongest of men," Fox said, "never recover from grief."

Justus reflected that the Lord Protector had always been able to endure the grief he inflicted on other people without flinching. More than once he had permitted the torturing of innocent people and the butchering of combatants and noncombatants alike, irrespective of sex or age. He wondered if Cromwell ever thought about the little town of Worcester and the fact that he had ridden off after the battle that he called his "crowning mercy," without giving any commands that would keep his ruffians, maddened like beasts by the taste of blood, from sacking and pillaging the town. Did he look back at the Cathedral towers as he rode through the orchards and fields of grain bordered by hedgerows covered with hop vines and honeysuckle?

How did the great general rationalize what was most

certainly going on back in the town? Did he think, "That's war," and that he had to be as ruthless as any general had ever been to earn the reputation of being the world's most clever military leader? Or did he look back and wonder about the townspeople hanging in the doorways of their own shops, the slaughtered men and butchered horses, and the orphaned children roaming the countryside, destitute, uncared for and hungry? Maybe that's why he couldn't sleep at night and why doors had to be locked and bolted the minute he passed through them.

When Justus finished his business he returned to London, and the very next day he heard that the Protector had fallen seriously ill. He was being brought to Whitehall in London, it was said. Groups of people gathered in the street to discuss the Protector's condition, and it was said that he was becoming weaker and weaker and that he was resigned to approaching death.

Several nights later the Lord Protector went into a coma, and about three o'clock the next day he died. By a strange coincidence it was the anniversary of the Battle of Worcester, September 3rd.

Almost immediately Cromwell was entombed in the Chapel of Henry VII in Westminster Abbey; the authorities didn't know what was going to happen. Anarchy could erupt like a volcano! They would wait and see what kind of funeral they should stage.

All over London, almost around the clock, people gathered in groups and talked about what was going to happen to the country now that Cromwell was dead. Military men conferred about plans to handle riots, which there was every reason to believe might occur. Mobs of apprentices gathered and muttered threats of violence if they were not fed and their wages promptly paid. They had heard the businessmen and shopkeepers talking anxiously about the state of the country and its future if Cromwell died.

Justus and the other men of the law watched the government. It was not long before they observed that the bureaucracy was going to resort to a centuries-old antidote invented by desperate tyrants. It reminded him, someone said, of ancient Rome, and Nero! The population was going to be distracted by a grand spectacle. A public funeral for the Lord Protector was being planned which would rival that of Philip of Spain! Sixty thousand pounds was allocated to be spent from the national treasury, as a starter, and the date set for November twenty-third. The innkeepers were told to prepare to house and feed hordes of people who would pour into the city from all over the kingdom. The shopkeepers were warned that they should replenish their stocks, for the visitors would certainly be interested in going home with cloth and shoes and household equipment. Artisans and craftsmen were kept out of mischief by immediate orders for vestments, ladies' gowns, men's costumes, jewerly and the trappings appropriate to national mourning. The apprentices didn't have to worry any more about the payment of their wages, because their masters had plenty of business.

The bureaucrats and military leaders knew that the spirit of democracy lay dangerously dormant in the British kingdom. Three months' preparation for a national pageant would provide a soporific and frantic activity at the same time. Each faction hoped that by the end of the celebration they would be in firm control of the government. And all the time the men in the *Sealed Knot* were cooperating with Edward Hyde, on the Continent, to bring back Charles Stuart to the throne.

Justus Walter didn't see the spectacle when it was finally ready. He was in Paris. He had taken advantage of Thurloe's preoccupation with other problems of security to scurry across the Channel without so much as a scrap of paper for a pass. John Cosin had sent for him; Lucy was gravely ill.

The clergyman received Justus in the home of the English Resident where he had just conducted the Sunday divine service in the little chapel.

"Where is she?" Justus asked.

"In an apartment in my home," Dr. Cosin said. "There is no question of poverty," he added hastily. "Her pension from the King has been paid in full, and it was by the King's command that William Erskine, his cupbearer, has taken care of her. She collapsed one day in my study and she is not recovering."

"Why did she come to Paris?" Justus asked.

"I don't know," Cosin said slowly, "I think that it was only partly because her son, James, was set up in a residence here with his guardian, Mr. Crofts. There is some other reason that she did not confide to me."

"Will you take me to her now?"

"Before you go," Dr. Cosin said, "I think that I should tell you that her papers are still safely in my keeping but I am watched constantly by spies because of them. It's possible that there may be one even among the servants of my household, but I still think that for your safety I should keep them."

"I am most grateful," Justus said.

Cosin murmured something polite and then led the way to his own house. Before they entered Lucy's bedchamber the clergyman said some words designed to prepare Justus for his sister's condition.

"She may not be able to speak, and she may not recognize you," he said. "Her heart is very weak, and her appearance has changed even in the short time that she has been with us. It is evident to us all," he said with compassion, because he knew that Justus would be shocked when he saw her, "that death is approaching."

"I can't believe it," Justus said in anguish. "She is so young. I can't believe it."

"The worst of all is that she doesn't wish to live. The physician tells me that even with her frail health she could live comfortably for many years if she were cared for by someone whom she loves."

"Can I do it?" asked Justus. "I am willing."

"No," said Cosin. "You could not do it."

"I see what you mean," Justus said. "I have never been the answer to all that she desires."

Lucy did recognize Justus, and she smiled at him, but when she tried to speak she was too weak. He saw that she had something that she wished to say to him. He bent over and kissed her forehead. "What is it, Lucy, that you are trying to tell me?"

"Justus," she whispered.

He put his ear close to her lips so he could catch the words.

"Justus," she whispered slowly again, "take care of him."

Tears came to Justus' eyes. Even in her illness she thought of her son!

"Yes, yes, dear sister, I promise. I will look after your little James. I will see that the very best is done for him."

"No," she said, "no, no, no." She was breathing with difficulty. "No, my son will be looked after—I mean—" Justus thought she would be unable to finish because her face contorted with pain.

"It's her heart," Cosin said. "She has excruciating pains in her chest. I'll get the nurse to administer the sedative medication," he said as he went out of the room.

"Stay with him—he will be lonely—and forgive him—" she said with effort, "my husband, Charles."

Justus was speechless. How could she expect such a thing of him!

"You are surprised, aren't you, Justus?"

That was putting it mildly, he thought. He saw that she had more to say so he didn't need to answer; he sat silently waiting.

"My death," she said, "will partly atone for any wrong that I have done Charles. Now, he will be free to make a good political marriage." She was silent for a moment and then said, "If you do as I ask, Justus, you will be rewarded. You will have a good post in the King's service before and after the restoration."

"I can't do it," Justus said. "You are asking more of me than I can do."

"You must," she said. "You must do this last thing for me—to expiate the wrong that I did Charles. I learned to hate him—I need his forgiveness."

He wanted to convince her that she had done no wrong but she seemed to be drifting away from consciousness—her eyes held his imploringly.

"Yes, yes, I promise," Justus said.

She didn't say anything else but she smiled as she drifted into a coma. During the night, she died.

Justus was beside himself all the next day. He paced the floor, paying no attention to Dr. Cosin, who tried to quiet him. Lucy had tricked him! He had promised to "look after" King Charles, the Merry Monarch, who at that very moment was enjoying himself with a new mistress in Brussels. He didn't know whether he could stand being in his presence without killing him, much less serve him!

After a while Justus sat down, exhausted by grief and exasperation. She had tricked him into a sacred deathbed promise! He feared that he would do what he had always done—what she demanded of him, no matter how unreasonable. "My stubborn sister, whose satellite I have been from the day I was born—gone—leaving me with that promise!"

When he had cooled down his legal mind began to work. What choice did he have? He could go back to London and take up his ordered, well-established life, or he could go to the King and offer his services. If

Charles refused, he could still go back to London—no harm done to the career he was engaged upon.

But if the King accepted he would be wagering his career and his life upon the future of a Pretender. On the other hand, it was almost certain that Charles would be restored to the throne—and soon. When that happened his own future would be guaranteed. He could be in high favor at the new court in London and reach the highest pinnacle of prosperity and success. He had nothing to lose!

But that was not what Lucy had in mind when she extracted that promise from him. He believed that she actually thought that he would be a good influence on Charles! It was too late for anything or anybody to have much influence on His Majesty. The trouble with him, Justus thought cynically, was that he didn't have the moral fiber to withstand the impoverishment of exile.

Justus realized that no amount of rationalizing was going to free him from the conviction that he had made a commitment—a solemn promise—to his sister and he would have to go through with it or feel guilty the rest of his life!

Very well, he thought grimly. He would go to that charming, dissembling, unfaithful libertine and he would try to see what Lucy saw in him. Forgive him—he wasn't sure that he could!

Lucy was interred in the Huguenot Cemetery in the Faubourg St. Germain. William Erskine, the King's cupbearer, made the arrangements and paid the bills. John Cosin offered up prayers. Justus Walter was the only member of Lucy's family that was there for her son was not allowed to come to his mother's funeral.

When the Duke of Ormonde received the news he went into the King's private chambers and asked permission to speak to him alone.

Charles was tired. He had puffs under his eyes and his large mouth drooped at the corners. When he heard what Ormonde had come to tell him he sat silently for a while and muttered, "First love—there is nothing like it to shackle a man!"

Ormonde saw that Charles was struggling for self-control. He looked away but not before he saw the tears gathering in the King's jaundiced eyes.

Then, after a few moments Charles said, "I will never again love any woman as I loved Lucy. There was none other quite like her. If she had only understood—if she had only been willing to do what I wished, everything would be different—for both of us. I am afraid that I will never be able to forget her!"

"Don't try," the Duke said gently. "It was a precious experience!"

The King saw no one the rest of the day. He did not join the debaucheries of the evening, and he stayed aloof all the next day. The next morning he appeared and he had a hard expression upon his dark face and his eyes glittered with an unnatural brightness.

"Summon Edward Hyde," he commanded his secretary.

When the Chancellor came the King wasted no time. "Begin negotiations for a marriage treaty with the court of Portugal," he said. "I am a free man, now."

BIBLIOGRAPHY

LUCY WALTER, WIFE OR MISTRESS, Lord George Scott (1947)

LUCY WALTER, G. Allan Heron (1929)

MEMOIRES DE MADEMOISELLE DE MONTPENSIER

THE GRAND MADEMOISELLE, Francis Steeholm (1956)

A LIFE OF JOHN COSIN, BISHOP OF DURHAM, P.H. Osmond (1913)

THE KING'S LADIES, D. Ponsonby (1936)

THE LIFE OF EDWARD, EARL OF CLARENDON, Autobiography

THE PRIVATE LIFE OF CHARLES II, A.I. Dasent (1927)

CHARLES II, Osmond Airy

KING CHARLES II, Arthur Bryant (1931)

CHARLES II IN THE CHANNEL ISLANDS, S.E. Hoskins (1854)

THE PERSONAL HISTORY OF CHARLES, Including the King's Own Account of His Escape and Preservation After the Battle of Worcester, as Dictated to Pepys, ed. by Sir Walter Scott (1846)

SYMONDS DIARY (Camden Society (1859))

ENTERTAINMENT OF CHARLES II, J. Ogilby (1662)

MEMOIRS OF THE COURT OF CHARLES THE

SECOND BY COUNT GRAMMONT, ed. by Sir Walter Scott (1896)
MEMOIRS OF THE COURT OF ENGLAND IN 1675, by the Baronne D'Aulnoy, ed. by G.D. Gilbert (1913)
THE BOSCOBEL TRACTS, OR CONTEMPORARY NARRATIVES OF HIS MAJESTY'S ADVENTURES FROM THE MURDER OF HIS FATHER TO THE RESTORATION, ed. by Sir Walter Scott (1846)
EXETER, Bryan Little
GLORIOUS DEVON, S.P.B. Mais
HISTORY AND ANTIQUITIES OF THE COUNTY OF SOMERSET, Vol. 2 Bridgwater
MEMOIRS OF LADY FANSHAWE
MEMOIRS OF SOPHIA, ELECTRESS OF HANOVER
OLD COURT LIFE IN FRANCE, Two volumes, Frances Elliot
OLD WORLD PLACES, Allan Fea (1912)
QUIET ROADS AND SLEEPY VILLAGES, Allan Fea (1914)
SOCIAL LIFE UNDER THE STUARTS, Elizabeth Godfrey (1904)
THE GROWTH OF STUART LONDON, N.G. Brett-James (1935)

ON SALE WHEREVER PAPERBACKS ARE SOLD
— or use this coupon to order directly from the publisher.

Elizabeth Goudge

MORE BEST SELLING PAPERBACKS BY ONE OF YOUR FAVORITE AUTHORS...

Elizabeth Goudge

A3548	BLUE HILLS	$1.50
A3586	THE BIRD IN THE TREE	$1.50
M4135	CASTLE ON THE HILL	$1.75
V2518	CHILD FROM THE SEA	$1.25
M4142	THE DEAN'S WATCH	$1.75
M4131	GREEN DOLPHIN STREET	$1.75
M4152	THE HEART OF THE FAMILY	$1.75
A3561	ISLAND MAGIC	$1.50
M2898	THE LOST ANGEL	$1.75
M4147	THE ROSEMARY TREE	$1.75
M4012	THE SCENT OF WATER	$1.75
M4156	TOWERS IN THE MIST	$1.75
M4160	THE WHITE WITCH	$1.75

Send To: JOVE PUBLICATIONS, INC.
Harcourt Brace Jovanovich, Inc.
Dept. M.O., 757 Third Avenue, New York, N.Y. 10017

NAME _____

ADDRESS _____

CITY _____

STATE _____ ZIP ____

I enclose $_____, which includes the total price of all books ordered plus 50¢ per book postage and handling for the first book and 25¢ for each additional. If my total order is $10.00 or more, I understand that Jove Publications, Inc. will pay all postage and handling.

No COD's or stamps. Please allow three to four weeks for delivery. Prices subject to change.

NT-4

ON SALE WHEREVER PAPERBACKS ARE SOLD
— or use this coupon to order directly from the publisher.

TAYLOR CALDWELL

MORE BEST SELLING PAPERBACKS BY ONE OF YOUR FAVORITE AUTHORS...

Taylor Caldwell

	Y4324	THE BALANCE WHEEL $1.95
	Y4151	THE DEVIL'S ADVOCATE $1.95
	Y4146	DYNASTY OF DEATH $1.95
	Y4605	THE EAGLES GATHER $1.95
	Y4062	THE EARTH IS THE LORD'S $1.95
	Y4326	LET LOVE COME LAST $1.95
	Y4607	MELISSA $1.95
	Y4091	THE STRONG CITY $1.95
	Y4155	THERE WAS A TIME $1.95
	Y4609	TIME NO LONGER $1.95
	Y4159	THE TURNBULLS $1.95
	Y4325	THE WIDE HOUSE $1.95

Send To: JOVE PUBLICATIONS, INC.
Harcourt Brace Jovanovich, Inc.
Dept. M.O., 757 Third Avenue, New York, N.Y. 10017

NAME

ADDRESS

CITY

STATE   ZIP

I enclose $_____, which includes the total price of all books ordered plus 50¢ per book postage and handling for the first book and 25¢ for each additional. If my total order is $10.00 or more, I understand that Jove Publications, Inc. will pay all postage and handling.

No COD's or stamps. Please allow three to four weeks for delivery.
Prices subject to change.   NT-7